D0055507

Bluff
Walk _____

Bluff
Walk

A John McAlister Mystery

Charles R. Crawford

Sunstone
Press

SANTA FE

The events, people, and incidents in this story are the sole product
of the author's imagination. The story is fictional and any resemblance
to individuals living or dead is purely coincidental.

Sunstone books may be purchased for educational, business, or sales promotional use.
For information please write: Special Markets Department, Sunstone Press,
P.O. Box 2321, Santa Fe, New Mexico 87504-2321.

Library of Congress Cataloging-in-Publication Data:

Crawford, Charles R., 1958-
  Bluff walk : a John McAlister mystery / Charles R. Crawford.
    p. cm.
  ISBN 0-86534-439-6 (Hardcover)
1. Private investigators—Tennessee—Memphis—Fiction. 2. Memphis (Tenn.)—Fiction.
I. Title.

PS3603.R3955B58 2005
813'.6—dc22
                              2004017075

Published in

WWW.SUNSTONEPRESS.COM
SUNSTONE PRESS / POST OFFICE BOX 2321 / SANTA FE, NM 87504-2321 /USA
(505) 988-4418 / ORDERS ONLY (800) 243-5644 / FAX (505) 988-1025

This book is dedicated to Alice,
my wife and best friend.

1 ———————————————————

"What have you got for me, John?" Amanda Baker asked.

"At least five million bucks," I replied with a smile.

"And how much do you want for it?"

"As usual, I'll let you decide."

Amanda Baker is one of the best divorce lawyers in Memphis. Thin, blonde and fortyish, her big blue eyes hide the mind of a combat general and the predatory instincts of a hunting lioness. Her clients give her a $20,000 non-refundable retainer up front, and that's just the beginning. The clients don't mind, since Amanda usually gets her fee out of the ex-husband in the end. Always the husband, because she doesn't represent men. She says it would be an issues conflict.

Her other clients are women who can't afford any lawyer, much less Amanda. Amanda takes their cases for free, and pays for their court and deposition costs out of her own pocket. It's not unusual for her to be in court on the same day with the wife of a chief executive officer of a prominent business and the wife of an unemployed roofer. With Amanda, it's full freight or nothing at all.

My name is John McAlister. I'm a private detective. I get paid when I can. On a good day, or a lucky day, I like to think I'm the best PI in the world, never mind Memphis. On a bad day, or an unlucky day, I sometimes feel like I couldn't detect the Mississippi River, even though it rolls past only a hundred yards from my office window.

Oh, yeah. I used to be a lawyer, too. I made more money then, but I didn't have nearly as much fun.

Amanda hires me on three or four cases a year. Our fee arrangement was reached some time ago. I get paid reasonable expenses plus what she thinks the result is worth. She passes my fee along to her rich clients, and pays me herself for her pro bono clients. I'm not asked to support her favorite charity.

My latest engagement for Amanda is the case of Jones v. Jones, Shelby County Chancery Court Docket No. 02-25437. Jack Jones III is what is known as a "Pillar of the Community," a title he earned by giving away large sums of inherited money. Jack's grandfather made money from huge cotton plantations in Arkansas and Mississippi, where thousands of sharecroppers hoed and picked cotton to enrich the original "Mr. Jack" while sinking further and further into hopeless debt at his company stores.

Mr. Jack died in 1920 at the age of eighty, after stroking out while screaming at hands who weren't hoeing the weeds out of the cotton to his satisfaction. Legend has it that the sharecroppers on both sides of the river held a celebration that Saturday night like nothing that has been seen since, and black preachers at services the next day called upon their flocks to kneel in thanksgiving for their deliverance. It's a good story, anyway.

After the old man's death, Jack Jones, Jr.--"Mr. Little Jack" in Delta parlance--sold most of the farmland. Jack, Jr. had been sent away to the University of Virginia, and was a thirty year old bank officer in Memphis at the time of his father's death. Everybody figured he would live quietly and well on his inheritance, maybe even keeping his job at the bank, since in Memphis it was important to "do" something even if you didn't have to.

But Jack, Jr. proved to be a chip off the old block. Through a combination of money, contacts and utter ruthlessness, he built a business empire that included banking, investments and insurance. His businesses not only survived the Great Depression, but thrived on it as they gobbled up failing competitors. He blew his artery in 1968 when he got overexcited at the news of Dr. King's assassination. His employees' celebration was more subdued but no less jubilant than the one when his father died. Mr. Jack would have been proud to know that his son was generally conceded to be the meanest son of a bitch in town at the time of his death.

Jack Jones III was not a chip off the old block. Upon his father's death, Jack had immediately quit his job as a loan officer at the same bank where Mr. Little Jack had started out. With the help of astute lawyers and financial advisers, Jack formed the Jones Foundation to preserve enough of the $50 million he had inherited from his father to insure himself an extremely comfortable life while at the same time very publicly donating large sums to charity. Since the Jones Foundation required only three or four hours of his time a week, Jack spent most of his time working on his handicap at the country club, collecting antiques for his Tudor mansion, and traveling. The speculation that he was homosexual was spurred by nothing more than the fact that he had never married or had a serious relationship with a woman until he was in his early fifties. Despite the rumors regarding his sexual orientation, he was always accompanied by a socially appropriate woman to all society events, and was considered one of the most eligible bachelors in town.

At the age of 52, Jack Jones shocked society by suddenly and unexpectedly marrying his secretary at the Jones Foundation, Betty Jo Talbot. Betty Jo was 30, divorced, and what was known in Jack's circle as pure white trailer trash. In truth, Betty Jo was a good-hearted country girl who looked a lot like Tanya Tucker. She had not been a debutante, but neither had she always lived off her daddy's or husband's money or gotten drunk before two p.m. every day playing bridge at the club.

Betty Jo and Jack had never dated or had any kind of relationship other than employer and employee. Then one week, he took her to lunch twice. The next week, he asked her to marry him. The week after that, they were married at Jack's home.

On their second anniversary, Jack told her it wasn't working out, and he wanted a divorce. He offered Betty Jo $250,000 and the Mercedes coupe he had bought for her birthday.

Much to his surprise, Betty Jo told him to stick it up his fat ass. She hadn't started out as a gold digger, but she knew that she was entitled to a lot more than Jack was offering. Besides, she had been about to tell Jack that she wanted a divorce when he beat her to it. Betty Jo was a healthy, lusty female, and except for two or three times that almost didn't happen, the marriage could have been annulled for lack of consummation.

Betty Jo moved in with her momma and momma's fourth husband and made an appointment with Amanda. Jack controlled the money, so Betty Jo didn't have the retainer. After hearing her new client's story, Amanda bent the rules on taking a domestic case on a contingency and agreed to represent Betty Jo for one third of the recovery.

The grounds for divorce aren't as important as they used to be in determining a settlement, but they are still legally relevant in Tennessee. Moreover, an adulterous spouse can get hammered more than may be strictly legal if the case is assigned to a judge who takes that kind of thing seriously. Jones v. Jones was assigned to exactly that kind of judge.

Amanda had a strong suspicion that Jack had married Betty Jo to dispel the rumors that he was gay, and maybe to produce an heir. When it got down to it, though, Jack hadn't been able to get it up with Betty Jo to pass along the Jones heritage. Amanda had concluded that Jack had planned all along to divorce Betty Jo after a suitable period. He had picked her instead of someone in his own social circle so that word of what marriage to Jack Jones was really like would not get around from an ex-wife who talked to people who mattered. In fact, Amanda heard that Jack was telling his friends that he had married Betty Jo out of physical attraction, but that in the end the differences in their backgrounds were too much for them to sustain a marriage.

Amanda called and told me my job was to provide physical evidence that Jack was gay.

"Good grief," I said, "it's the twenty-first century, who cares if Jack's gay?"

"Obviously, Jack cares, and he cares who knows. And Judge Sanders will care," Amanda replied.

"What kind of proof?" I asked.

"Pictures. Preferably videos. Sanders will roast Jones if I can prove he's gay, but he'll roast me if I go in with unsubstantiated charges. Besides, if I can show visual evidence to Jack's attorney, we'll settle and never have to go to trial. Jack can keep his secret for all I care if he'll do right by Betty Jo."

"Pictures aren't easy, Amanda," I said.

"Hey, that's why I'm calling you, John. A picture is worth a thousand words, and in this case a lot more money. See what you can do."

Which is why I found myself driving around Jack's neighborhood that afternoon. A call to the Jones Foundation had confirmed that Jack was in town but not available until tomorrow to discuss a contribution to the Pets Without People Society. I told Betty Jo's successor that I would call back.

Jack's neighborhood was built in the late 1950s at what was then the eastern edge of town on one and two acre lots with houses to match. A private security car drove by me the other way as I cruised past Jack's estate, but didn't pay me any particular attention that I could tell.

A circular driveway curved under a canopy of oaks and past beds of azaleas and annuals. The azaleas were long past blooming, but white, pink and grape-colored crape myrtles thrived in patches of August sun. The grass was the deep green that comes only from constant watering and fertilizing. From the cab of my air-conditioned truck, the yard looked like it was inviting you to sit down under its trees and read a book and drink iced tea. Accept the invitation, though, and the heat and humidity would have you sweating buckets in ten minutes.

The house was not as big as you would expect, only six or seven thousand square feet, with an attached four-car garage that was designed to look like a stable. The windows were leaded, and the roof was a light blue slate that blended well with the stucco walls and dark brown Tudor accents. Other than the tall pines that could be seen over the roofline, the backyard was hidden by a ten foot tall field stone wall. It was easy to imagine a pool, poolhouse and more landscaping, with maybe a tennis court thrown in. Betty Jo must have thought she had come a long way when she first saw it.

At ten that night, I parked my white truck by a drainage ditch that bisected Jack's street three houses down from his yard. The removable utility company logo was affixed to the driver's door, and a whip antenna completed my vehicle's disguise. As long as I didn't leave it there too long, it would not alarm either security or the police. If I had to come back the next night, I would have to arrange a drop off.

I hopped the wire fence around the ditch and dropped into it. As I picked my way down the ditch without a flashlight, clouds of mosquitoes rose from the shallow puddles left by yesterday's thunderstorm. I had sprayed myself liberally with insect repellent before setting out, but I had to consciously resist the urge to slap the little bloodsuckers as they whined around my head.

A black patch suddenly separated itself from a puddle in front of me, causing me to jump sideways against the concrete ditch wall. The world's biggest water moccasin turned out to be a raccoon, which churred at me and waddled off down the ditch. My heart rate slowly returned to normal, and I continued down the manmade creek until it reached the utility line that marked the boundary between the backyards on Jack's street and the next street over.

I slipped off my soft backpack and pulled out cotton gloves and a hat with a roll down mosquito net. Along with my long pants and long-sleeved shirt, I now had head to toe covering that would provide camouflage and protection from bugs and poison ivy, but cost a heavy price in sweat.

I put my backpack on and scaled the head high wall and then the wire fence, and was in the unlit corner of the backyard of the French provincial home three doors down from Jack. There were no people and no dogs, just the soft glow of a television through a downstairs window. I crossed through the shrubs along the fence without incident, and had an equally uneventful trip through the next two yards. Either nobody had a dog, or they had brought them inside out of the heat.

At the boundary of Jack's place, I discovered that the field stone wall I had seen from the street extended all the way around the sides and back of his yard. I knew I could make a running leap and get my hands on top of the wall, but I also knew that it might have glass shards embedded in the cement on top. I pulled my pack off, leaned my back against the wall, and put my feet against a tree that grew a convenient three feet away. By placing my palms against the wall and alternating pressure on my feet and back, I climbed up the wall far enough to reach backwards over my head and gingerly feel along the top. It was flat and smooth and about a foot wide. Better safe than sorry.

I got back down, retrieved my pack, and levered myself up on to the wall. Both Jack and his neighbor had planted magnolias and pines along the wall, and they provided a perfect screen for my careful stroll down the wall toward the houses.

I walked the wall till it ran flush along the side of the four-car garage, and stopped and reconnoitered. Because of the magnolias, I couldn't see anything of Jack's yard except the faint glimmer of lights. I could smell the chlorine of a swimming pool, but I couldn't tell if it was in his yard or the neighbor's.

I had a choice of dropping off the wall into the yard, or trying to get above the magnolia screen. I opted for height. One of the pines I had seen from the road grew almost against the wall, and I could see its first thick branch sticking out over the yard some ten feet above my head. I shinnied up the tree, thankful for the long sleeves and gloves on the rough, resinous bark. I stopped about half way up when I had cleared the magnolias and peeked around the trunk, but couldn't see anyone. I got to the limb and kept going until my feet were even with it, and then twisted around the trunk so I could stand on it. It was not a quiet process, and I could only hope that the hum of air conditioners covered the noise of crumbling bark and my rasping breath.

Another limb grew a convenient distance above the first one, giving me a place to rest my butt. I was twenty feet above the ground, and my first move was to strap the opposite end of the safety belt I was clever enough to wear around the tree trunk. It would be hard to explain to Jack's gardener the next morning why I was lying under his tree with a broken back.

I then took in the set for the movie I hoped to film. The back yard featured a huge flagstone patio that flowed around a swimming pool and through meticulously groomed flower beds. There were soft electric lights in the plantings and along the edges of the patio, and lights glowed underwater in the pool. The lights didn't illuminate very far into the heavy night air, and I knew that their effect on someone on the patio would be to make things outside their reach even darker.

The back of the house itself had more leaded windows, including a massive bow window in the kitchen. Upstairs, in the middle of the house and slightly below my perch, a row of six adjacent windows looked out from what

I assumed to be the master bedroom. I pulled out my video camera, turned up the magnification, and peered in.

The room looked like a photograph from *Architectural Digest*. Paintings that appeared to be the real thing hung on the walls, antique furniture was tastefully spaced, and a king size rice bed with the spread turned back at one corner was centered on a carpet that must have cost more than a new Mercedes. I could read the time on the gold clock that stood on the night stand by the bed. I told myself I could afford a room like that if I didn't spend so much on expensive video equipment, but I'd have a hard time writing it off as a business expense.

I checked the camera on the back yard, took a swig of water to replace some of the fluid I had sweated out, and settled back to wait. It was ten forty five.

I knew there was a big chance I was wasting my time. I had spent days and weeks in similar circumstances before coming up with anything, and sometimes had discovered nothing at all. On the other hand, I didn't have a lot of choices. I could follow Jack, and might even see him with another man in a public place, but the chances of finding him in a compromising position where I could film him were remote. The best I could hope for would be to see him going into a motel room with someone and coming out later, but that could be explained as some kind of business meeting. I was betting that Jack would feel most at home on his own turf, and I was betting on the strength of the sex urge. Jack's attorney had surely given him the standard advice to be chaste during the pendency of the divorce proceeding, but Jack would as surely ignore it. Everybody else did. I could only hope he didn't pull the curtains too soon.

The night was full of the sounds of a Southern city in the summer. Mosquitoes whined around my ears, and crickets chirped in the grass. Traffic noise was muffled by the humid air and the dense vegetation. Air conditioning units started and stopped, and the occasional dog barked.

It had been a long day, and the fatigue helped my brain slip into neutral and make the waiting easier. Even so, by twelve thirty the ache in my ass and the vision of a cold beer were tempting me to call it a night. I checked the time by looking through my videocam at the clock on Jack's bedside table, and told myself I would wait another fifteen minutes. I waited what I thought was fifteen minutes, and then another estimated five, before I looked at my watch. It was either keeping different time than Jack's clock, or it had only been ten minutes. I circled my left arm around the tree trunk, and stood up to relieve my back and butt.

While I was reaching my right arm and the camera over my head to stretch, I heard a car pull up to the house and stop. There was the sound of a garage door opening and closing, and then a short period of silence. I eased back on to the limb.

A shaft of light spilled out over the yard as a door on the side of the garage opened. I heard low voices, and Jack Jones himself walked down the softly lighted path toward the pool. My heart rate increased. The prey was in the kill zone, and I aimed my weapon at him.

Jack was wearing a white Brooks Brothers shirt, starched pleated khakis, and an alligator belt with moccasins to match. He still had a full head of gray hair, and a golf course tan. Except for a softness under his chin, his features looked young. I had a very, very good camera.

A much younger man was with Jack, which was not unexpected. His appearance was a bit of a surprise, though. I don't know what I had expected, but it was not someone who dressed almost exactly like Jack, and who carried himself with the same patrician air.

The young man sat down in a chair, and Jack disappeared inside the pool house. He came back in a couple of minutes with two martini glasses and a pitcher on a tray, which he set down on a small table beside the other man. Jack poured, and he and his friend touched glasses and sipped. I was too hot to enjoy a martini, but I thought Jack probably mixed a good gin and tonic, too. I could hear the sound of their voices and make out a word here and there, but I couldn't follow their conversation. Halfway through the second drink, though, I noticed Jack's hand resting on the other man's thigh. It was more than enough for me, but I knew Amanda would want all she could get. I didn't have to wait long.

Jack swiveled around in his chair, put his arm around the other man's shoulders, and gave him a long, lingering kiss. I had never seen two grown men kiss each other on the mouth, much less filmed it from twenty feet up a pine tree at one in the morning. The discomfort I felt from the pine branch under my butt and the heat quickly became nothing compared to what I felt as I looked through the camera.

First on the patio furniture, and then in the pool, Jack proceeded to provide all the evidence anyone could want concerning his sexual orientation. Long before Jack and the other man walked naked through the back door and into the house, I had turned off the camera and was trying to identify constellations through the pine needles.

2 ———————————————

I was in Amanda's office in a Front Street high rise the next morning at ten, eager to get rid of the videocassette.

"That was quick," she said, "and you thought it would be hard."

"I got lucky. At least I think I did," I replied.

"What do you mean? Didn't you get the proof?"

"Oh yeah, I got it," I answered. "But there is such a thing as too much information."

"Look," she said, "if you've got the proof I want on that tape, I'll send it over to Morrie Friedlander, Jack's lawyer, this afternoon and we'll settle this case tomorrow. Betty Jo can live comfortably and Jack can go on with his lifestyle. All it will cost Jack is some money, and he's got plenty. For that, we can both see some things we'd rather not."

"Hey," I said, "I don't do domestic relations anymore for anyone but you, and I never did it because I like to see other people have sex."

"Okay, I'll bite," she said. "Why do you do it?"

"I like working with you, the money's good, and I enjoy setting up the shots. I guess I'm just getting where I don't like pulling the trigger on that kind of subject matter," I replied.

"As long as you'll at least mention the money, I'm willing to accept the other bullshit, maybe even believe it," she said. "But I think you're leaving out part of the reason. Now let's watch a movie."

"I saw the live production," I said. "That's more than enough."

I walked out of Amanda's office building on to Front Street and past the bums and winos in Confederate Park. An old man who looked like one of my great uncles gone far out of control stood behind a tree, holding a bottle in a paper bag in one hand and his penis in the other as he watered the grass. A hot, dry wind blew across the river from Arkansas, swarmed up the bluff that kept out the floods and riffled the leaves of the cottonwoods in the park.

I went south, past the old courthouse and the fire station, the river visible on my right as I came to streets that ran across Front and dead ended into Riverside. The river was low in late summer, with sandbars sticking up here and there and barge traffic carefully picking its way through the channel.

I crossed Beale into the old warehouse district where I keep my combination office and apartment. A brass sign at head height was screwed into the hundred year old brick at the corner of the street and the alley that was my official address. It read "John McAlister, Investigations."

I turned right down the alley that ran perpendicular to the river, the walls of the buildings looming close on either side. Fifty feet down the alley, I climbed the outside metal staircase the three stories to my door, past the potted plants and barbecue grills of my neighbors. Another brass nameplate beside the only door at the third and last landing proclaimed my business address again. I don't get much walk-in traffic, but the signs help people find me once they've called for an appointment. The location is pretty obscure, but my clients generally see that as a plus.

I let myself into my office, an 18 by 22 foot rectangle with a 14 foot high ceiling. The walls on three sides were solid brick, with a door in the back wall that led to my living quarters. The west wall was a long series of windows that started three feet up from the floor and ran almost to the ceiling. The shades on all the windows were up, and the river was visible over the tops of the magnolias that grew along the bluff. If I leaned out over the balcony off my living quarters, I could see Cybill Shepherd's house perched on the bluff to the south. I knew, because I had done it more than once. I still hadn't seen Cybill, though.

I checked my answering machine, but there had been no calls since I had left an hour before to see Amanda. I pulled my active files out and flipped through them, but I didn't have the energy to make phone calls or do much of anything else. I was physically and emotionally drained from the night before. I took the phone off the hook, lay down on the old leather couch across from my desk, and was asleep in less than a minute.

I didn't wake up until four o'clock, when the westering sun began to heat up the room despite the air conditioning. I pulled the shades, then went into my apartment and put on workout clothes.

I ran the mile over to the YMCA, and put in a hard hour with the free weights, working my chest and shoulders. I had hit a plateau on the bench press, and wanted to go up at least ten more pounds. It didn't happen this time. I jogged back to my place, and noticed that the light on the answering machine was blinking on the office phone as I went back to my living space. The nap and the workout had made me feel almost human again, but I decided that I would wait until the next day before I even listened to the messages.

I got a Samuel Adams beer out of the refrigerator and put it in the freezer to really cool off while I took a shower. After I got out, I put on a t-shirt and shorts and rescued Sam from the icebox. I had just taken the first swig when the buzzer on my door sounded. I looked through the peephole and opened the door. Amanda had a strange look in her eyes. "Where the hell have you been?" she asked. "I've called at least three times and gotten no answer."

"I've been at the Y," I said, "but tell me again when it was that we got married."

"What are you babbling about?" she asked.

"Look, you've never even been to my office, and all of a sudden you show up acting as if I'm supposed to share my schedule with you," I answered.

"Then you don't know?" she asked.

"Know what?" I responded.

"Jack Jones is dead."

"You're kidding me!" I said.

"No," Amanda said slowly as if I were a child, "I am most definitely not kidding you. He died at three forty five this afternoon at Morrie's office while watching your video. Morrie called and told me after the ambulance had left."

"Good God," I said. "Did he have a heart attack?"

"Morrie said he grabbed his head, then fell over on the floor. He thinks it was a cerebral hemorrhage."

My throat had closed up, and my bowels were churning. I sat down on the couch and stared at Amanda.

"John, did you know who the young man was with Jack last night?" Amanda asked.

"No, did you?"

"Not until Morrie told me. It was Chip Blakeney, Sam Blakeney's son," Amanda said.

"Sam Blakeney, the banker?"

"Sam Blakeney the banker," Amanda answered. "Also Sam Blakeney Jack's roommate at Virginia, and Sam Blakeney Jack's regular golf partner."

"No shit?"

"No shit," Amanda said.

"So what happens now?" I asked. "I mean to Betty Jo's case?"

"Jack and Betty Jo were still married at the time of his death, so she'll take a spouse's elective share and get something like ten or twenty percent of his estate regardless of whether he cut her out of his will," Amanda replied. "I've got to look at the statute. Her percentage depends on how long they were married."

"What about you," I asked, "what do you get since there wasn't a settlement or award?"

"I could tell you that's none of your business, but I won't," Amanda said. "My fee arrangement covers this possibility. I'll get a third of whatever Betty Jo gets."

"Congratulations," I said. "You're a rich woman. Or maybe I should say a richer woman."

"Fuck you," she said. "I didn't come over here to be congratulated."

"Then why did you come?" I asked.

"I really don't know," she answered. "I guess I'll leave. I'll send you a check when I get my money. And there'll be a lot for you. It was your tape that did it."

I had never before seen Amanda looking anything but calm and professional, with a slight air of useful bitchiness. Now, inspecting her more closely, she seemed different. Her blonde hair, usually perfectly coiffed in a shoulder length pageboy, was sticking out here and there, and her makeup was smeared.

She turned to go back out the door.

"Sit down for a minute," I said. "Let me get you something to drink."

"Like I said, I didn't come over here to be congratulated, and I don't feel like celebrating. This isn't that kind of a case," Amanda said, as she turned back to me.

"Look, I'm sorry," I said. "I didn't mean to be an asshole. I just don't know what the appropriate response is here. I mean, I'm glad Betty Jo is going to get some money, and I'm glad you're going to get some money. Hell, I'm glad I'm going to get some money. On the other hand, I'm sorry Jack died. It wasn't what any of us intended."

Amanda sat down on the couch and ran her fingers through her hair. That explained part of her appearance. "I'm sorry, too," she said. "I don't know how to react, either. But I'm trying to fight this overwhelming feeling that I'm responsible for his death. It's been eating at me since Morrie called. Don't you feel that way, too?"

I looked down and noticed the forgotten Sam Adams bottle in my hand. I took a long pull, decided there was no point in confessing the wave of guilt washing through me, and said, "I'm not sure what I feel, but I know in my head that neither one of us is responsible for Jones's death. Your head is better than mine, so you must know it, too. You were representing your client, and I was doing a job. Jack stroking out over the tape is not a foreseeable effect of that."

"I don't know, John, I'm having a hard time going with my head on this one."

"Your head has gotten you a long way," I said. "You ought to stay with it."

3 _____

The heat wave broke the second week of September, bringing the highs down into the mid-eighties and lowering the humidity. It was a temporary respite, and there would be more days in the nineties, but the emotional worst of summer was over.

I had the windows open in my office and was sitting at my desk on a fine blue sky Thursday morning, sipping coffee and watching a barge of gravel work its way up the river when Amanda called. I hadn't heard from her since she had delivered the news of Jack Jones's death, and I knew it would be at least several months before Betty Jo, then Amanda, then I received any money from his estate.

"I've got a case I want you to take, Jack," Amanda said. "Don't worry, it's not a divorce. It's a missing person case."

"Who's missing?" I asked.

"The son of a client," she said. "She's sitting here in my office. I was wondering if you could come over now."

"Now? You must think I'm not very busy," I replied.

"Can you come or not, Jack? It's important," Amanda said.

"No time for levity this morning, huh? Give me fifteen minutes."

I was wearing khakis and a white buttondown shirt, and added a tie and seersucker coat before heading out. Amanda was not a believer in casual day.

Ten minutes later, Amanda's receptionist led me into her office. Amanda was seated behind her glass-topped desk, and in one of her red leather client chairs sat an overweight black woman who appeared to be in her forties. She was wearing orange stretch pants that didn't look like they could stretch any further, and a t-shirt with a picture of a basketball star dunking the ball. For shoes, she was wearing purple house slippers without any heels.

"Ms. Tuggle," Amanda said formally, "this is John McAlister. John, Ms. Tuggle."

"How do you do, ma'am?" I said.

Ms. Tuggle nodded at me, but didn't say anything or offer her hand. I sat down in the other chair and waited.

"Ms. Tuggle's son, Thomas, is missing," Amanda said. "Ms. Tuggle, why don't you tell John about it."

"I done told you, why I got to tell him, too?" she asked.

"Because," Amanda replied patiently, "John is the one who will look for Thomas, not I."

Ms. Tuggle took a deep, ragged breath, and began to speak in an angry voice. "I never had nothing good in this life but Thomas, and now he gone, too. How this white man going to change that?"

"I don't know that I can, but I'm sure that I can't if I don't know what's going on. If you don't want to tell me, I'll go enjoy the rest of my day. It's entirely up to you," I said. I looked across the glass at Amanda and shrugged with my eyebrows.

"Goddamit, Lucy, tell the man the story," Amanda said, in a voice that had made more than one philandering husband fear for his retirement plan and club membership.

"Fuck you, Amanda, don't you be cussin' me," Tuggle hissed back.

"I see you girls know each other already," I said.

"You shut up," Amanda said to me, "and you quit being so pig-headed stubborn and tell the man what you know," she added, jabbing her finger at Amanda.

"I know he gone, and he ain't comin' back, that's what I know," she said, her eyes still defiant but her voice breaking.

"Tell him, Lucy, just tell him," Amanda said quietly.

"'Bout three weeks ago, Thomas was over at my house on a Friday night like always, eatin' supper and drinking wine with me when the police come knocking on the door. They said Thomas been dealin' crack, and started to read him his rights, like they do on TV. Thomas, he been drinking a lot, and he say he ain't had nothing to do with crack, and that the policeman is a lying nigger. The other police, he white, he shoot Thomas with one of them cattle prod guns. Thomas jerk like he havin' a fit and fall down on the floor and start throwing up on the black cop's shoes, and so he get mad and whack Thomas on the back two three times with his night stick. I started in after him with the bottle of wine but the white cop pull his gun and say "freeze, nigger." I know I ain't doing no good against a gun with a bottle of Thunderbird, so I do what he say. Then they each grabs aholt of Thomas and drag him out my house and th'ow him in the police car."

"When did you see him next, Ms. Tuggle?" I asked.

"I ain't never seen him again," she said with a sob. I was afraid for a moment that she was going to break down, but she pulled herself together and went on without any prompting.

"He called me next day and said they set bond on him of twenty thousand, and he already paid it and was out. He said he be over the next Friday night like always for dinner, but he didn't come. I tried to call him three four times, but he never answer, and when he didn't come over the next Friday night, I got my friend to carry me over to his house. Thomas wasn't home, and his neighbors say they ain't seen him in a couple of weeks. "

"I've been over to the neighborhood and asked around, too. Nobody has seen him," Amanda added.

"Have you called the police," I asked, "or is that a stupid question?"

"You're right, that's a stupid question," Amanda said. "They are obviously looking for Thomas, too. He missed his first hearing."

Ms. Tuggle spoke up, "No, I ain't called the police, 'cause that sho' wouldn't be what Thomas wanted me to do and they ain't nobody else to call 'cept Amanda."

"When you went over to the house, did either one of you go inside?" I asked.

"I don't have a key," Ms. Tuggle said.

"What about a court order to get in?" I asked.

"Another stupid question," Amanda said. "That would involve filing a missing person's report with the police."

"And the police would want to come with you to the house, right?" I asked them both.

Now they both gave me the blank stare.

"Look," I said, "if Thomas is wanted for crack dealing and bail jumping, the cops can get into his house anyway. We might as well go in and see what we can find."

Lucy looked at Amanda, and Amanda said to me, "No cops."

"Okay. What line of business is your son in, Ms. Tuggle?" I asked.

"He's in a good line of business, but I don't know what it is. I know it ain't no crack business."

"Do you know the name of his bail bond company?" I asked.

"He probably used Ajax Bond, that's who he got to help me last year when I got in a fight with that woman who used to stay next door. She a crack 'ho and the police arrest me for assault. What kind of justice is that?"

Lucy Tuggle was obviously a member of that large subculture who knew the practical aspects of the criminal justice system from personal experience. A good bail bondsman was an essential part of existence, and probably sent a card at Christmas.

"What about a lawyer, Ms. Tuggle? Had Thomas ever used one before?"

"The last time he was in trouble, he had some no account cracker who didn't know what he was doing. I went down to the trial to testify as a character witness, and he wouldn't even put me on the stand, made me stay out in the hall. I don't even remember his name, but Thomas promised me when he got out of the penal farm that he wouldn't never use him again."

I could imagine Lucy Tuggle's effect on a jury, and knew that Amanda could, too. I purposefully did not look at Amanda as I asked why Thomas had been sent to the penal farm.

"I don't remember," she answered.

"You don't remember?" I asked. "It might in some way help me find Thomas."

"No, I don't remember."

I looked at Amanda for help, but she offered none.

"Is there anything else you can tell me that might help me? Names of friends, other family, business associates?" I asked.

"I don't know his friends and we got no other family. I don't know nothing about his business."

"Ms. Tuggle, you understand that I'm not a policeman. If there's anything that might help, I would like to know it," I said.

Apparently, she had not heard me.

Before I could say anything else, Amanda added, "I have Thomas's picture and address, John. I'll give them to you before you leave. Lucy, I'm sure John will do everything he can to find Thomas."

Lucy conveyed her doubts in my ability by snorting, heaved herself up out of her chair, and shuffled out of the office.

As the door closed behind her, Amanda turned to me and said, "No cracks from you, buddy."

"You don't know me as well as you think you do, Amanda," I said. "If we were having a be polite to Ms. Tuggle contest, I'd be the clear winner. I believe you were the one who called her pig-headed."

"It's one thing how you treat her to her face, it's another what you say after she's gone," Amanda said.

"Well, I won't say she's a vision of loveliness and I plan to ask her out," I said, "but she is a mother concerned about her son, and I feel bad for her, even if I can't relate to sitting around with my mom getting shit-faced on cheap wine. Maybe with Dad."

Amanda curled one side of her lovely lips, but only asked, "Do you feel bad enough to look for Thomas?"

"First, tell me how you know her."

"Lucy and I grew up together," Amanda said. "She comes to me when she has a problem."

"You mean you went to private school together and swam at the country club while your mothers played tennis?"

"You know what I mean, smartass. Lucy's mother was our housekeeper. We're the same age and played together when we were kids."

"Sort of like in *Gone with the Wind*, huh?" I asked.

"Yeah, just like that. Now, I have to be in court in thirty minutes. Will you help Lucy or not?"

"I'll see what I can do. But you know the two likeliest scenarios as well as I do. First, Thomas has skipped town for a while. He's in Chicago or Detroit and he'll be back for Christmas. Second, his crack buddies have killed him. If so, his body will show up any day and the case will be solved, no thanks to me."

"Maybe you can find out if he left town. That would ease Lucy's mind," Amanda said.

"Everyone I talk to about Thomas will be about as forthcoming as Lucy. Besides, if he's alive, he'd have gotten in touch with her."

"Well, he hasn't."

"Which means . . . "

"Not necessarily," Amanda said.

"99% is not enough?" I asked.

"John, I've given you a lot of good business over the years. You owe me this," Amanda said with a look that was both exasperated and pleading.

"Amanda," I said, "you know I'll do it. I just hate to see us both waste our time."

She gave me a relieved look, and murmured a quiet thank you.

"Okay, okay," I said. "So tell me what you know about Thomas."

"I don't really know much," she said. "Lucy had him when she was fifteen, which would make him about twenty-seven, since she and I are the same age. Her mother quit working for us right after Thomas was born, and we didn't stay in touch. I was a freshman in high school, and I remember feeling that Lucy was much older."

"When did you see her next?" I asked.

"Not till I was in college. My mother heard that her mother had died, and she asked Lucy if she wanted to work for us. I was home one summer while she was our maid, and she brought Thomas over now and then. He was a cute little boy. But by the time I came back for Christmas break, Lucy was gone. Mom said the silver and booze kept disappearing, so she finally let Lucy go. Lucy ended up the way you saw her today."

"I bet I hadn't thought of Lucy in ten years," she continued, "when she called me one day after I had started practicing law. She said she had heard I was a lawyer, and asked me if I would help her in a dispute with her landlord. Since then she'll call me every two or three years with some problem."

"Did you get her off the assault charge she mentioned?" I asked.

"No, that's the first time I heard about that one, but it doesn't surprise me. She's always had a temper."

"What did Lucy tell you about Thomas?"

"Not much. I know he graduated from high school, she was real proud of that. The last time I saw her she just said he was a businessman, and doing real well."

"What's going on with the Jones estate?" I asked, changing the subject. "Do you see any problems?"

"No, but it won't happen any time soon. What does that have to do with Lucy?"

"I don't expect to get paid on Jones till you get paid, but I'll make you a deal. You pay me for Tuggle, and then when Jones comes in you deduct the Tuggle fee and pay me from that."

"I'll pay you for Lucy anyway," she said. "I'm not asking you to work for free."

"I know you're not, but this is the way I want to do it. Maybe the PI society will give me the do-gooder award."

"You're not the one feeling guilty about Jones now, are you? Is this atonement?" she asked.

"That's just the way I want to do it, okay?" I said.

"Okay, would you like an advance?"

"An advance is always nice."

"How about a thousand?" she said.

"A thousand is always nice."

She pulled a checkbook out of her drawer and wrote a check. She handed it to me along with a legal sized envelope and said, "Now I have to go to court. You find Thomas, Jack. I'm counting on you."

4

I went to the bank and deposited my check, and then sat down outside on a bench and opened Amanda's envelope. Inside was a Polaroid of Lucy standing in front of a Christmas tree with one arm around a slender young black man with a light complexion. Lucy was dressed about the way she had been at Amanda's office, but Thomas had on a smart blue blazer with gold buttons, a striped button-down shirt, and gray slacks.

Thomas's address and phone number was on a separate piece of paper. I knew from working a previous case that the address was on a street in a neighborhood of affluent African-American professionals and business people. I strolled over to the public library and checked the city directory to see if it listed a business address for Thomas, but all it had was his home, the same as Lucy had given me.

I picked up a sandwich at the Front Street Deli and returned to my office. I ate lunch while I returned phone calls and went through the mail. In one envelope was a check for $800 from a client that I had decided was never going to pay. This was looking like one of those days that it did pay to get out of bed.

About two thirty, I headed down to the Ajax Bail Bond Company. It was located across the street from the Criminal Justice Center, on the north edge of downtown, at 201 Poplar Avenue, the main thoroughfare from the river out to the affluent suburbs of Germantown and Collierville. The Justice

Center is an imposing gray stone building built in the early 1980s to relieve prisoner crowding. It was nicknamed the Glamour Slammer because of the supposed amenities it would offer prisoners. Ask any local businessman who has spent his 48 hours there for a first-time DUI and he'll tell you how glamorous it is.

Ajax had a blinking blue neon sign that operated even in the afternoon. It was in a one-story brick building separated from its neighbors only by firewalls. A liquor store occupied the space on the west, and a pawnshop was on the east. It was a complete urban strip mall, offering liberty, the pursuit of happiness and the means for financing both.

Black men, young and old, loitered on the sidewalk in front of the three businesses. Almost all smoked cigarettes, and some sucked liquor or wine from bottles hidden in paper sacks. Women strolled back and forth across Poplar to and from the jail, some carrying babies or holding children's hands, obstructing traffic and not seeming to notice. Visiting day.

Cars waited more or less patiently for a gap in the pedestrians. Memphians don't blow horns unless someone is about to run into them.

I walked in through the propped open door of Ajax Bond and stopped to let my eyes adjust to the dimness. When I could focus, I saw I was in a square room divided by a waist high wooden counter. There were rows of file cabinets covering the back wall behind the counter, and two metal desks with rolling chairs. On my side of the counter there were cheap vinyl-covered chairs and stacks of magazines on end tables. A strong odor of disinfectant filled the air. In one of the chairs a man sat looking at me.

He was dressed in blue jeans and a tight white t-shirt that showed an athlete's torso. He wore a semiautomatic pistol in a holster high on his right hip, and a gold watch on his left wrist with an intricately braided gold band. His hair was cut short, but not shaved. He wore half lens reading glasses, and a book was closed on his left forefinger.

"May I help you?" he asked without much feeling.

"I understand you wrote the bond for a man named Thomas Tuggle," I answered. "I'm trying to get a lead on him and thought you might help."

"You're not a cop. I've never seen you before," he said. "Unless you're a Fed. But I'd say you're a lawyer."

"Neither one. I'm a private investigator," I said as I handed him my card.

He took it, stuck it in his book as a bookmark without looking at it, and placed the book on the counter.

"Are you the owner?" I asked.

"Yeah, I'm the owner," he replied.

"I'm John McAlister," I said, and stuck out my hand.

He looked at my hand for a second, then took it softly in a big dry hand.

"Henry Jackson is my name," he said. "So you're looking for Thomas. Well, me too."

"So you did write his bond?" I asked.

"Yeah, I wrote it and I regret it. He missed his court date last week and I'm looking at nine thousand dollars if he's not back soon," he replied.

"I thought it was twenty thousand for the bond, which would leave you eighteen grand since he paid you two," I said.

"I reinsure half my risk, but I still don't want to pay nine. What's your interest in Tuggle?" he asked.

"Missing person case," I said. "The family hired me."

"You're bullshitting me, right? If Thomas even has a family, they're not the type to hire a PI to look for him."

"His mother is his family. She said you would know who she is."

"Oh, God, yes, I remember her now. I bailed her out on an assault. But don't tell me she hired you to find Thomas."

"Well, a friend of the family got me involved," I said.

"A white friend, huh? Noblesse oblige and all that," he said.

"Maybe. I'm working for the money."

"Yeah, me too. If I don't find him I lose a lot of it. What have you found so far?"

"You're my first stop. I've got a picture and an address, and that's it."

"You don't have shit. You working contingency or hourly?" he asked.

"Hourly," I said.

He laughed. "You don't have shit and you don't give a shit, right?"

"Well, I've got my reputation to think of."

"I've never heard of you," he said.

"I try to keep a low profile, you know," I said.

"Must be real low," he said. "Well, it's early, not much going on. I might as well tell you what I can about Tuggle. Even a blind pig finds an acorn now and then."

He apparently shared Lucy Tuggle's assessment of my abilities.

"Sit down," he said, gesturing to a chair covered in aqua blue vinyl. He went behind the counter and poured himself a cup of coffee from an old-fashioned electric percolator with a glass bulb on top. "You want some?" he asked.

"No thanks. Too late in the day for me," I replied.

"Man, I'm just getting started. I open at two in the afternoon and close at two in the morning. I wish the police would just arrest folks between nine and five."

"Must be tough on your social life. Now what can you tell me about Tuggle?"

He knelt and opened the bottom drawer of one of the filing cabinets, pulled out a file folder and sat down at one of the desks.

"Thomas Jefferson Tuggle," he read from the file. "He must be the last black man in America to be named after a signer of the Declaration of Independence. Born November fifteenth, nineteen seventy-seven, arrested four times, served four months of an eleven month, twenty-nine day sentence at the penal farm for receiving stolen property. Always showed up for hearings in the past. Rated a very good risk."

"Maybe he was scared of a crack rap," I said. "That would carry a lot bigger jolt than receiving stolen property."

"They would have never made a crack dealer rap stick on Thomas. He knew that," he replied.

"Do you think he was dealing crack?" I asked.

"Thomas dealing crack? Man, you weren't lying when you said you didn't know much about him. Thomas doesn't deal crack, he's the Designer."

"He's the what?" I asked.

"The Designer, man. Like designer clothes and shoes," he said.

"He has a line of designer clothes?"

"No, no, Thomas sells them. Hilfiger, Polo clothes, Nike shoes, all sorts of sports stuff."

"I assume he's not a licensed distributor," I said.

"No, he's a thief. Or at least he gets other people to steal it for him. Kids go into department stores and grab a whole stack of jeans and run out to a car waiting for them. Or somebody breaks into a truck or a train car, or even a warehouse, and gets the stuff. You know what they say, man. Memphis is America's distribution center. Anyway, the thieves bring it to Thomas because he gives them a fair price."

"How does he sell it?" I asked.

"On the black market, no pun intended. He's got a van that he drives into the neighborhoods. He pulls up at a store or playground after dark and sets up shop. Word goes out real quick that the Designer is on the scene. He sells at a forty percent discount off retail and still makes a killing."

"Free enterprise at work, huh? So what do you think has happened to him?" I asked.

"It beats the hell out of me," he said, shaking his head.

"My first guesses are out of town or dead," I said. "What do you think about those options?"

"If it weren't Thomas, I'd say you were right," he responded. "But Thomas has got a thriving business and this crack rap was bullshit. I don't think he'd leave town. A real crack dealer might. I've had four skip out on me during the last twelve months. I don't write them anymore."

"What about the dead choice?"

"It's more likely, but I'm having a hard time believing that one, too."

"Why?" I asked. "You don't think Thomas was dealing crack, but the police do. Even if he's not, here's a guy who was driving around in war zones with all kinds of cash, and everybody knew it."

"I see your point, but Thomas was an urban legend, almost a hero. Some crackhead might off him for his cash, but the average gangbanger would no more shoot him than he would Jesse Jackson. And if a crackhead had shot him, the cops would have found the body the next day. Somebody like that is not going to hide a corpse, at least not well."

"You seem to have a pretty good handle on this crack stuff," I said.

"I ought to. One way or the other it supplies a good chunk of my business. People get arrested for buying it, selling it, using it, stealing for it, whoring for it, killing for it."

"Did you ever use it?" I asked.

"Do I look stupid?"

"I was just wondering what people see in it."

"If you want to find out, you can go out there on the sidewalk and buy some right now. And if you're like nine out of ten people, it'll be the first day of the end of your life."

"My curiosity doesn't extend to that personal risk," I said.

"Then maybe you're not as dumb as you look," he said.

"I appreciate that," I said. "I think."

"What else can I tell you?" he asked. "Business will start picking up soon."

"Does Thomas have a lawyer?" I asked.

"Not as far as I know. He had Clyde Johnson when he got sent to the penal farm the last time he was arrested. But I called Clyde a couple of days ago and he said he wasn't representing him and hadn't heard from him in years."

"Did Thomas say anything about why he might have been arrested for crack?" I asked.

"Just that he had no idea why. He figured it was some mistake. The cops make them sometimes."

"Well, thank you for your time," I said. "You've got my card there in your book if you think of anything else."

He turned the book on the counter over, opened it to my card, and stuck the card in the pocket of his t-shirt. He was reading a law school casebook on securities regulation.

"Are you going to law school?" I asked.

"Yeah, I'm in my last year. Does that surprise you?" he asked.

"No, but it impresses me. Working a full time job and getting through three years of grind would take more energy than I have."

"How do you know? Did you go to law school?" he asked, pulling my card out of his pocket and looking at it for the first time.

"Yeah, but I don't practice anymore," I said.

He looked at me questioningly, but didn't say anything.

"Are you going to stay in this line, do criminal work?" I asked.

"No, man, I'm going to get as far away from it as I can," he replied. "I want to do corporate and securities work. I'm tired of whores and thieves."

5

By the time I got back to the office, it was after four. I put in a call to an acquaintance at the DA's office, but didn't get anything but her voice mail. I decided to wrap it up for the day.

I put on my workout clothes and ran over to the Y. I did weights and then stayed on the treadmill too long trying to impress the twenty five-year-old aerobics instructor who was on the stationary bike next to me. Just when I knew I couldn't go on, she got off and left with some guy even younger than she was with tattoos and an earring. I walked home slowly, and decided right before I got there that I probably wasn't going to puke.

I showered and drank a beer, and then made a sandwich, my second nutritious meal of the day. After I ate, I cleaned up and made a pot of decaffeinated coffee. I got a light blanket and took a cup out on the balcony.

The air was at least ten degrees cooler than when I had come in an hour before, and a strong breeze from the north added to the chill. Despite the city glow, the stars were out in a navy blue sky. Reflections from the lights on the M-shaped Hernando DeSoto bridge shimmered and danced on the black, shifting surface of the river. Interstate 40, from Los Angeles to the Carolina coast, and Interstate 55, from the Gulf of Mexico to Chicago, both crossed that bridge. On the river, barges cruised up and down, south towards Natchez and New Orleans, north towards St. Louis. Despite all the traffic, I was far enough removed that the noise was only a distant rumble.

I sat down on a reclining lawn chair covered with a plastic and foam pad, and pulled the blanket over me. I sipped my coffee and let my mind wander over the day. I tried to think about the Tuggle case, but my inclination for analytical thought was non-existent.

Despite a half-hearted effort not to let them go there, my thoughts drifted to my ex-wife. She was in business school at Vanderbilt when I was in law school. Mutual friends had fixed us up, knowing that I was from Memphis and that she had accepted an offer from Federal Express. She was from Michigan, short, vivacious and brunette, with a direct way about her that was new and different for a southern boy. There was never any doubt in my mind that I loved her more than she loved me.

Neither one of us had much money, but she was determined to get as much as she could, and made no apologies for her attitude. It was the go-go eighties, and she could have joined an investment banking firm in New York or a Silicon Valley company, but she thought an established but innovative company like FedEx fit in better with her life plan. I wasn't established or innovative, but I must have fit in somewhere, so we got married two weeks after graduation.

We moved into a one-bedroom apartment in midtown, and I took the bar exam and then started as an associate with the Lipscomb Riley firm. It wasn't the largest firm in the city, but it was one of the oldest and most prestigious. Kathleen started immediately at FedEx.

I went straight to the commercial litigation team at Lipscomb Riley, working on commercial disputes between Fortune 500 companies that generated rooms full of documents and shelves of deposition transcripts. The name of the game was wearing down the other side and evaluating your chances before trial with endless discovery requests and pre-trial motions on every conceivable issue. In the eight years I was at the firm, every major case I worked on but two settled before trial, and one of those settled immediately after closing arguments to the jury. The party on the other side got nervous and made a settlement offer, but our client almost beat him to it. We won the other case at the trial level, but the last I heard it was still on appeal.

Toughness, and even meanness, were virtues, and I aspired to both. By my fourth year, I was traveling around the country taking depositions and interviewing witnesses while bolstering my billable hours with time in cabs and on airplanes. I was making money for myself and even more for the firm, and I was determined to be a partner.

Looking back, I can't logically explain my determination. It had a lot to do with trying to live up to Kathleen's expectations, but it was also just a matter of getting caught up in the race. There was a seven-year partnership track, but I realized early on that making partner didn't mean you stopped working. The partners, especially those in their thirties and forties, worked just as hard as the associates. They had nicer cars and bigger houses, but they were fatter and balder. All I knew was that I was going to win the race. I didn't question whether it was worth running.

Kathleen was running the same race in the corporate world. She quickly became a favorite of her boss, and traveled the world, making presentations and gathering and analyzing data. We had part of most weekends together, but little time else except when we were asleep. Still, I was in love and couldn't imagine being without her.

When Kathleen's boss, a guy in his early forties, was relocated to Los Angeles to head up a Pacific Rim project, we had even less time. The company leased an apartment for her in LA, and she started staying there during the week if she wasn't traveling to Asia or Australia. At first, she came home most weekends, but pretty soon it was every other weekend at best. I went out there as much as I could, but that wasn't much.

On a Thursday morning in early December, three members of the firm's management committee came into my office and shut the door. It was a year before I was due to make partner, so I thought there wasn't any reason for them to be there except to fire me. I was wrong. I had made partner a year early, only the second person to fast track in the history of the firm.

After they left my office, I picked up the phone and started to dial Kathleen. I was full of pride and success, and I couldn't wait to share it. But then I decided to surprise her. I was supposed to fly out to LA for the weekend on Friday anyway, so I changed my ticket and left that afternoon.

It was a clear, cool night in California. The taxi dropped me at her place about nine. Her car was out front, so I knew she was home. I used my key and let myself in.

The front room was dark, but there was a diffused light from a glow in the bedroom. I was halfway across the room before it registered on me that the light was from the candles that Kathleen liked to light before making love.

Then I heard her voice, saying things she hadn't said to me in years.

I should have left then, but I couldn't help myself. I edged up to the door of the bedroom, and saw her astride her boss, her head thrown back and her breasts in his hands. It was an image I knew I would never get out of my head, but it was what she was saying that tore my heart out.

They never saw me. I left quietly and took a redeye back to Memphis. I called the next day and said that work would keep me from coming out for the weekend. I never told her I had been there that night. A month later, she asked for a divorce.

I fell asleep in my chair sometime before midnight, and woke up chilled and shivering at two a.m. I went inside and got in bed without really waking up.

6

Right at dawn, sleeping on my stomach, I woke up to a warm weight on my butt and two strong hands making lazy circles on my back. I lay still, and pretended I was still asleep, till the hands left my back and bare feet slid down the outsides of my legs. Soft breasts with hard nipples pushed against my back, and hair tickled my neck and the side of my face.

"Wake up, love, and turn over," a husky voice whispered in my ear.

I did as I was told, and smiled into blue eyes. She looked down at me. "Have you been awake all this time or do you have to go to the bathroom?"

"Awake," I answered.

"Good," she said, reaching into my nightstand, "I don't want to wait any longer."

Later, holding an armful of warm Dutch flight attendant, I asked her how long she was in town.

"Just till day after tomorrow, then back to Amsterdam. I'm too tired to go back to my place. Can I sleep here?"

"You know you can, but I have to get up," I said.

"Not till I go to sleep," she said, tightening her arm around my chest.

Mary Arenduyk had been on the Amsterdam to Memphis flight for nine months, and shared an apartment below me with four other attendants, two or three of whom might be in town at the same time. I liked her, and she liked me, and we had agreed that it probably wouldn't get beyond that, but it was still fun. I didn't ask her about men in Holland, and she didn't ask me about other women in Memphis. For me, there weren't any, but I didn't see the point of forcing the issue.

After her breathing slowed and her arm relaxed across my chest, I slipped out of bed and showered. Then I dressed quietly, and had coffee and cereal on the balcony before going into the office.

I made phone calls for an hour or two on other cases, then turned my attention to Tuggle.

It was likely that the police had known Thomas was a fence, especially since he had served time, but for some reason they had decided he was also into crack. Maybe he was, but his bondsman thought the idea was ridiculous. Looking at it objectively, I had to agree with Jackson. Thomas had obviously devoted a great deal of time to his stolen garments business, which appeared to be hugely successful. I had practiced law and worked as a PI long enough to know that many courses in life weren't dictated by good sense, but Thomas's success indicated he had some sense. A crack dealer's life was violent and usually short, and not as profitable as Thomas's venture. Thomas would be in the ideal position to compare the two industries, and I doubted he would choose to diversify into crack.

I called an acquaintance in the district attorney's office and explained my situation. She would not confirm my suspicion that the probable cause for Thomas's arrest came from an informant. She did confirm Jackson's statement that Thomas did not have an attorney of record, but represented himself at the bail hearing. And she gave me the names of the arresting officers.

I had to decide where to concentrate my search. I could try to see if Thomas had any associates or friends who might know his whereabouts, but they were even less likely than his mother to be candid. Besides, I felt pretty confident that if Henry Jackson had not heard anything from his clientele, it was unlikely that I would have any better luck.

The unconfirmed informant was the obvious best potential source of meaningful information, but identifying him or her and then getting them to talk was going to be a challenge. If they even existed. The arresting officers might not even know the name of the informant, and their supervisor probably wouldn't tell me. The police would have their own investigation into Thomas's disappearance, but their purpose in finding him would be to arrest a bail jumper, not to ease his mother's heart. I doubted very much that they would want to give out any information that might let me find him first.

One possibility was to have Amanda enter an appearance as Thomas's attorney of record, and ask for the government's case against him in order to defend it. I didn't know enough about criminal law to know if this was practical, or if she would even be allowed to represent him without proof that he had hired her. I would ask her about the feasibility of doing it that way, but I didn't think it would reveal anything fast. In the meantime, I decided to give it a shot my own way.

I looked in on Mary, who was still sleeping heavily. I left her a note, and then walked the block to the parking garage where I kept my truck. I drove down Union Avenue through the medical center and past every fast food outlet known to man to the west precinct station house, parked, and walked in. The police probably wouldn't tell me anything, but I figured it wouldn't hurt to ask. And if I asked in person, instead of over the telephone, it might be a little bit harder to say no.

Except for the police cars parked around, the station looks like any other business on the street. It doesn't look much different in the public areas inside, either, except for the uniforms, and it smells better than the fast food restaurants, since all arrested suspects go directly to the Criminal Justice Center downtown without a stop at the precinct.

The civilian receptionist took my card and request to speak to a detective and politely asked me to take a seat. I sat down and flipped through a fitness magazine. I had just decided that the text wasn't much but that some of the pictures were pretty good when a door opened and a voice said "Mr. McAlister?"

I looked up and saw an angular white man well over six feet, with his wet looking dark blond hair cut just on the long side of a flattop. He was wearing grey pleated slacks, a starched blue button down shirt and an expensive-looking tie that matched his light green eyes. An empty tan leather holster was attached to the belt on the left side of his waist, positioned for a cross draw with his right hand.

"Yes," I said, standing up. He stuck out his right hand and introduced himself. "I'm Lieutenant Steiner, detective squad. I understand that you asked for a detective?"

I nodded my head as I shook his hand. "Come on back to my office," he said, leading me through the door.

I followed him down a couple of halls, breathing his cologne and another half familiar scent all the way. A surreptitious sniff at my hand revealed that I smelled like both odors now, too.

He turned into a small office that contained a metal desk and a swivel chair, and was lined with filing cabinets. It was an internal office, so there were no windows. There were no photographs on the walls or desk, just a pile of folders on one side and a spread open newspaper on the other side. On the newspaper there was a greasy looking rag and a short pistol barrel cleaning rod with a dirty cotton patch stuck in the end. An open bottle of Hoppe's gun oil lent its fruity smell to the room and answered my question about the mystery odor. A Smith & Wesson Chief's Special with the three inch barrel and an open cylinder lay on the paper beside a box of .38 Special hollow points.

"Sorry for the mess," he said, sitting down behind the desk and waving at another chair. "I was at the range this morning and I didn't get a chance to clean my weapon there."

"No problem," I said. "I've always liked the smell of Hoppe's. It reminds me of my father. He would always use it to clean his shotgun after he went duck hunting."

"You duck hunt?" he asked, running the rod through each one of the chambers in the cylinder.

"Sometimes," I said. "I don't belong to a club, but I'll go two or three times a year with friends. Sort of for old times sake. What about you?"

"No, I'm out at four in the morning freezing my ass off enough in this job not to want to do it for fun."

I could have asked him about his golf game then, or whether he was a University of Memphis basketball fan, and kept on talking for another fifteen or twenty minutes about nothing. But I didn't say anything for a minute while he peered through each of the five chambers.

He then set the gun down on the paper with the cylinder still open. "So, how can I help you?"

I explained about Thomas, and told him the name of the two arresting officers. "I was told they were working out of this precinct, and so I thought you might be able to tell me something that would help me find Tuggle," I said. "I assume you're looking for him, too, so I figured you wouldn't mind telling me what you know," I lied. "I'll be glad to tell you what I know, but it's not much."

"I'm familiar with the Tuggle case," he said. "But you go first."

I had already decided that, despite Lucy's wishes, talking to the police wouldn't harm Thomas. She had the ingrained distrust of the police that was almost a genetic code in many of her race, even though the mayor and about half of the force were now black. The police were already looking for Thomas, and they might let something slip that would let me find him first. If I found him, I could then decide what to do about the law. And I doubted that I knew anything that they didn't.

I told him that I was working for the family, and that I had talked to Thomas's bail bondsman. I told him that Jackson didn't think Thomas was a crack dealer, but I didn't mention his other business. Basically, I told him that I didn't have anything.

When I had finished, he said, "That's it so far, huh?"

"Yeah, it's not much, and I don't know if it's going to get any better," I said.

"You realize if you find him that you have a legal obligation to advise us, right? If you don't, you'll be an accessory," he said.

"I hadn't really thought about it like that, but I guess you're right," I said.

"Now," he said, "you said you're working for his family. Do you mind telling me exactly which family member?"

I didn't see any point in not answering, so I told him I was working for Thomas's mother.

"If a crack dealer's mother is paying you to look for him, she's probably doing it with money he made selling crack," he said. "That bother you?"

I started to tell him about Amanda, but decided not to. I didn't want him calling her and asking her questions.

I shrugged. "I don't have any indications that's where she's getting my fee."

He smiled and began to load his revolver.

"I'm serious," I said. "His mother doesn't think he's a crack dealer, which I admit doesn't carry a hell of a lot of weight, but neither does his bondsman. His bondsman said he wouldn't have put up the bond for him if he thought he was."

Steiner was picking rounds out of the cartridge box using the oily rag to cover his fingers. He didn't want fingerprint oil to get on the shells and then transfer to the insides of the cylinder and cause rust. He filled all five chambers, and then gently closed the cylinder using the oily rag over his hand. Holding only the checkered walnut grips, he slipped the little gun into its holster and snapped the strap.

"Everybody else is going around with fifteen shot semi-automatics these days. You feel comfortable with a five shot revolver?" I asked.

"You know what they say," he replied, grinning. "It's not what you got, but how you use it. No, really, the guys out in the patrol cars need the firepower, they never know what's going to pop up. But I'm comfortable with five shots in my job because I know where they're going, and most of the people who'll be shooting at me with their Berettas and Glocks have no idea how to hit anything with a firearm. They watch television, they think you just point the gun in the general direction of someone, pull the trigger, and they fall over dead. They need fifteen shots to have a chance of connecting, and they're still most likely to shoot some innocent passerby."

"You know this from experience?" I asked.

"Yeah," he said and grinned again, with a sparkle in his eyes.

I smiled back at him automatically, but I didn't like that grin. When I didn't say anything, he asked, "What else do you know about Thomas Tuggle?"

"Jackson, his bondsman, told me he had served time for receiving stolen property. I've got his picture and his address. That's about it."

"That's not much." He screwed the top back on the bottle of Hoppe's and stuck it in a shoebox with the rest of the cleaning material. He put the top on the box and put it away in a drawer. Either he hadn't heard about oily rags and spontaneous combustion, or he didn't care. At least he put the cartridges in a separate drawer.

I figured it was his turn, so I asked, "Why did the police think Thomas was dealing?"

"We had probable cause to believe that he was," Steiner replied.

"Can you tell me what that was?" I asked.

"No, I really can't. It will come out in the court proceeding, if there ever is one," he said as he wiped his hands on a wad of tissues.

"Can you tell me if it was an informant?" I asked, hoping for some type of indication that it was, even if he wouldn't tell me whom.

"I really can't say one way or the other," he replied evenly. If he gave some hint as to the answer, I didn't pick it up.

"Do you have any ideas where he might be?" I asked. "I mean in general."

"I couldn't tell you if I did," he replied. "I tell you what I think, and you tell his mother, and she tells him, and he goes somewhere else. Then I'm the dumbass."

"You think that's why she hired me?" I asked. His statement implied that I was the dumbass, and he didn't want me to pass it on.

"Probably not. It's a lot of trouble for a little bit of information, but you never know."

"Well, I won't take up any more of your time," I said, standing up. "Thanks for talking to me."

"Are you licensed to carry?" he asked, as he stood up, too.

"Yes," I said. "Why do you ask?"

"Because looking for a crack dealer can be dangerous work. He's not going to stop and let you explain that you're not a cop, that his momma just wants him to call home. He's going to shoot you dead. If you're licensed to carry, do it. Better yet, forget the whole thing and let us find him."

"I've never heard of a cop telling a private citizen to carry a weapon," I said.

"You're a PI, so you cross the line. If you're going to persist in acting like a cop, you'd better be ready to defend yourself. If you do get a line on Thomas, the best thing you can do is call me."

"Even if he can't shoot straight?" I asked.

He gave me the same disturbing grin. "He doesn't have to shoot straight if he puts the muzzle against the back of your head."

As I drove back downtown, I tried to figure out if I had learned anything. It was pretty easy to decide that I hadn't. I then tried to decide if Steiner had learned anything from me that would be useful to him in finding Thomas. Other than the fact that I was looking for him, too, I couldn't think of anything I had said that would help him. I didn't figure the police would have the resources to follow me around just on the off chance it might help them catch one accused crack dealer. I also figured that they weren't doing much proactively to find him in the first place. They probably assumed that he had blown town and that their best chance of getting him back would be when he got arrested the next time in another city and the outstanding warrant showed up on the computer. Call it a wash.

I had thought about asking Steiner what he knew about Thomas's wholesale to the consumer business, but, even though I assumed he knew about it, I concluded that it was probably not a good idea. Amanda was going to be pissed anyway if she found out I had talked to the cops at all, much less suggested to them that Thomas was engaged in a lucrative criminal enterprise.

I got back to the office around five, and found a note from Mary saying to call her if I wanted to go out for dinner. I checked my voice mail and flipped through the bills and offers for credit cards that the mailman had left me, then went into my apartment for a beer.

I sat on the balcony facing west, and watched the earth spin me away from the sun. Cicadas hummed from the stand of magnolias beneath my window, and the direct sunlight on my face was still hot but not as heavy as August. It was barely fall by the calendar, but during the day it was still more summer than autumn.

I was going nowhere fast on the Tuggle investigation, and I wasn't sure how to pick up the pace. I would talk to Amanda tomorrow about her trying to get information on the police's case against Thomas, especially the identity of an informant, but I thought there should be something else I could do.

I finished my beer and went inside and called Mary. I told her to be ready in ten minutes and dress casual. When I stopped by to get her, she was dressed in sandals, blue jeans and a white t-shirt that almost came down to her navel. It was obvious she was not wearing a bra.

"Am I okay for where we are going?" she asked. I loved it when she didn't use contractions.

"If you were any more okay you'd cause a riot," I said. I saw from the look in her eyes that she was trying to understand this remark, so I quickly added, "You look perfect, great."

She smiled, gave me a quick kiss and picked up her purse and a margarita in a plastic cup. I declined a drink for the road, and we went down to the garage where I kept my pickup.

We headed out of downtown on Third Street just as full dark came on. As we got further into south Memphis, knots of young black men stood on street corners, talking and jiving and listening to boom boxes. Hookers cruised the sidewalks, and cop cars cruised the streets, but both groups looked like it was still too early to really get down to business.

Then the road ran under an Illinois Central railroad overpass, and dropped down off the last Chickasaw Bluff onto the Mississippi Delta. In daytime, the levee that snaked down the side of the river for hundreds of miles would have been visible on our right, and we could have seen the end of the hills from the east on our left. Even at night, though, and in a vehicle going sixty-five miles per hour, there was a strong sense of utter flatness, of uninterrupted space. Of no place to hide.

Casino gambling had come to northwest Mississippi in the 1990s in a big way, and now ranked behind only Vegas and Atlantic City as a gaming destination. We were soon in the midst of thousands of other people from the city who were making the short trip down the highway to try their luck. Billboards and gas stations appeared in the cotton and soybean fields that lined the road, and then we could see the casinos on our right along the river. By law, they had to be on the water, but the requirement was interpreted very loosely, and a small canal that ran around the casino and connected to the river was enough. The fields along the river had been owned by large farmers who already had plenty of money, but who had sold or leased parts of their land to the gambling interests and suddenly climbed several more notches on the wealth scale.

The casinos had brought jobs and money to Tunica County, one of the poorest in the country, and offered another form of entertainment to the region, gaming and Vegas type shows. They had also provided some people with the opportunity to discover they could not resist the temptation to bet, even if losing the money meant their children would go hungry.

Mary hadn't said a word since we crossed into Mississippi, but had sat with her window wide open and her legs pulled up under her, breathing in the cool night air and the smells of the drying vegetation in the fields. Despite several months off and on in Memphis, it still had the newness and excitement of a foreign country to her. This sense was heightened by the vast differences between her urbanized, sophisticated country, and a place like Memphis that was set down in the middle of vast stretches of forest and farmland, and held areas within the city limits that it was worth your life to drive into at night. The Netherlands were already old and settled when Chickasaws were the only human residents in what is now Memphis. In the town's early days, bears had roamed the streets at night, picking off free-ranging pigs and stray dogs. The nighttime predators were still there, but they weren't just looking for a meal anymore.

Mary felt me looking at her, and turned and smiled at me. "I like this," she said.

"I like you," I said.

She put her hand on my thigh and turned back to the window. She still hadn't asked where we were going, and made no comment as we rode past the last turn off for the casinos.

The traffic thinned out as we left the gambling crowd behind. We went through the town of Tunica and headed on down, deeper into the Delta, till we got to an intersection with a two-lane state highway and turned right, west toward the river. In a few miles, the highway came to the levee and turned south. We stayed on it for less than a mile, paralleling the levee. I slowed and turned off on a gravel road that ran up and over the levee and into a stand of trees. No other cars were visible, but a haze of dust in the headlights showed that we weren't the only ones to come this way.

We came out of the trees into a cotton field that stretched away on both sides as far as you could see in the starlight. The taillights of two or three other vehicles showed ahead of us. A ground fog was starting to form in the field, and I shivered in the damp breeze that came through Mary's window. She must have felt my leg shake, because she patted it once and rolled up her window.

The field eventually came to an end in another stand of trees. We could see lights shining through the trunks and branches. We pulled into an open place in the trees that served as a parking lot, stopped between two other pickups, and got out onto a surface that was part gravel, part dust and part flattened beer cans. Dozens of cars, trucks and motorcycles were parked helter skelter around us. Light and honky tonk music shot out at us from a building barely visible through the trees.

As we got closer to the source of the lights and music, we could see an old one story structure made of gray, weathered boards with a rusted tin roof. It sat out over black water, supported by pilings that stuck up a good ten feet out of the water, its floor higher than our heads. A ramp made out of wide planks ran from the shore to an uncovered porch along the right side of the building. A frame without a door stood at the end of the ramp, and a neon sign affixed to its top proclaimed "Dude's Joint."

Dude's was built over an oxbow lake, formed when the river changed channels and left a semicircular lake, full of the fish and other creatures that lived in the Mississippi. Cypress trees dotted its shoreline and grew out in the lake, their knees sticking up here and there out of the water like shark fins. It filled in some each year with mud and vegetation, but the annual flood helped scour it back out and replenished its marine life. It would probably disappear altogether eventually, but not in my lifetime. It had been six months since the last flood, and after a hot, dry summer the mud along the shore gave off a fetid odor of garbage and dead fish.

Dude's had been at this location for more years than I could remember. It was only open for business when the water wasn't high enough to cover the parking lot or the road across the cotton field, and the building itself was washed off its pilings every ten or fifteen years when a big flood came. The walls were always rebuilt out of some cheap material, plywood or pressboard or the lumber from abandoned farm buildings that made up this incarnation. Since 1953, when a corner of the outdoor deck collapsed and three drunken patrons had drowned, the floor had been made of stout lumber, but it still creaked and groaned under a full load of customers.

The place had always drawn an eclectic crowd, ranging from bikers and rednecks to fraternity boys from Ole Miss and slummers from Memphis. The mix made for an interesting crowd and more interesting fights. The only thing you didn't see was any black faces. Dude didn't believe in that kind of diversity.

Years ago, I had asked a bartender who Dude was, and had gotten only a shrug and shake of the head in reply. I knew who the current Dude was, though.

The mud stink was masked by the smell of beer and cigarette smoke as soon as we stepped off the ramp onto the porch. Men and women sat in metal folding chairs around small wooden tables made out of scrap lumber. The end of a chair leg occasionally fell down into a crack between the floor decking, adding to the confusion and hilarity. Naked light bulbs were strung along wires that ran from the building on the left to poles at the side of the porch, and a bar stretched along the side of the deck by the building. Four bartenders worked furiously to keep up with the waitresses bringing orders from the tables and the people stacked up two deep shouting their own orders and passing money over the heads of the people in front of them.

I had to pull Mary in front of me and guide her with a hand on her left shoulder as we weaved our way through the crowd toward the back of the deck. The cool wind through the truck window had accentuated Mary's figure, and several of the men we passed couldn't help staring at her. I didn't blame them.

As Mary came abreast of a table halfway down the forty-yard long platform, a large hand attached to a beefy forearm shot out and grabbed her thigh. I pushed on her shoulder with my left hand and kept walking, slamming my right thigh up as hard as I could into the locked out elbow. I heard a grunt of pain above the music and crowd noise at the same time the arm and hand windmilled up past my face and back over the shoulder of a man with a red beard wearing a camouflage baseball cap and t-shirt. I had a fleeting glimpse of a fountain of beer shooting into the air as his hand impacted a cup held by a person sitting beside him, then we were into the crowd and out of sight.

It had happened in a second, and as I looked over at Mary I realized that she wasn't even aware that she had been grabbed. I took a few quick looks over my shoulder to make sure the guy with the hand wasn't coming, but I didn't see any sign of him. The crowd was so thick that he might not have realized what happened, either.

The deck ran a few yards past the end of the building on its left. A yellow rope was strung waist high from the rail of the deck to the corner of the building. Behind the rope were four large tables, three of which were surrounded by small, boisterous crowds. One person sat alone at the fourth table.

A dark, wiry man about six feet tall wearing a western style shirt, jeans and cowboy boots, and a belt with a rodeo buckle, stood by the rope. He had a soda can in his left hand to hold the tobacco juice from the bulging cud in his cheek, and a lit cigarette in his right hand. His eyes looked like they had decided to go ahead and get it over with and not wait around till his habit killed the rest of him.

"This is a private area," he said, not looking at Mary but keeping his zombie eyes on me. "You'll have to find a table somewhere else."

"Have you tried the patch?" I asked with my best sincere smile.

"What do you mean?" he asked me back.

"You know," I said. "The nicotine patch."

"I don't want to quit," he retorted.

"Not to quit," I said. "So you can get more nicotine into your body."

"Look, bud, ya'll will have to go sit somewhere else," was all he said, though I thought I had seen something flash in his eyes for a second.

"I came to say hello to Tommy," I said, gesturing with a nod of my head to the table in the far corner with the solitary figure.

"Everybody wants to say hello to Tommy. My job is to make sure that he gets a quiet evening," he said.

Mary was holding on to my left arm, smiling up at Smoky's face, but he hadn't looked at her once. I was beginning to think that he was either a great bodyguard or that something other than his eyes was dead, too.

"If Tommy wants a quiet evening, who are all the people at the other tables?" I asked.

"Just a few friends, partner. Now you and the lady need to move along."

"Well, I'm another friend, and Tommy told me to drop by any time," I said. I got a business card out of my wallet and held it out to him. "I'd appreciate it if you gave him my card and told him I'd like to give him my regards."

He took a deep drag on the cigarette and then reached out for the card. As he took it with his thumb and forefinger he twisted his hand down, trying to catch my hand with the glowing ember of the cigarette sticking up between his index and middle fingers. Someone had done that to me before with a cigar and I still had a round scar at the base of my thumb. Once burned, twice shy, and I had my hand six inches back from his by the time the tip of his smoke punched through empty air. I kept my forearm up, ready to block the left jab that was the next move, but the soda can never moved. For the second time I thought I saw a spark in his eyes as he waited for my reaction, but when I made no move toward him they faded back into blackness.

He stuck the cigarette back into his mouth, and said, "Wait here. Don't come past the rope." He took two backward steps, then turned and walked back to the far table. I had been wondering, only partly academically, where he kept his business, but I still couldn't see any sign of a weapon.

"John, I don't care where we sit," Mary said. "Are you going to get in a fight with that man?"

"No, I don't think so. Not once he's talked to the man at the table."

I could see him bend over the seated figure, hand him my card and point over at us. Then he straightened up and walked back. He lifted the yellow rope up to head height, and gestured back behind him. "Tommy says come on over," he said.

He watched me as we walked under the rope, and I watched him right back. The fact that I couldn't figure out where he kept his gun made me more, not less, leery of him. I resisted the urge to say I told you so.

Before we got to the table in the corner, Tommy Traylor stood up and yelled, "John, you old sonofabitch, come on over here!" A few heads turned at the other tables, but they all went right back to partying.

Tommy was smiling broadly, but his lips stayed together, covering his crooked teeth. He gathered me into a big bear hug, whacking my back hard with his right hand. The top of his bald head glistened pinkly against my chest as I pounded on his wide, fleshy back with my open hand. I had learned from previous encounters that being hugged by Tommy was less embarrassing if you returned his manly backslapping instead of just standing there with your arms trying to reach around him.

"Goddam, son, you need to put on some weight. I can get my arms clean around you," he said, grabbing my shoulder and beaming up into my face. "Sit down here and have a plate of swamp chicken with me," he said, gesturing at a plate stacked with fried meat.

I half turned to introduce Mary, but before I could say anything he grabbed her and gave her the same hug, without the back beating. Mary, who had learned to expect the unexpected on our dates, hugged him right back. Tommy swiveled his head toward me, and said, "Son, I hate to hurt your feelings, but I'd a lot rather grab aholt of her than you."

"I'm relieved to hear it, Tommy," I said, as he turned back to Mary.

"Now, what's your name, sweetheart?" he asked, holding her back away from him.

Mary didn't talk a lot but she liked to speak for herself. "My name is Mary Arenduyk," she said, holding out her right hand. The gesture seemed superfluous after the friendly mauling she had just received, but Tommy took it in both of this and shook it up and down. "I'm Tommy Taylor," he said. "And I sure am pleased to meet you. Where are you from? England? You don't talk like us."

"The Netherlands," Mary said. "But that's close to England."

"Well, you sure got a pretty voice. Now sit down here with me," he said as he pulled out a chair for her.

A waitress came up to the table as we took chairs on either side of Tommy. Beside Tommy's plate of food was an open quart bottle of Jack Daniels' Black Label that was half gone and a large foam cup that was full of sour mash and crushed ice. The waitress looked like a biker's girl with her oily jeans, black t-shirt and a tattoo on each forearm. She had bottle blond hair and a face that might have been pretty before the injury that broke her nose and left a four inch long scar across her left cheekbone. Harley wreck or abusive boyfriend, take your pick.

She leaned on Tommy so that one of the large, sagging breasts under her t-shirt rested on his shoulder. "What are your friends drinking, Tommy?" she asked.

"What do you want, Mary?" Tommy asked. "Some wine, a beer?"

"May I have some of your whiskey, please?" she asked him back.

"Well, sure you can. Do you want a Coke with it?"

"No, thank you, just a cup of ice like you have," she said.

"You heard the lady, sweetie," he said to the waitress.

"I'll take a Bud, please," I said.

"A cup of ice and a Budweiser," Tommy said unnecessarily. "And bring 'em some munchies while they decide what they want for supper." Tommy reached up and stroked the breast laid out on his shoulder, and the waitress bent down and kissed him on top of his bald head before carrying our order into the kitchen.

"Is this true love, Tommy? You didn't even introduce us," I said.

"What? Oh, you mean Jessie?" he said. "She's real pretty, ain't she?"

"Yes, she's very attractive," I said with a totally straight face.

"She has beautiful eyes," Mary said. I hadn't even noticed Jessie's eyes, but I had never heard Mary say anything she didn't mean. Tommy responded to Mary's obvious sincerity and began to engage her in conversation. Jessie returned quickly with my beer, a cup full of ice for Mary, and a bucket full of more crushed ice. She held a stack of paper plates and two big platters, one of hush puppies and one of UFOs (unidentified fried objects) with a bowl of horseradish dipping sauce in front of Tommy. He gave her a quick smile, but still didn't offer any introductions.

Tommy poured a good four or five ounces of whiskey into Mary's cup, then began heaping a paper plate full of food for her. I listened to him identify the battered covered objects for her: tomato, pickle, chicken, zucchini, shrimp, turtle, and oyster.

"You decide what you like best then we'll get you a whole plate," he said.

"What is your favorite?" Mary asked, as she took a big swallow of whiskey.

"I call it swamp chicken, but it's really soft-shelled turtle," he said. "A soft-shell will eat anything it can get, dead or alive, so its meat can be a bit strong. Most white people won't eat it, but I've always been partial to it. Now a nigger'll tell you that an alligator snapping turtle tastes better 'cause they don't eat as much dead stuff. But I won't eat a snappin' turtle. You know why?"

Mary shook her head and drank more whiskey.

"Because a snappin' turtle can live to be a hundred years old, maybe older. It just don't seem right to me to eat something that lives so long. Kind of takes 'em out of the food category for me, you know?"

"That is a very interesting way of thinking," Mary said, nodding her head. "Would you show me which of these on my plate is turtle for eating?"

"That's a piece right there," Tommy said, pointing with his fork. "But like I said, you may find it a little strong."

Mary picked up the chunk Tommy indicated, dropped it and her fingers in the sauce, and stuck the whole piece in her mouth. She chewed twice, swallowed, licked her fingers, then took a swig of blackjack. She smiled, then reached for another piece.

"Then again, you might not," Tommy said.

I watched the two of them discussing food and drinking whiskey, Tommy enjoying Mary's appetite and throwing out country witticisms that Mary laughed at even though she didn't understand half of them.

Except for less hair and about forty more pounds, Tommy looked about the same as he had when I'd met him twenty years earlier in high school. His fat kept his face smooth and shiny, and his eyes twinkled like blue neon bulbs.

In school, he'd been one of the few remaining country boys in a community that was changing rapidly from farms to suburbs. Jokes about his height and his accent seemed not to faze him. He was friendly and outgoing and talked to everybody from the principal to the janitors and from the homecoming queen to guys like me who didn't hardly talk to anybody. He was nicknamed Tiny Tommy, or TT for short, and I never heard him object to it. But he had introduced himself to me as Tommy, so that's what I called him.

No one ever knew for sure about the darker side of Tommy, but I saw the first hint of it my sophomore year. He and I were in the same gym class, and a bunch of us were changing clothes when two senior football players grabbed Tommy and threw him into one of the big wire cage lockers. One of them stuck a ballpoint pen through the latch, trapping him. Then they pulled out their dicks and began to piss on him through the wire. Tommy put his hands over his face and tried to turn away from them, but the locker was too tight. "There's some tee tee for you, TT," one of them said, and they both laughed so hard their urine came out in spurts.

I hardly ever acted without thinking, even then, but this was so outrageous that I yelled to them to stop. One of them yelled back over his shoulder, "Shut up, you little fucker, or we'll shit on you."

They were finished by then, anyway, and they zipped up and walked out, still laughing. The rest of the boys in the locker room walked out quickly, laughing nervously or frowning with shame and disgust.

Tommy was stuck tight in the locker, urine dripping off his chin and nose and puddling at his feet. I got the pen out of the latch, and pulled the locker open, wetting my hand in the process.

Tommy squeezed out of the locker and immediately began taking off his clothes. He wouldn't look at me. "Well, hey, they got me good, didn't they," he said with a sound that could have been a laugh or a sob. "Yeah, yeah, that was a good joke all right," he said in a steadier voice.

"Tommy, that wasn't any kind of a joke," I said. I was so mad and so embarrassed for him that I could hardly talk. "I'm sorry I couldn't stop it. Let's go to the principal right now and tell him what happened."

Tommy was stripped off by now, but he looked at me and said, "John, I appreciate you at least trying. Now I'm going to take another shower and find some sweats that I can wear to class."

"Do you want me to go ahead and tell the principal?" I asked.

"There ain't no need to tell the principal. Them boys was just having some fun," Tommy said.

"Come on, Tommy. That's not right. They ought to be punished."

He stared up at me intently, and said, "It happened to me, John, not you. I don't want the principal to know, you got it?"

It was one of those three or four things that happen to every kid, when he learns the world is made up of the strong and the weak, and that fairness is not a universally held ideal. It took weeks for it to fade in my mind, but in the meantime Tommy was his usual self, talking and laughing with everyone, showing up at all the games, pep rallies and dances as if he was the biggest man on campus.

About a month after the locker room incident, on a warm fall day, a police car pulled up in front of the school while most of the senior class was sitting outside eating lunch. The students watched curiously as the two cops, acting on an anonymous tip, went in the building and met the principal, who was coming out of his office with a bolt cutter. The principal guided them to the locker of one of the boys who had peed on Tommy, and snipped the combination lock off. In a brown paper grocery sack, the policemen found eight one ounce sandwich bags of marijuana. Subsequent tests would show that one of the bags was covered with the boy's fingerprints. That bag, in addition to the marijuana, contained some bread crumbs and mayonnaise residue.

They walked back outside, and the principal pointed to the owner of the locker. The two cops walked over to him and announced that he was under arrest for possession of illegal drugs with intent to sell. They made him lie flat on the sidewalk while they roughly searched him and handcuffed him. Then they yanked him up, read him his rights, and threw him in the back of the patrol car.

Some of those present said he worked his mouth open and closed like a fish, but no words came out. Everyone else sat in stunned silence. As the police car drove off, the principal said loudly, "That is what happens to drug pushers. Let it be a lesson to you."

The football player's father had held him back a year so he would have a better shot at playing college ball for a big program. The strategy had worked and his son had already accepted a full scholarship at the University of Alabama starting the next fall. His father couldn't have known that the same strategy would result in his son being tried as an adult and sentenced to five years. We never saw him again.

The other boy who had degraded Tommy was one of the wealthiest kids in school. His family lived on a twenty-acre estate outside of town, complete with horses that no one ever rode. It was next door to the small working farm where Tommy's parents continued to try to eke out a living.

About a month after the other player was arrested, the rich kid was on his way home from a dance about two in the morning. He turned off the main road onto the long tree-lined drive that led to his house, and punched the accelerator on the Trans Am he had gotten for his sixteenth birthday. Halfway down the drive, going eighty miles an hour, the low-slung car hit a six-inch thick dead limb that had fallen from an overhanging tree and lay diagonally across the road. The car went airborne and veered to the left, twisting on its axis in mid-air and impacting a foot thick oak while it was upside down and ten feet off the ground. Every one agreed that it was a miracle the driver survived. He came back to school three months later, walking with a cane, dragging his left foot and carrying a towel to mop up the drool he couldn't stop.

I was fifteen years old, and there were some things I couldn't even imagine yet, so it was years before I suspected a link between Tommy and his tormentors' misfortunes. We had never been close friends, and that didn't change. He went his way, and I went mine. After graduation, I went off to college, and Tommy took a job at a local manufacturing plant. I didn't see him for years, until one night Kathleen and I were pulled over by a sheriff's car as we came back from a client's Christmas party out in the county. I knew I had been speeding, and I was nervously trying to remember how many drinks I had had and figure out whether I should take the breathalyzer test. I rolled the window down as the deputy walked up beside me, and a familiar voice said, "Would you step out of the car please, sir?"

Before I could get out, Tommy was shining his light on me, and then asked, "Shit, John, is that you?"

We stood out in the cold on the shoulder of the road for half an hour, catching up on old times, me talking too much out of relief that I wasn't going to spend the night in jail. He stuck his head in the window to say hello to Kathleen, but she stayed in the running car for warmth. He had joined the sheriff's department three years earlier and thought it was a great job. He was impressed that I was a lawyer. We promised to stay in touch, but of course didn't.

A couple of years later, just before Kathleen left me, Tommy called me at the office one day. The area of the county in which his parents had farmed had developed like everywhere else. They had both died within the last few years. Tommy, as sole heir, was receiving offers from developers who wanted to build subdivisions. Tommy had received one offer from a man who didn't want to buy the land, but wanted to go in with Tommy as partners to develop it themselves. He promised that Tommy would make at least twice as much money this way.

Tommy told me that he had checked the guy out through the sheriff's department and couldn't find anything of a criminal nature against him. But he wanted me to see what I could find out about him.

I asked the head of our real estate section what he knew about the developer. He had me pull the door of his office shut, said not to quote him, and told me the developer would be indicted before the end of the year on a variety of federal charges.

When I called Tommy back and told him not to do the deal, he said he had already decided that it was the way to make the most money. He had all the documents and was just about to sign them. He appreciated my advice, but thought he would go ahead and deed over the property to a limited liability company that the developer had formed. I told him I couldn't say why, but it would be a big mistake. A lot of cops, like a lot of lawyers, think that their ability to judge character is infallible. Tommy had decided the developer was honest, and he didn't want to believe he might have been wrong. He pressed me for more information, but I told him that was all I could say. Tommy hung up the phone still undecided on what he was going to do.

A week later, the headline on the business page of *The Commercial Appeal* announced that the developer had been indicted on sixty counts of bank and mail fraud. Tommy called me that afternoon and thanked me for my advice. After I told him he was welcome, and he told me to send him a bill, he asked, "John, what happens if a person has signed a deed, but it was never recorded. It's no good, right?"

"If you mean is it legally binding between the parties, sure it is," I said. "It just wouldn't be effective against another purchaser who didn't know about it."

"Well, what if the seller found out that the buyer was a lying, thieving sonofabitch and changed his mind before the deed was recorded, and just took the deed back. Then there wouldn't be any proof that he had made the transfer, would there?"

"Under the statute of frauds, there has to be some writing to prove a transfer of real estate, but the buyer could testify that there had been one and that the seller had taken it back. Besides, all deeds are notarized, so the notary could testify that there had been a deed."

"Let's just say that the notary is a real good friend of the seller and not worry about what she'll say."

"Tommy, what are we talking about here, man?" I asked. "If you went ahead and did the deal with this guy, we can file a petition to set aside the deed for fraud. The other things you're talking about are illegal. You're a cop, you know that."

"John, I'm just talking hypothetically here, you know," Tommy said. "Don't get all excited."

"Tommy, I can't give you advice on how to break the law," I said.

"John, let me just ask you one more hypothetical question. Okay? For old time's sake?"

"Okay, Tommy."

"If this fellow who had been ripped off filed a petition, like you said, but this other fellow, the crooked one, was in a whole lot of other shit, probably going to file bankruptcy, maybe go to jail, how long would it be before he got his property back?"

"I won't lie to you, Tommy, it could be a long time. The bankruptcy trustee would probably try to keep all of the assets intact to pay off all the other creditors, so he would fight tooth and nail to keep the property."

"Hey, John, I appreciate your advice. Like I said, send me a bill."

I never heard anything about the developer claiming that he owned Tommy's property. Maybe he decided that it would just get him into more of the same kind of trouble he was already in, or maybe Tommy persuaded him that it was not in his best interest to swindle a cop.

In any event, Tommy decided that I was a great lawyer, even though all I had done was give him some inside information. He sold his property a few months later for over two million dollars, and our firm handled the closing for him. He promptly quit the sheriff's department and went into business for himself, but he was always vague about what that business was. He only told me that he had figured out some ways to make money if you had money while he was working for the sheriff. My firm didn't do any legal work on his new ventures.

By now, Tommy and Mary had finished off the platter of battered meat and vegetables, and Tommy was starting in on the hushpuppies. Through a mouth of cornmeal, he gestured at me and said to Mary, "Did you know that this fellow here you're with tonight used to be one of the best lawyers in Memphis?"

Mary only smiled, first at him and then at me.

"It's the truth," Tommy said. "And now he's one of the best private investigators around. Why, hell, just last month he got the goods on some rich faggot, nobody knows how."

"Hey, come on, Tommy," I winced, "that's supposed to be confidential. How did you know about that? And don't say faggot."

"Confidential?" he asked loudly. "Hell, son, something that good ain't gonna stay confidential for long. And don't go correcting my grammar. I just called him a name, you're the one who took the movies of him engaged in unnatural acts."

"You may have a point, Tommy," I said.

"Course I have a point," he said. "The man was a faggot, so I call him a faggot. Besides, you don't try to get me to quit saying nigger anymore."

"I gave up on that one after about the hundredth try," I said.

Mary reached out and put her hand on Tommy's arm. "Tommy," she said, "I don't like those words either. You are too nice a man to use them."

Tommy looked at her for a minute, and then said, "Mary, if you don't like them words, I won't use them in front of you, and I'll try not to use them at all." Tommy turned to me and said "See, John, you just need to learn how to ask."

"I don't think I could ever ask like that," I said.

Jessie brought my catfish surrounded by hushpuppies, French fries and slaw. While I ate, I told Tommy about Thomas Tuggle. Tommy hadn't heard of Tuggle by his real name or his street name. He had been out of the sheriff's department for several years, and figured Thomas's troubles had probably been with the MPD. Mary listened to my story intently, her eyes darting back and forth between Tommy and me.

"John," Tommy said when I had finished, "this is kind of a funny sounding case, don't you think? I mean, whoever heard of hiring a PI to track down a, uh, black crack dealer?"

"He's not a crack dealer, Tommy. His bondsman admits he's a crook, but says he's not that kind of crook."

"Some of the guys on the MPD may think their shit don't stink, but I never heard of 'em arresting a dealer who wasn't a dealer."

"Whether he's a dealer or not, his mother wants me to find him," I said.

"Are you sure you're going to get paid for this?" he asked.

"Yes, I'm getting paid."

"Well, I'll make a couple of calls, see if any of my old buddies know anything that might help you." I knew from past experience that Tommy's old buddies weren't just from the sheriff's department, but were also people he knew in his current businesses.

Just then Tommy's bodyguard walked up to the table and bent over and whispered in Tommy's ear as he pointed over to the rope where two men stood. "Okay, tell 'em I'll be with 'em in a minute," Tommy said.

The man straightened up, looked at me, and then walked back toward the rope.

"Tommy, I got to ask you," I said. "Where does he keep his gun?"

"Promise not to tell?" he asked.

"Promise," I said. "It's just professional curiosity."

"He keeps a small frame Glock nine millimeter in the front of his jeans. He hides the handle behind that big belt buckle and the barrel sticks straight down."

"That sounds slow to me," I said. "He'd have to flip the buckle back with his left hand before he could pull the pistol out with his right."

"Believe it," Tommy said, "it's not slow."

"I hope he doesn't get in too much of a hurry. You know a Glock doesn't have a safety, don't you?" I asked.

"Really? We were still using revolvers when I was with the department. They didn't have a safety, either, but I sure'n hell wouldn't point one down my pants."

"Maybe that's what makes him a good bodyguard," I said. "A total lack of concern for his personal well-being."

"I don't know why he's good, but he is," Tommy said. "He's one mean fucker."

"I believe it. Listen," I said, "I know you've got to see some other folks. We appreciate your hospitality. Give me a call when you're going to be in town and we'll get a drink."

Tommy tried to persuade us to join one of the other tables until he finished his business, but it was almost midnight so we begged off. He gave us each another hug, and we walked away past the bodyguard and the two men he was bringing up to Tommy's table.

As we started down the ramp to the parking lot, the red-bearded man who had grabbed Mary on the way in pushed himself off the left handrail and blocked Mary's path. He stood less than a foot in front of her, thick and heavy in the chest, shoulders and belly, swaying slightly and breathing beer fumes. He didn't seem to see me, but grinned and reached out and grabbed Mary's left breast.

In some situations, there is nothing that needs to be said. He opened his mouth, but I closed it with a punch that I brought across my body from down around my knee. His head popped up and sideways, and his body followed. He hit the guardrail with his stomach and flipped over it, turning a complete somersault in the air and landing face down in six inches of water and mud ten feet below. He made a pretty good splash.

Three or four people looked over the rail at him, but nobody seemed very excited. When we got to the end of the ramp, I turned and saw that he was up on his hands and knees, coughing out mud, blood and beer. Sometimes persistence doesn't pay.

As we drove across the misty field toward the levee, Mary said, "John, I don't think I understand what you do for a living."

7

Mary flew back to Holland the next morning. Her crew was out of rotation for a week, and she didn't know when her next trip to Memphis would be. It was another gorgeous fall day, but her leaving made an ache that I didn't want to deal with in an empty apartment.

I threw my waders and flyrod in the back of the truck and headed across the bridge into Arkansas. By noon I was standing in thigh deep water in the catch-and-release area at Cow Shoals on the Little Red River, working a tan sowbug through a run filled with rainbows and brown trout. Deep blue sky, red and yellow leaves on the trees, falling through the air and spinning on the river, clear, cold water flowing over rocks and moss beds and pushing and chuckling past my legs, the rhythm and concentration of casting and drifting a fly, was far more than enough for the next six hours.

I stayed on the river till the stars were coming out. All the heat went out of the day with the setting of the sun. Cold, damp air began to flow over the top of the water like another layer of the river, creating a peaceful in between world that was more of the water than of the land.

Suddenly, a big fish broke the surface just upriver from me, and slipped back into the water with a muted splash. I began to ease up toward it, but my left foot caught on an unseen rock below the surface. I struggled for balance, lost it, and ended up on both knees, my right hand and the rod in it pointed up and my left hand out flat on the surface of the water. The water was an inch below the top of my chest waders, but what felt like a gallon of ice cold liquid had splashed in during my fall. I carefully got to my feet, and started to shiver. It was time to go.

On the way home, I stopped in Wynne at a 24-hour gas station/ice cream shop/sandwich shop. The Little Red is in the foothills of the Ozarks, but here I was back in the Delta, with ricefields pushing up against the outskirts of town. I filled up the truck and then went inside. I knew that nothing fast would be open downtown by the time I got home, so I ordered the safest looking sandwich and a bag of chips. I wanted a beer, but I still had an hour to go, so I got a Diet Coke.

I sat at a plastic table and ate my sandwich, wanting to get it over with and get back on the road. To save myself from looking at row after row of junk food, I picked up the local paper that someone had left on the table. Among the articles about high school football and crops, there was a brief story on the second page that caught my eye.

Two local men had been out on the St. Francis River some miles east of town. They motored up into a patch of flooded timber alongside the river, scouting for a place to duck hunt when the season opened. One of the men saw a grayish bowl-shaped object floating on the surface of the brown water. Curious, he reached out from the bow with a paddle and lifted the thing up and onto the middle thwart of the boat. It was only when he flipped it over with his hand that he recognized it as the top third of a human skull, with part of the right eye orbit still attached.

The men resisted their first impulse to knock the grisly relic back into the water, and brought it back to the landing. The sheriff's office had then dragged the area where the skull piece was found, but came up with no other pieces of a skeleton or corpse. The hunters' find had been sent to Little Rock for a full pathology report. A sheriff's deputy was quoted as saying, "It don't look that old, but turtles and stuff has picked it clean, so we can't tell nothin' about it." I was glad that I had declined any of Tommy's swamp chicken.

I rammed the pickup east on Highway 64, over Crowley's Ridge and across the Arkansas side of the Delta. Despite the cool temperature, the bugs were thick in my headlights. I had killed at least fifty big moths and lots of smaller ones with my windshield before I hit I-55 and headed south. I turned on the wipers and sprayed the window a few times. That traded me a collage of inch square spots of no vision for an entire forward field of sight dimly seen through an opaque yellow goo. I made the Hernando Desoto at eleven thirty, and turned off on Front Street toward my apartment.

I passed the office tower where Lipscomb Riley, my old law firm, had its offices. Lights were on in several of the windows, where lawyers were preparing for trials or closings the next day. I started to think that I was glad that I didn't work those hours any more, then remembered I had been on the job at midnight more as a PI than as a lawyer. It was more a question of whether you would rather spend that time in an office or twenty feet up a pine tree in the backyard of a prominent pederastic philanthropist.

After Kathleen left me, I had continued on at Lipscomb Riley as if nothing had happened. Divorce was not unusual in our office, and since we didn't have kids, sympathy was limited to a few banal words of encouragement and promises to fix me up with friends. It didn't cause me to undertake any conscious self-examination of my life. I did notice, however, that my temper was more likely to flare up at unexpected moments, and that I was drinking more than I had.

That summer, I was in a deposition in our offices. My client, Rick Babbage, was the owner of a small but successful local chain of frame shops. A national franchiser of frame shops had sued him in federal court, alleging that Rick was infringing on one of its trademarks. We had quickly concluded there was no substance to their allegations, but that the lawsuit was designed to sap Rick's energy and financial resources to soften him up for a lowball buyout offer.

The franchiser hired Max Schaeffer to prosecute its case. Max was the perfect choice for anyone who wanted to drive the other side crazy. Most lawyers would agree to scheduling and other routine issues as a matter of course. With Max, nothing was agreed to. Instead of a phone call, he filed a ten-page brief. His presence was even more obnoxious than his methods. Fat and oily-looking, he had a deep, fruity voice that sounded like a bad sports announcer's. He could talk, and talk, and talk, and not say a damn thing. The worst part was he seemed totally oblivious to the fact that everyone at the bar thought he was a pompous, overbearing windbag.

Rick had paid us a $25,000 retainer, but we burned through it in two months fighting Schaeffer's slash and burn tactics. Rick was determined not to give in, but he was already having trouble meeting payroll. He was into us for another $20,000, and it was only a matter of time before the firm had to withdraw from the case unless he could get his bill current.

It was Schaeffer's deposition of Rick, but we were taking it in our offices. His office was out east, and I think he liked to come downtown so he could bill his client for the drive. We were in the Lipscomb conference room, named after one of the deceased founders of the firm. The room was dominated by a large bronze bust of Mr. Lipscomb that rested on a chest high marble pedestal.

It was late in the afternoon of the second day of the deposition, and Max had spent the entire day asking Rick the same questions he had asked him the day before in slightly different words. Meanwhile, the clock ticked away, costing Rick $200 an hour that he couldn't afford and that I didn't know if I would ever get. I had explained to Rick at lunch break that I could object and adjourn the deposition, but that Schaeffer would surely file a motion to resume the deposition and for Rick to pay his attorney fees spent in drafting the motion. I would have to respond to the motion in writing, and argue about it in court. Even if we won, it would cost Rick more than just gutting it out through the rest of the day. He took my advice philosophically, and had patiently answered Max's inane and repetitive questions all afternoon. Personally, though, I found my own patience waning as I thought of all the other work I needed to be doing and how much of Rick's money and my time Schaeffer was wasting.

We took a break, and the court reporter headed for the bathroom. "Max," I said, as he stood up and began to walk around to our side of the table to the door, "do you think we can wrap up by six today?"

"Six is fine with me," he said. "Let's start back tomorrow at nine."

"What? Don't tell me you want more? You've been asking the same goddamn questions for two days now!"

"Yes, I want more," he said in his annoying voice, emphatically jabbing the air in front of my chest with two short fingers. "This man here has violated the federal rights of my client and must be brought to account for his actions."

"Save your bullshit for the courtroom!" I yelled back. "You could have taken this deposition in three hours, and now you want three days!"

I felt Rick's hand on my arm, and heard him saying my name, but I ignored him in the rising tide of fury that was sweeping over me.

"Counselor, I'll take four days if I need them," Max hissed back. "And there's not a damn thing you can do about it," he said as he jabbed his fingers into my shoulder.

I slammed both of my palms into his fat chest, knocking him back a step. His right heel caught on the leg of a chair, and he fell backwards, his mouth open and arms reaching frantically for support. His back, then his head, hit the marble sculpture stand. Mr. Lipscomb got into the fray, tipping off the stand and falling four and a half feet to land nose to nose on Schaeffer.

It was a spectacularly gory scene, with blood oozing out of the back of Max's head and gushing from his ruined, flattened nose onto the antique Oriental rug and walnut parquet floor. The court reporter chose that moment to walk back in to the room. She couldn't see Max's head past his stomach, but she could see Mr. Lipscomb's bloody bust lying under his armpit, the empty eyes staring our way. She didn't even scream, she just fainted dead away across Rick's lap.

Rick looked at the court reporter lying across his lap with her skirt bunched around her waist and her butt stuck up in the air, then at Schaeffer, then at me. "John, he said, "I didn't know getting sued could be this much fun." Then he started laughing.

Schaeffer recovered with nothing worse than a mild concussion, some stitches and a broken nose. He never could get the nose reconstructed right, though, and his blocked nasal passages ruined his fruity baritone, making him sound like Winston Churchill with a bad cold. He threatened to sue me and the firm, but one of our older litigators, who was a good friend of the governor, visited him, showed him Rick's affidavit swearing that Max pushed me first, and threatened a counterclaim. He told Max (truthfully) that the carpet he had bled on cost $50,000, and that (not quite so truthfully) the bust of Mr. Lipscomb, which now had irremovable bloodstains, had been appraised at $400,000. He had a hard time coming up with any damages to me, but he did mention emotional distress. He also said we would file a claim with the disciplinary board. We didn't hear any more from Max, although several lawyers from other firms called and offered to buy me drinks.

Rick Babbage got lucky, too. The franchiser that was suing him ran into financial difficulties and couldn't afford to continue its acquisition through litigation strategy. They filed a voluntary non-suit, ending their case. Max ended up suing his client for $50,000 in unpaid legal fees.

Nothing changed at the firm. If anything, my reputation as an aggressive litigator only increased, even though pushing a fat guy down didn't have anything to do with lawyering skills. What my partners didn't know, though, was that I had barely controlled a consuming urge to kick Schaeffer's unconscious, bleeding body into a pulp.

I took some long overdue vacation time and visited relatives and friends I had lost touch with since starting law school. I was supposed to be gone a week, but I stretched it to two. I was back in the office early on a Monday morning, and by noon knew that I couldn't stand it any longer. I delivered my resignation letter by the end of the day, stayed on for a month helping transition files, and then walked out for the last time on a Friday afternoon. I was thirty-three years old, divorced and unemployed. It was the happiest I had been for a very long time.

Thinking back on all this, my apartment never looked so good. I had made the right decision.

8

I called Amanda the next morning, omitting any word on my visit with Lieutenant Steiner, but telling her about the rest of my investigation. She seemed unimpressed, and I couldn't blame her. She didn't think much of my idea for her to enter an appearance as Thomas's lawyer so she could find out why he had been arrested. The prosecutor had no obligation to provide any information since Thomas had skipped out on his bail, and she didn't think he would do it voluntarily.

"Give him that cute little smile, Amanda," I said. "Maybe he'll change his mind."

"John, are you really trying to find Thomas or not?" she asked, exasperation in her voice.

"Yes, I'm trying to find him," I replied. "There's just not a hell of a lot to go on."

"Would it help if I paid you more?" she asked.

"Now I'm starting to get pissed. It's not about money. I'm doing everything I can, but I'll tell you that I still think he's dead or in another city."

"Then try another city," she said.

"Amanda, I'm just wasting your money."

"No, John, remember your deal. It's your money, your pro bono case. I guess you just didn't set your penance for Jack Jones very high."

"Amanda?"

"Yes, John?"

"Fuck you."

I got the truck out of the parking garage and stopped in a nearby alley. I opened the built-in tool box in the back and pulled out the stick-on utility company door signs, fake whip antenna, and a clip-on pocket identification badge. I quickly screwed on an old government license plate I had purchased from an acquaintance who dealt in all things automotive. Dark glasses and a baseball cap with the utility logo completed my disguise. I had found that this was the best all around way of blending into the environment anywhere in the city. I could pass unquestioned at any time of day or night anywhere, from Jack Jones's toney neighborhood to places a white man rarely went unless he was on official business. I was probably breaking some laws in the process, but I doubted that the penalties were very high.

Thomas's neighborhood was set in an area of small, wooded hills in southwest Memphis. Some of the affluent blacks in the city had moved out to the white enclaves in Germantown and East Memphis, and many still lived in the old stately homes along South Parkway that they had begun to buy from whites in the 1940s. But a growing number of the black elite were living here, in this brand new subdivision they had started.

I cruised past Thomas's house, checking out the neighborhood. The houses were all new, and the lawns were immaculate. Most of the kids were in school, but I saw a few little ones playing in driveways and yards. The only other white guy I saw, from a lawn fertilizer company, was hosing down a yard with chemicals from a tank on the back of a truck. It didn't look like a case of environmental racism.

Thomas's house was a two-story affair that didn't fit into any of my few architectural classifications, except maybe heavy red brick. It looked like a few extra loads had been delivered, and the masons had decided to go ahead and stick them somewhere instead of sending them back. The front door was covered by a narrow brick portico that rose up all the way to the roof-line, and the empty flower beds in front were bordered by low walls made of the same brick. Two brick columns about five feet tall flanked the entrance to the driveway. The house sat on a decent-sized lawn bisected by a circular washed concrete drive. It wasn't as grand as the Jones estate, but it was still nothing to be ashamed of, especially if you hadn't inherited money.

The driveway ran past the front door, but an offshoot of it ran along the side of the lot to an offset garage with doors that didn't face the street. Despite the obvious expense, the whole place looked incomplete with no plantings or other touches that would signify home. It looked, in fact, like a rich bachelor who wasn't at home much lived in it.

I pulled onto the apron of concrete by the garage and killed the engine. Both garage doors were down, but the backyard was separated from the driveway by only a low wall made of the same brick. The masons had made it back here, too.

I was betting that the police had obtained a search warrant and quietly snooped Thomas's house at night after contacting his alarm company and getting his alarm turned off. I was also betting that the cops hadn't bothered to call the alarm company and tell them to turn it back on, either because it was just one more thing to do or because they thought they might want to come back without calling the company. But I wanted to hedge my bets.

I put on my baseball cap and identification badge, and grabbed a clipboard. The door must have been inside the closed garage, so I walked around front and rang the doorbell. For a second, I had a funny feeling that, despite Amanda's fruitless phone calls to Thomas and face to face chats with the neighbors, the man himself was going to come to the door. A timed three minutes of doorbell ringing convinced me my hunch was wrong.

I walked over to the next door neighbor's house and rang the doorbell. It was another red brick house, but with a landscaped yard and blooming pansies in the beds, and a basketball goal and two kids' bikes in the driveway. It looked like people lived here.

After I rang the bell, a woman in her forties opened the wooden door, stared out at me for a second through the glass security door, and then opened it too after she saw my badge, cap and clipboard.

"Good afternoon," I said.

"Good afternoon," she said back. "How may I help you?" Her voice, demeanor and appearance all indicated upper middle class.

"Your neighbor here, Mr., er, Tuggle," I said, looking down at my clipboard, "seems to be having some kind of trouble with his water meter. It's showing up on our computer. We've been trying to call him, and I rang the bell just now, but he's not at home. I was wondering if you happen to know how we could get hold of him."

"No, I'm afraid I don't," she said. "I haven't seen him for several weeks. We don't know him very well anyway. He's single and we have kids, so we've kind of gone our separate ways."

I listened hard to her voice, but I could not detect any hint of disapproval, of wild parties and loud music, of suspicious looking guests committing illegal or immoral acts on the lawn.

"Do you think some of the other neighbors might have an idea?" I asked.

"No, I don't think they would. We know all of them and everybody is kind of wondering where he is."

I didn't want to step out of my role as a utility company worker, so I didn't ask her any more questions. Lucy had said she asked the neighbors about Thomas, and so had Amanda. The neighbors probably figured that one of them would notify the cops if it was necessary. Besides, I wasn't really trying to get information. I was just doing advance damage control.

I had decided that I would go into Thomas's house, and I didn't like it. Creeping around in someone's back yard would get you into trouble with the cops, but not like breaking and entering. If you didn't get shot, getting caught meant at the very least you were going to lose your license, and there was a real chance of spending a few months at the penal farm. The fact that Amanda could get into the house legally if Lucy would just file a missing person report didn't help my attitude. I was taking the risk for the illogical reason that Amanda had all but said I was dogging it on the case because of money. Since everything I got paid on Tuggle was a reduction on the Jones fee, she believed I wasn't giving it my best shot. Or, at least she wanted me to think she believed it. Either way, I was pissed, and so I was a little reckless. The fact that Amanda had inherited more money than she could ever possibly make practicing law, and so could afford a lot more charity than I could, angered me even more.

"Well, thanks anyway," I said. "I'm going to look in the back yard and see if he has a leak."

"Okay," she said, and shut the door.

Now, when she saw me in the backyard she wouldn't even consider calling the cops. If the alarm was still on and I tripped it going into the house, she probably wouldn't call the police, either. I would get in the truck and drive away immediately at least five minutes before the police arrived in response to the call from the alarm company. If she came out the front door before I got in the truck, I would tell her I must have set off the alarm when I was looking for the leak. Either way, when the cops arrived they would find the house secure, bolts locked, and no apparent problem. The neighbor would come out and tell them that a utility man had been there, that he must have set it off, and that the owner had been out of town for several weeks. The cops would probably drop it there, but they might call MLG&W and ask if a truck had been called to the address. It wouldn't matter, though, because by then I would have stopped somewhere out of sight and removed the antenna, utility company decals, and government license plate, and thrown them, along with my cap and badge, into the built-in toolbox in back. I would be driving one of hundreds of plain white pickups.

I walked back to my truck, and pulled a shovel out of the back. I stepped over the low brick wall and into the backyard, and walked around the back of the house. The grass was thick Bermuda, mostly turned tan at this time of year. There were no trees near the back of the house, but a cluster of locust, persimmon and other scrub trees grew along a board fence at the back of the lot, 100 feet behind the house. There were no houses behind Thomas's, just more scraggly trees of the type that grow up in a field that is slowly going back to woods. I smelled fresh paint and new brick and mortar.

There was a patio hidden away inside the U-shaped back of the house. French doors, out of sight of both houses on the side, led into the house. I leaned my shovel against the wall, pulled a thin tool out my shirt pocket, and went to work on the dead bolt. It took about three minutes before I got it turned over. I took a deep breath, twisted the knob, and pushed the door open. I was hit by a breath of stale air, but no beep-beep-beep of an alarm system.

And no smell of a body, which I didn't expect if the cops had been in already, but you never know. I walked quickly to the kitchen, and saw the alarm panel by the door into the garage. It showed no signs of life. If the phone didn't ring in the next two or three minutes, I was home free.

I started in the kitchen, but there wasn't much to see. There was a wall mounted portable phone, but no answering machine. There were a few glasses and dishes in the cupboard, and some cheap cutlery in a drawer, but no pots or pans. The refrigerator contained three quarts of Colt 45 malt liquor, one of them half empty. There was a bottle of Absolut vodka in the freezer, and a can of frozen orange juice concentrate. That was it for groceries. There was none of the usual kitchen clutter of calendars, notes and refrigerator magnets, and no dirty dishes in the sink or dishwasher. The garbage can held an empty quart of malt liquor, and a white paper sack and foil wrapper from a barbecue chain.

I walked through an empty dining room and living room, no furniture, nothing on the walls, no rugs except the wall to wall carpeting, and up the carpeted staircase to the second floor. There were four bedrooms and a walk-in attic. There was nothing in any of them. I went back down the stairs and paused to go through the mail that lay in a heap against the inside of the front door where it had fallen after being pushed through the mail slot. There were bills for utilities, cable and telephone, but the rest was junk. I pocketed the phone bill and went into the den where I had started. A big screen television stood against one wall opposite a brown leather couch and recliner. There were a few sports magazines on a coffee table in front of the couch, but no mailing label on them. They were probably bought at the same place where Thomas got his supply of Colt 45. The oldest issue was September of the same year, which had probably been available on the newsstand by mid-August. An end table flanked both sides of the couch, and a lamp sat on each table. They were both on timers, set to go on at seven p.m. and off at eleven p.m. There was a boombox CD player in the corner, and a stack of CDs by musicians I didn't recognize. There was no telephone in this room.

I went into the master bedroom. It was big, with a vaulted ceiling, and a king size bed with some kind of shiny black wood frame and headboard. The bed was covered with a white, puffy duvet and four big white pillows. A long, waist high dresser with gold handles hugged one wall, and a huge entertainment center stood against the opposite wall. They were both made out of the same wood as the bed. A thick layer of dust covered their horizontal surfaces. A telephone sat on the dresser, but again, no answering machine. A walk in closet held neat rows of suits, sports coats, slacks and shirts, with rows of highly polished but dusty dress shoes, each with a shoetree, and neatly arranged pairs of athletic shoes.

I went back out to the bedroom, and quickly searched the drawers in the dresser. They were full of socks, silk t-shirts and underwear, a few athletic clothes, and nothing else. A jewelry box on the top of the dresser held two chunky gold rings, a diamond ear stud, and a silver chain bracelet. The top of the entertainment center was already open, but I went over and opened the bottom cabinet. There were a few action hero-type videos, and a cardboard box. I pulled the box out onto the floor and quickly riffled through the papers in it, report cards, high school diploma, house deed (no mortgage) dated last summer, and a lease agreement on a new Lexus. There were no business records, no certificates of title or leases on any vans, no financial records, no checkbooks.

Toward the bottom, I found two things of interest. The first was a box of Federal .40 caliber hollow point pistol ammo. I flipped the box open and saw that fifteen rounds were missing. That was just right for one of the high capacity magazines that were legally sold before further manufacture was outlawed during the Clinton Administration. They were called pre-Hillary clips. I felt in the back of the cabinet and underneath the bottom, but didn't locate the pistol that went with the ammo.

The second item was a stack of color photographs still inside the paper envelope from the developer. They were all taken inside with a flash, and bore an automatic date of December 25 of the previous year. I quickly realized that the picture Amanda had given me was from this same roll. They were all of Thomas and Lucy, either together or alone, except for one picture of Lucy and another man. They were both sitting on a ratty looking sofa, holding beer cans and smiling at the camera. The man was African-American, mid to late forties, with a receding hairline, and mustache and a goatee. Although he was sitting down, he looked tall. He was wearing a tan work shirt, blue jeans and lace up boots, and somehow looked like he belonged outdoors. He looked too good for Lucy.

I stuck the photograph inside my shirt, the ammo back in the box, and the box back inside the cabinet. I took a quick look around to see if I had missed any obvious hiding places or left anything out of order. Then I walked back out through the den and into the kitchen. The garage was the only place left, but I had to make it quick. I was timing myself, and I had already been in the house just over thirteen minutes. I had planned to be back out and in my truck in fifteen, and I was running late.

I turned the handle on the deadbolt and stepped out into Thomas's two-car garage. There were no windows, so I flipped on the light. His garage was a lot like his house. There were no stacks of stolen clothes or shoes, and no van. Except for the Lexus coupe and a green rolling curbside garbage can, there was nothing to see. There were no tools or lawn mower, no boxes or camping or sports equipment. I looked in the garbage can first, but saw nothing except a few empty malt liquor bottles. I walked up to the Lexus carefully, not wanting to set off any alarm. I peered in the window, but didn't see a blinking light that would indicate an alarm. If the car had been sitting there as long as Thomas had been missing, the battery had probably worn down and the alarm wouldn't work. But I hadn't come with the right tools for breaking into a car, and even if I had I couldn't take the risk that the alarm might still be in action. Thomas's neighbor might believe I set off his house alarm from outside by accident, but if his car alarm worked by blowing the horn over and over, I was going to have a hard time explaining. I pulled the pen light out of my pocket, and shone it through the window of the car. Nothing. I got down on my hands and knees and looked under the car, then went around back and wrote down the license plate number just in case it might come in handy.

As I headed back to the kitchen door, I kicked something that skittered across the concrete floor. I bent and picked it up and it crumbled in my fingers. It was a piece of dried mud, with a short piece of grass stalk embedded in it. I started to drop it back down, then stuck it in my shirt pocket.

I closed the garage door behind me, walked through the kitchen into the den, then peered out the French doors at the back of the house. There was nobody in sight, so I slipped out, relocked the deadbolt, picked up my shovel, and walked back around to the truck. The neighbor wasn't out in her front yard, and there were no SWAT teams with M-16s waiting for me. I drove out of the driveway at 10 miles per hour, and headed out of the neighborhood. Easy as pie, I thought, if you didn't mind the huge sweat rings and the thumping pulse. I also thought that I had just used up one of my free parking cards. The next time I went into an office or residence the odds against me would have increased.

I made a quick stop in the service alley behind a strip shopping mall and returned the truck to normal. As I headed back downtown, I tried to figure out whether my burglary escapade was successful. I could tell Amanda and impress with her with how hard I was working the case. She wouldn't want to hear the details, because it could implicate her in a crime, but I was damn well going to tell her. Other than that, I had a photograph, a piece of mud and some idea of how Thomas lived. He had the money to pay cash for what had to be at least a $400,000 house, lease a recent model Lexus, and buy some real furniture. He dressed well, but he still drank malt liquor. He paid no attention to his yard or neighbors, and obviously wasn't interested in grocery shopping or cooking. He could just as well have lived in an apartment or condominium. Maybe he had bought the house as a way to invest some of his illegal money, or maybe he had bought it to impress Lucy. Or, I thought, maybe he bought it so Lucy would feel good knowing he had it.

Wherever he had gone, he hadn't driven his car, but I knew he might have driven the van that Henry Jackson had mentioned he used in his business or taken a cab to the airport. I also knew that he kept his home life and his work strictly segregated, at least as far as keeping any indications or records of work at the house. Which meant that there was another address where he maintained his business. I doubted that he kept a large inventory, but he would have to have some place where he could collect his goods and load them into the van. He also obviously needed a place to keep the van. He couldn't have the suppliers he did business with coming to his new house, either. It was possible that he operated completely out of his van, doing all of his buying as well as his selling from it, but I doubted it. There would be some deliveries to him that were more than one van full. I was also beginning to wonder if he had any employees. It sounded like a big operation to be run by one man.

9 _____

When I got back home, I called Amanda's office. I told her secretary
that I wanted a few minutes of her time the next day, and was told that she was
in trial for the rest of the week and was taking no further appointments till the
following week. I asked for her voice mail, and left her a message. I figured she
would call me despite her trial schedule.

It was after five, but I didn't feel like working out and I wasn't hungry
yet. I took off my utility worker clothes and boots and showered, washing off
the breaking and entering sweat. I put on a pair of jeans, a turtleneck sweater,
and my running shoes, and headed out into the twilight.

It was another beautiful evening, with the sun settling toward the far
horizon over Arkansas, painting the river as it went. I walked north on the
mall, past tourists who were looking for Beale Street or waiting on the trolley,
and bag ladies and homeless alcoholics and schizophrenics who sat on benches
or wandered slowly down the street. The weather seemed to have put everyone
in a better mood. The smell of barbecued pig blew through the air from the
Rendezvous, followed closely by the odor of fresh baked bread from the bakery
near downtown. My stomach and mouth let down like the breasts of a nursing
mother who hears her baby's hungry cry. It was a great evening for a stroll.

I went all the way up the mall to Poplar, past the ugliness of the sixties
architecture of city hall and the federal building, and turned east toward the
jail. The scene was pretty much the same as it had been when I last visited Ajax

Bond, except that the pedestrian traffic in and out of the justice center building was slowed this time of day. In front of Jackson's and the liquor store, though, the crowd was even thicker. As I walked down the sidewalk by the liquor store, I had to step out into the street to go around a group of men who were passing a wine bottle. One of them looked at me, tapped his pocket with his hand, and asked, "Hey, man, you looking for something?"

"No thanks," I replied, and kept on.

"Hey, man, I got whatever you need, you know what I'm sayin'," he called after me.

"Don't be no fool, man," I heard one of the other men say to him. "He might be a cop."

"He ain't no cop. I know who's a cop and who ain't a cop."

They were discussing exactly how the first one knew I wasn't a cop as I stepped back up on the sidewalk and into the open door of Ajax Bond. Inside, the scene was the same it had been on my first visit, except Henry was doing some business. He was standing behind the counter, completing a form with a ballpoint pen while a young white woman with big blonde hair answered his questions. She was wearing white high heel shoes, tight black jeans and a white blouse with the first three buttons undone. Her arms were crossed and resting on the top of the counter, and her breasts rested on top of her arms. The result was that her cleavage was enhanced and her breasts bulged out of the top of the blouse at Jackson. He apparently didn't notice, though, so I pretended like I didn't, either.

Jackson looked up and recognized me, but just said, "I'll be with you in a minute."

"Now, sign right here," Jackson said, as he turned the form around and handed the pen to the woman, "and it'll be five hundred dollars."

The woman leaned over the counter a little more, looked up at Henry and said, "Where do I sign?"

"Right here," he said, pointing.

"Oh, I see," she said, not moving. Henry kept his eyes on hers. "The thing is, honey, I can't really spare five hundred right now. Could we work out some other arrangement?"

"No, baby, I'm not interested in anything you got except money," he replied.

"Why don't you let me prove you're wrong?" she asked, running her tongue around her lips.

"Sweetheart, I don't want to offend you. Let's just say you're not my type."

"Why not? You don't like white women, or you just don't like women at all?"

"No, I like women, and I don't really care what color they are. What I don't like is being this far back in the line."

I expected her to be mad, but she just smiled and said, "It doesn't wear out, you know."

"It does for me," Jackson said. "Now, you want the bond or not?"

"Yeah, I want the bond," she said, finally giving up. She signed the form, and then pulled a wad of bills out of her front pocket. She peeled off five hundreds, laid them on the counter, and then stuck the rest of the money back in her pocket.

"I thought you couldn't spare five hundred," Henry said.

"What I meant was I would rather use it on something else," she said. "Besides, we weren't just talking about work and money. You keep the five hundred, but if you ever want something else, you just call me. My number's on your form." With that, she smiled at Henry, ignored me, and walked out the door.

"I admire your restraint," I told Jackson with a grin.

"Restraint, hell. I wouldn't touch that if I was wearing a body condom. She may look okay, but it's a fifty-fifty shot she's got the bug."

"Nobody's perfect," I said.

"Hey, man, even if she was perfect, I'd go for the five hundred. You start writing bonds for drugs or sex you can kiss your business goodbye. Now, what can I do for you?"

"You remember me, don't you?" I asked.

"Yeah, I remember you. You were asking about Thomas Tuggle. But I'll be honest, I don't remember your name."

"I couldn't expect you to," I said, holding out my hand. "Not when you have to spend all your time turning down sex. I'm John McAlister."

He grinned and took my hand. "I knew it was one of those Mac names. Did you find our mutual friend Thomas yet?"

"What do you mean, Mac names," I said. "Jackson is just as British Isles as McAlister."

"Maybe so, but you came by yours honestly. My grandmother always claimed our people were owned by Andrew Jackson. She couldn't be proud that her ancestors were famous, so she had to be proud that her ancestors were owned by a famous person."

"Too bad your last name's not Jefferson," I said. "Then maybe you could claim a famous ancestor."

"Yeah, I read that Thomas was open-minded when it came to the bedroom. Now, how you doing finding our Thomas?"

"I'm working on it. I was hoping you might could help me a little more."

"More? I wish I could."

"Do you have any idea where he might store his inventory, take deliveries, park his van?"

He opened the same file cabinet and took out Thomas's file. He flipped it open and read out Thomas's home address.

"That's his home," I said. "Did he give you a work address or a telephone number?"

"That's the only address I got."

Then he read me a phone number that was the same as the one on the phone bill I had taken from Thomas's house. "No other number?" I asked. "Cell phone, beeper?"

"No, man, that's all I got."

"Do you think you could find out, maybe?" I asked.

"Maybe," he said.

"Why haven't you tried to before now?"

"Look, like I said, I hate to lose nine thousand dollars, but there's worse things can happen."

"Like what?" I asked.

"Like maybe getting killed," he said.

"Killed? For what?" I asked. "You said yourself he's not a crack dealer. Besides, you got that big old Beretta stuck on your butt."

"Let's just say I make it a general policy not to go after skips myself. If I'm out looking for some dude has skipped out on me, I'm not here taking care of business. I leave that to the police and the bounty hunters."

"Then what's the Beretta for?" I asked.

"For personal security. In case you haven't noticed, this is a tough neighborhood. I do a lot of cash business, and my clientele has, how should I say, evidenced a predisposition to break the law."

"Yeah, but there's always a dozen cops and sheriffs cars parked right across the street. I mean, the jail is right there."

"You think that means anything to a crackhead who needs a fix?" he asked, looking exasperated. "Hey, I'll bet you right now if you go stand outside my door for five minutes, somebody will try to sell you rock."

"They already did," I said.

"See what I'm telling you."

"Well, I can understand you not wanting to get killed," I said. "It's not high on my list, either. But maybe you can help me find him, and you won't have to leave your business."

"I'll have to think about that one," he said.

"What's to think about?" I asked.

"Two things. One, I help someone find a skip, and the skip finds out I helped, I could still get killed. Two, it's not great publicity for my business to go around handing people over to the cops."

"Two things back at you. One, you're not turning him over to the cops, you're just helping his momma rest easy at night knowing her boy is okay. Two, how can you run this business if your customers don't know you'll come get them if they leave you holding the bag?"

"Don't tell me how to run my business," Henry said with an edge in his voice. "Some of them you can go get, fine. But some you just write off on your tax return as bad debt and go on with your life. Otherwise, you're not going to have any more life. No bail bondsman will admit that, but it's the truth."

"Why do you write that kind in the first place?" I asked.

Jackson shrugged. "Money. They usually have a big bond to meet, so they pay me a big fee. I make more, but I stand to lose more if they don't show up and don't get caught again. I take a few of them, but not on a regular basis."

"But you don't think Thomas is one of them, do you?"

"No."

"So do you think I'm trying to find him for the cops?" I asked.

Jackson wrinkled his forehead, and stared at me for a few seconds. "I don't know what to think about you," he said. "I've never had a PI come in here and tell me he's looking for a fugitive so his mother won't worry about him."

"Well, it's not the kind of case we studied in detective school, but it's the job I got now."

"Detective school, huh? Look, let me think about it. I'll give you a call."

"I'd appreciate it very much," I said, handing him another business card. "How's law school coming?"

"It's going okay. My grades are good, but I'm ready for it to be over."

"Have you got a job lined up yet?" I asked.

"No," he said shortly. It didn't seem like this was his favorite question.

"What will you do with this business once you start practicing?' I asked.

"Sell it. You want to buy it?"

"No," I said. "I've done my time with the thieves and the whores."

It was totally dark when I left Ajax. There was a full moon rising over the eastern part of the city, and the temperature had cooled enough that I appreciated my sweater. I stopped at the Rendezvous and sat at the bar with a half order of ribs and a couple of draft Michelobs. It was almost nine when I left, and a heavy drizzle had settled over the city, blocking out the moon and stars and fuzzing the lights and sounds of downtown. I felt like the heavy food and the beer had done the same thing to my mind, and I walked slowly back toward home.

I turned down the alley toward my apartment, and was half way to the stairs when two figures stepped out from underneath them heading my way. I quickly turned and started running for the street. But the alley was now blocked by another figure closing in on me. Before I could think about stopping, he raised his hand and pointed it at me from about fifteen feet away.

As his hand came up, I skidded down face first on the bricks. A four foot long cone of yellow and red muzzle blast flared out from his hand, and a sound like the ripping thunder from a close lightning strike smashed my ears.

I heard a scream and a voice from behind me, "No, no, you stupid fuck, you hit Jimmy!" I was back up and running hard at him just as he pulled the gun back down from the recoil. The muzzle blast had ruined my night vision, but I knew it had done the same to his. I faked to the left, went to the right, and was past him as he hesitated, my head down and running hard for the mouth of the alley. I heard the same voice yelling again just as I turned the corner onto Front Street. "Shoot him! Shoot him now, you dumb fucker!" A shot chunked into a car parallel parked on the street, but I was already around the angle and into dead ground.

I ran pell-mell down the sidewalk, turning at the first side street and doing my best Carl Lewis all the way to the lights of Beale Street, not looking back once. There were no more yells behind me, and no more shots.

I pulled up just before I hit the lights, sucking deep breaths into my lungs and fighting to keep my dinner down. My ears were keening with the explosion that had blown over my head, and my eyes still had spots in front of them from the flash. I knelt behind a parked car, and looked back the way I had come. Nothing. When my breathing was under control, I walked into one of the clubs and went straight to the bathroom. My palms were scratched and covered with grit, and there was a small scrape on my left cheek. One of the elbows was out of my sweater, and the knees of my pants were dirty but not ripped open. The damage was a hell of a lot less than it could have been. I cleaned up as best I could, and went out and sat at the bar.

The adrenaline was beginning to drain out of me, and I was getting the shakes. When the bartender asked me what I wanted, my teeth were chattering so hard I had to stick my tongue between the teeth on one side of my mouth to get an order out. He gave me a close look, decided I wasn't too drunk to serve, and brought me a Beefeater on the rocks. I picked it up with both hands, and took slow sips, keeping it to my lips till half of it was gone. I usually reveled in the clean, minty odor and texture of good gin, but this one tasted like water. I put it back down on the bar, taking deep breaths and holding them for a second while I pretended to watch the football game on the television set above the bar. When I wasn't shaking anymore, I picked the glass back up, drained the rest of the gin, threw a bill down on the bar, and walked out.

There were a few people moving up and down the street, but not many on a weekday night. None of them looked like they wanted to kill me. I walked slowly back toward my place, and saw what I expected when I was only halfway there. Three patrol cars were parked at the entrance to the alley, their blue lights dimmed by the drizzle. As I walked up to them, an unmarked car pulled up, and a man in plainclothes got out from behind the wheel and walked into the alley. A patrolman came out and backed up one of the cars so its lights were shining into the alley.

I knew my appearance wasn't great, but neither was the light, so I decided to risk talking to the cops to see if they had found anything. I didn't see them talking to any witnesses, so I doubted there was anybody who could place me at the scene except the three guys who had been there.

I walked up to the three patrolmen and plainclothes guy. They were standing in a semicircle, adding to the illumination from the car's headlights with flashlights they were shining on the pavement. Patches of blood lay like purple neon on the wet paving stones.

"Excuse me, officer," I said to the group, "I live up there. Is it okay if I go past?"

One of them turned around to me and briefly shone his light on my face, then snapped it off. He asked to see my driver's license, which I pulled out of my wallet. He looked at it quickly under his light, then gave it back. "Sir," he said, "this is a crime scene, and I need you to wait here for a few minutes while we look around before I can let you past. I know it's late, but it won't be long."

"That's fine, officer," I said. "Can you tell me what happened? I'd like to know since this is like my front yard."

"We got a call from someone saying they heard gunshots. It looks like someone was hit, but we haven't found anyone yet. Did you hear anything?" he asked.

"No, but I was down on Beale Street, having a drink. Do you think it was a robbery? I've always kind of worried about that when I've been coming in at night."

"We don't know yet, but I doubt it. It looks like whoever was hit took off, and I can't think why a victim would do that. Now, sir, I have to get back to work. I'm going to ask you to stay right here until we're through."

"That's fine, officer."

I leaned against the alley wall, watching them look around. I saw a light coming in from the far end of the alley, and a patrolman walked up to the plainclothes.

"Lieutenant, the blood trail goes all the way down to the next street, and then stops at the curb. It looks like whoever it was got into a vehicle and drove off."

"Did you find any cartridge cases?" the lieutenant asked the patrolman. I knew the answer before he gave it. The shooter had taken both shots from this end of the alley, but he was also using a revolver, so there would be no ejected cartridges anywhere. The image of the muzzle blast was still burned into my optic memory. It had shot out not only from the end of the barrel, but also sideways, where the front of the cylinder aligned with the back of the barrel. The cylinder wouldn't turn if it fit too closely, so part of the blast always escaped between the cylinder and the barrel. It was why you didn't steady a revolver except by putting another hand on the grip.

"Here's where a bullet hit," called one of the cops. He shone his light on a paving stone with a white gouge out of it, and a streak of red on it and the stone beside it.

"Hey, I found something over here," called another cop by the wall on the far side.

They all walked over to him, and shone their lights on whatever he was looking at.

"What is that thing?" I heard one of the cops ask.

"Man, I don't know," the cop who found it said. "I'm just a patrolman, I find things, the lieutenant tells me what they are."

I saw the plainclothes squat down, so he wouldn't get a knee wet, and look at something on the stones, then stand back up with a grunt. "I'll tell you what it is, children. It's the last joint of a man's big toe, a white guy with fungus nail. And it's fresh, still seeping blood."

"No shit," said one of the patrolmen, squatting down and fixing the object in his flashlight. "You're right, lieutenant. It's a fucking toe!"

"Man, that's gross," I heard one of the other patrolmen say.

"Gross or not," the lieutenant said, "go get an evidence bag out of the trunk and stick it in it after we put the chalk down and get some photos. Don't forget to put a glove on before you touch it. The rest of you guys keep looking around. I'll bet a dollar you find a piece of a shoe."

"Aw, Lieutenant, I don't want to touch that thing, even if I got two gloves on," the patrolman said.

"Don't be a pussy, Miller," another patrolman said. "I'll do it myself. How'd I ever get such a weenie for a partner?"

Another unmarked car pulled up behind the patrol cars, and a man stepped out, paused briefly at the curb, and walked up to the group in the alley.

"Hey, Julian, what are you doing here?" the lieutenant asked. "I got this covered."

"Yeah, I see. I was in the area when I heard the call, so I stopped by. It's a slow night. Did any of your Sherlocks notice there's a bullet hole like a fucking crater in the black Buick pulled in to the curb where they're parked?" he said as he pointed back down the alley.

"Not yet, but we would have gotten to it," the first one said. "Hey, Miller," he yelled, "go check out that Buick."

"So what have you got, Randy?" the new arrival asked. "All I heard on the radio was a shots fired report."

"So far, all we got is the same. Plus a blood trail up the alley and a piece of somebody's big toe. No cartridge case and no bullet. I bet we can dig one out of the Buick, but it'll be torn to hell by the metal unless it's a solid."

"No witnesses?"

"No witnesses. We've talked to the people in the apartments around, and nobody saw anything. Most of them heard the shots, but only one or two even knew what they were."

"Who's the citizen over there?" he asked, nodding toward me.

I was standing in the deep shadow outside the car lights, and I was pretty sure he couldn't see my face.

"Just some guy heading home. We made him wait till we had secured the scene. What's the deal with all these questions? This is my investigation, Julian. Don't you have anything better to do?"

"Hey, I was just curious. Like I said, it's a slow night. I think I'll go get some coffee." Steiner walked back to his car and drove off.

"Excuse me, officer," I said. "Would it be all right if I went on into my apartment? It's at the top of the fire escape."

"Hang on one minute, sir," he said. "Hey, Rich, you checked out the fire escape when you talked to the residents, didn't you?" he asked a patrolman.

"Yes sir," he said. "It's clean."

"All right, sir. You can go on. Just stay on this side of the alley so you don't step in the blood."

I was pretty sure the men waiting for me hadn't been in my apartment or office, but the first thing I did when I got inside was unlock the bottom left hand drawer of my office desk and fill my hand with walnut and blue steel. I checked the load, then methodically went through office and apartment, first making sure I didn't have any visitors. I then checked and double checked the locks on all the windows and threw the auxiliary deadbolt on the outside door. If Mary flew in unexpectedly tonight, she'd have to knock.

The lock on the outside hadn't shown any signs of being tampered with, and I couldn't find any evidence inside that someone had been in. That didn't keep me from dragging one of the leather wing chairs I had kept from my law practice over to the door and wedging it under the knob. So much for the fearless detective refusing to cower behind locked doors.

I set the alarm system, and went into the bathroom. I wrapped the .357 in a towel so it wouldn't get damp and put it on top of the toilet tank. I stripped off and got in the shower after I locked the bathroom door. I needed a long, hot soak, but I found myself hurrying to get out. The shower is a vulnerable, insecure feeling place when someone has just tried to kill you, even if the chances of them coming back that night are slim to none.

I put on sweats and a t-shirt, got a beer out of the refrigerator, and sat at the computer. I was continuing to calm down, but I still kept the pistol near me. It was a great comfort.

I took a couple of pulls on the beer, and then started a new document entitled "What the Fuck Happened?" I began to type an account of the last hour's events, so I could get it all down before I forgot anything. It was one of the few lawyering skills that I had found carried over to detective work.

I couldn't remember seeing anyone on Front before I had turned into the alley. No one walking, riding in a car or sitting in one. So put the shooter crouched down between two cars parked past the alley entrance, or sitting in one with the interior dome light turned off and the door cracked.

The two under the stairs would have seen me as soon as I turned up the alley. There was a streetlight there, so they could probably have seen my face in profile as I made the corner and began to walk toward them. They hadn't waited for me to get halfway to them so they could make a positive i.d., but so their friend could block the entrance. I had wheeled back so quickly when I had seen them that there wasn't much I could say about their appearance except for what I could tell from their silhouettes. They were about the same height, right around six feet, and one of them was wearing a ball cap. One had been wearing a knee length coat of some kind, and the other either had a very bulky torso or was wearing a bomber-type jacket. That was it. No clothes or skin colors, no glint of glasses or jewelry, no sign of a weapon.

The shooter was shorter than the other two by a good three inches, and I had seen a reflection on his face that indicated glasses. I tried to relive the moment when I had skidded into the bricks and the pistol had crashed over my head, but came up with very little on his appearance. Dark, receding hair, white skin, but no facial features. The hands that gripped the revolver were pitch black, which meant he was wearing black athletic gloves to contain his fingerprints and control the recoil. The revolver itself was big and silvery, a stainless steel or nickel finish. Probably stainless, since they didn't make a lot of nickel finishes anymore. It had a six-inch barrel and, judging from the noise and muzzle blast, was at least a match for my .357, and was probably a .44 Special or Magnum. Maybe Dirty Harry was after me.

The only other thing I had to go on was the voice of the man who had yelled at the shooter. My ears were still ringing from the increment of permanent nerve damage they had just suffered, but I could distinctly hear that voice. It was a white voice, Southern, not redneck, but obviously blunt in language. The first thing it had yelled at the gunman was "no" right after the first shot. Had he meant no, don't shoot again this way because you hit Jimmy, or had he meant don't shoot at all? Either way, I was grateful, since the yell had confused the shooter long enough for me to get past before he could recover and pump one into me at point blank range. The voice was then immediately exhorting him to shoot me, which argued that his initial words were aimed at self-preservation, not at sparing me, but I couldn't rule out that he decided instantaneously that since I was getting away they might as well shoot me.

The only other voice I had heard was Jimmy's when he yelled after his big toe was shot off. I couldn't tell his race from one yell, but the police lieutenant had found the toe of a white man.

So what did I have? Three white guys set me up in my home alley. It was obviously premeditated, but was it premeditated at me? They could have been waiting for anyone to walk into the alley to get mugged, but it seemed like a lot of forethought and firepower to lift a wallet and a watch. Maybe they were waiting there to collect a gambling debt from one of my neighbors and picked me by mistake. Most likely, though, I told myself, they were waiting for me, and I was extremely lucky they hadn't gotten me.

The obvious question, though, was why were they waiting? I could think of a lot of pissed off ex-husbands who probably wouldn't mind picking up the paper and reading that I had been killed, but I doubted that any of them were serious enough about it to try to kill me in cold blood, or even hire someone else to do it. I had been shot at before, by a neurosurgeon who objected to my filming him entertaining his children's French nanny on the pool table in the den while Mrs. Neurosurgeon and the kids were out of town. I had gotten careless, stepping up too close to the open sliding doors to make sure I had the light right, figuring he was too involved in the moment to notice me, and stepped right on a cat that was lying there. The cat yowled and jumped, and I tripped over him and fell headlong into the den, my shoulder crashing into the edge of the door and knocking it out of its grooves and over with a smash onto the flagstone floor. He and I were both up and running at the same time, I for the safety of the darkness and my truck and he, it turned out, for his pistol. I was almost to the fence at his back yard when I heard the first blast and wood splinters flew out of the fence in front of me and to the right, and I was halfway over the fence when the second bullet hit the video camera and showered me with bits of plastic and glass. The bullet had ruined the camera, but not hit the film. After Amanda watched the movie, she bought me a new camera as an expense before she paid me my fee out of the four million settlement she got out of the doctor.

The point, though, was that I didn't worry about the surgeon coming around to try to kill me later. He knew what was going on when he saw me sprawled on his floor with a video camera, and he decided he would shoot me. Those guys don't get paid the big bucks for being slow thinkers, so he probably figured he could nail me and claim he thought I was a burglar. My camera, or at least its film, would disappear before the cops showed up. It was a quick but cold-blooded decision, with a lot riding on its outcome, but once the decision was made, attempted and had failed, there was no reason for him to come back and try again.

Now, though, I had no idea why anyone would want to kill me. A revenge killing was possible, but not likely. As for current matters, I was working several cases, two ongoing domestic relations matters for Amanda, an employee theft investigation for a local business, and the Tuggle case. The way I saw it, the only way my being permanently removed from any of those cases would benefit anyone was a possible delay while someone else was hired. Also, I was pretty sure that neither of the suspected husbands in the domestic relations cases had any idea I was on their trail, and I didn't think the thieving employee did, either. As for Thomas, I was pretty sure he was dead or gone.

Why hadn't I told the police what happened? Because, I answered myself, you don't know why it happened. Until you do, you have a lawyer's trained reticence to reveal information. Plus, I didn't see how it could help them catch the guys who did it, and I didn't want to be the object of the cops' attention. Getting on the police shit list was not a good career move for a PI. While getting shot at was not a crime, it didn't usually happen to the average citizen. When it did, the police typically asked themselves whether the shootee was really an average citizen, or whether he was involved in some activities—usually criminal—that would make people want to shoot at him. Nobody likes the authorities looking into their affairs, especially if you're someone like me who has to bend the rules from time to time and depends on a license from the state to conduct his business.

Why was Steiner, the cop in charge of the Tuggle case, at the crime scene? Coincidence, I decided. His explanation for his presence made a lot more sense than any possible connection with the Tuggle case. Most likely, he didn't even know where I lived. I had stayed back in the shadows when he arrived because I didn't want to start him on any speculations, especially if he looked at me closer and saw my scrapes and torn and dirty clothes. But it still seemed weird that he had been there.

I saved my description of the night's events, and turned off the computer. I knew I had just created evidence of my crime—obstructing justice or something like that—in not telling the police what happened, but I judged the importance of having a record more important than the remote possibility anyone but me would ever read it. And if I did turn up dead, maybe someone would read it, and use it to figure out who and why.

I made a last circuit of the doors and windows, then put the .357 on my nightstand and got into bed. I was tired, physically and mentally, and went to sleep faster than I thought I would.

10 ——————————

At six thirty the next morning, I pulled into the drive of a house right across from the country club's golf course. The house was not as big as Jack Jones's pile, but its red brick and white columns made it every bit as imposing. The driveway was made out of the same weathered brick, and a matching walk bisected the lawn and ran at least 75 yards from the front porch to the street. The drive wound past the end of the house and ended in a pull around circle with a two-car garage on the other side. I parked in the middle of the circle and reached over and retrieved my pistol from the glove compartment. I got out of the truck and clipped the unfamiliar weight on the back of my belt under my tweed sports coat. I didn't really need it right now, but I wanted to get used to carrying it and I didn't want to leave it in the truck.

A head high ornamental metal gate flanked by brick columns led into the back yard. It was locked with a brass deadbolt, so I glanced behind me to make sure no one had pulled into the drive, put both hands on the top, and levered myself up and over. I made a little noise in the process, but not much. I paused for a second, waiting to see if a Rottweiler would come charging up, then walked out past the holly bushes that hid the back yard. The lawn here stretched another 75 yards to a brick wall that was visible in pieces between the vegetation that grew along it. There was an old, unused looking tennis court with no net set over against one side, and a brick and lumber gazebo against the other. A piece of lattice was missing from the gazebo. The grass was cut, but there was a scattering of early leaves from the ginkgoes and maples that grew in several clumps around the yard. The few flowerbeds were choked with tall, bare roses and lilies, with an occasional weed poking up here and there. Closer to the house, there were a few pieces of wrought iron furniture on a brick patio that lay flush with the ground. More weeds grew out of the patio where the mortar had worn away between bricks, and rust spotted the furniture. Like many old two story brick houses that have been added onto, the back of the house was covered with white boards. The paint was just beginning to peel on the boards. Three wide brick steps mounted from the patio to the back door, which opened onto an enclosed sun porch.

I had just put my foot on the first step, when I noticed someone sitting at a small table on the sun porch with her back to me. She was wearing a white bathrobe, and had a white towel wrapped around her hair. I waited till she put her coffee down, then reached out and knocked sharply on the glass. She jumped straight out of her chair, banging into the table and sloshing coffee out of her cup as she tried to turn around at the same time. The towel fell off her head, and her hair fell down over her eyes. She brushed her hair up, peered out at me, and said a bad word that I could hear through the glass. I gave her a little wave and pointed at the door.

I could hear her trying to turn the lock, and then the door swung back suddenly and Amanda was standing there, shooting Godzilla death rays at me with her lovely blue eyes. "You no good sonofabitch!" she hissed. "You scared the shit out of me! Why didn't you knock on the front door like a normal person? Why didn't you call? I know I locked that gate! How did you get back here?"

She was ready to say a lot more, but she was swinging her hands around so much that one side of her robe dropped open, revealing a lovely shower fresh breast with a surprisingly large nipple. While she struggled to get covered up, I stepped past her, saying "Good morning to you, too, sweetheart," and poured myself a cup of coffee from the pot setting on a hot plate on the table.

She turned around, and for a second I thought she was going to hit me. I sat down in the chair on the other side of the table, and waited while she took a couple of deep breaths, pushing her chest out against her robe, holding the air two or three seconds before releasing it in a relaxation technique I had used myself. It was fun to watch Amanda relaxing, especially since I knew what was on the other side of that terry cloth.

She sat down, poured more coffee, and took a sip. Then she said, "Okay, why are you here?"

"Because you won't return my calls and I need to talk to you."

"John, I'm in the last week of a three week trial. I'm not returning any phone calls unless they have to do with this case. I don't have time and I can't afford the distraction. You used to be a lawyer. You ought to understand that."

"You're the one who's so hot to find Thomas Tuggle," I said. "Surely you can spare me ten minutes. Besides, who ever heard of a divorce trial that went three weeks? How many people did he screw?"

"It's not who he screwed, it's where he hid the money. Look, John, I didn't go to bed until two this morning. I have an important cross-examination at ten a.m." She gestured to a coffee-stained deposition transcript lying on the table. "I have eighty more pages of that to read before then."

"Okay, just give me five minutes." Before she could answer, I pulled the picture I had stolen from Thomas's house out of my pocket and placed it on the table. "Do you know this guy with Lucy?"

She picked it up and studied it for a minute. "No," she said slowly, "he looks familiar somehow. I think I've seen him, but I can't place him. Where did you get the photograph?"

"It was in a box in Thomas's house," I said.

"In his house? Shit, John, you know better than to tell me that," she said, tossing the photo back at me.

"Hey, you asked, I told you. Next time, don't ask."

"Well, don't tell me anything else like that."

"There's not much else to tell about Thomas's house. But don't give me anymore shit about not looking for him hard."

"I didn't tell you to break into his house."

"Was that statement for the record, counselor? I know you didn't tell me to break into his house. But you did say find him. I'm just doing what I can."

"So what else have you done?" she asked. Her fingers were tapping on the table, and there was a tic in her left cheek muscle. It must be some trial, I thought.

"I've talked to some people, but I haven't had any real luck yet. What about you? Any legal avenues that will get us information on who informed on Thomas?"

"No, that's a dead end. He skipped out. The district attorney's office won't tell us anything, even if I enter an appearance as his attorney."

"Can you think of anything you might not have told me about Thomas or Lucy that would help me?" I asked.

"No, John, I've told you everything I can think of."

"Well, since I'm here, do you want me to give you an update on the Becky Murphy and Celeste Scott cases?" I asked.

"John, I really don't have time," she said, looking down at the unread deposition transcript.

"Okay," I said. Then, as an afterthought, I asked, "Can you think of anything unusual about those cases? I'm not having a lot of luck on them either. Anything peculiar about the husbands?"

"No," she said. "They're the usual adulterous assholes. I just need you to prove the adulterous part."

"I'll do my best. Now I'll let you get back to work."

"Thank you. And thanks for the report on Thomas. I'm sorry I jumped down your throat. I'm under a lot of pressure in this trial. I really want a good result for my client, and it's not been easy going."

"I'm sorry I scared you," I said, standing up. "Listen, don't you ever get tired of it?"

"Tired of what?" she asked.

"The constant conflict, the bullshit, other people's problems, staying up till two a.m. and getting up at six a.m. during a trial."

"No, it's the only thing I know how to do well. I can't afford to get tired of it."

"I assume you don't mean that from a money standpoint," I said.

"No, I mean it from a standpoint a lot more important than that."

"Well, good luck with the trial. I'll show myself out," I said.

"No, I'll let you out. You might tear your clothes if you have to climb over my gate again." She took a key off a hook by the door and walked barefoot onto the patio, her feet bare and her hair wet and dark blonde in the cool morning air. She stopped a moment and looked around. "This place is really going to hell," she said. "I need to get a good yard crew back here and have some painting done."

"It's a big place for one person," I said. "Did you ever think about selling it and getting something smaller?"

"Sell this place? No, I never thought about it. It's where I grew up."

She opened the gate, and I walked through. Before I got to my truck, I heard her pulling the gate closed, and the sound of the deadbolt turning. I half turned around to say goodbye, but caught only a glimpse of bare calf and a flash of white robe framed briefly by black iron bars.

On the way back downtown, I stopped in at the Barksdale Restaurant and treated myself to a real breakfast. I felt like I deserved it for not getting killed the night before. I sipped coffee and read the paper until my country ham, eggs and biscuits arrived. I packed them in on top of last night's ribs, and decided I'd better stop the daily dose of pig meat before I keeled over from clogged arteries and saved whoever was trying to kill me the trouble. I waved at the owner on the way out, and said, "Next time I'm just getting the pancakes."

"That's what you always say," he called after me.

It was another gorgeous fall morning, the air just cool enough to smoke through your lips, and the trees were hitting full peak on the colors. I forgot for a moment that someone had tried to kill me the night before, but I remembered it as soon as I got into the pickup and the revolver dug into the small of my back. I unclipped the holster from my belt and laid it on the seat beside me.

I headed down Peabody, avoiding the worst of rush hour on Union and enjoying the tunnel effect created by the trees that arched over the street from the yards of the old homes. I turned onto Linden out of the residential section, past the backside of the medical center and the newspaper's offices. A few nineteenth century homes, some of them antebellum, stuck up here and there on side streets, mingling with the dilapidated shotgun cottages and warehouses. They had at one time been the pride of cotton merchants and other elite Memphians, but most of them now served as flophouses for street people and crackheads. They were like sick old people in a bad nursing home, tired of living but afraid to die.

When I got back downtown, I unlocked the double deadbolts on the office door and stepped in. I drew my revolver and began to check all the rooms, but I started feeling silly so I put it on top of my desk. It was a Smith & Wesson Model 27, a big tool and a heavy one, even with the short 3 1/2 inch barrel. It was the original model chambered specifically for the then new .357 magnum cartridge. My great uncle Stan McAlister, who was sheriff in a Missouri Bootheel river town, bought it used in 1947. It was more gun than he could afford, but he invested in it on the theory that when he needed a gun he needed it bad, so he'd better get the best.

When I graduated from high school, Uncle Stan called my father and asked us to come up and see him. It was a two-hour drive up I-55 and across a state highway through the cotton and beanfields to the little town where he still lived. Most of the buildings in the town square were vacant, but a few people, mostly black, wandered in and out of the places still open for business. A crowd of black kids ran back and forth playing on the courthouse lawn, and a group of old white men sat on green wooden slat benches screwed into the sidewalk. Their eyes watched our car as we went by. I remember Dad saying that half the town would know about our visit before the end of the day.

Uncle Stan lived in a small, neat white house two blocks off the square. Black children playing in the yard across the street stopped for a minute and looked at us as we pulled into the curb and got out of the car, then went back to their game. We stepped up onto the porch, and Dad knocked on the screen door. The wooden door behind it was open, and Dad called in, "Uncle Stan, it's me, Johnny."

Uncle Stan, a spare, wiry figure with a bright red face, a full head of white hair, and piercing blue eyes, appeared out of the shadows and opened the screen. He didn't ask us in, but came out on the porch and grabbed my Dad's hand in both of his. "By God, Johnny, it's so good to see you," he said, looking Dad up and down. "And this boy," he said, turning to me, "I haven't seen him in years. He's all growed up. Sit down, sit down," he said, gesturing at two cane bottomed, ladder back chairs beside a rocker.

Uncle Stan went back into the house, and came back with a six-pack of Budweiser tall boys in cans still attached by the plastic holder. He pulled two off, handed one to Dad and one to me, and got one for himself. The others he set down on the floor by his chair. He and Dad spent an hour talking about relatives living and dead, during which time the other beers disappeared. Then he got up from the rocking chair, and went inside. He came back carrying a green tin box about a foot square in one hand, and another six-pack in the other.

He offered Dad and me both another beer, but I declined when Dad did. Uncle Stan set the box down on the floor, and helped himself to another. Once he had gotten it open, he said, "Johnny, if it's all right with you, I want your boy to have my old Smith. It's still a fine weapon, and I have no need for it anymore. But I'm too old to teach him how to use it, so you'll have to do that. I always thought you had more sense than most of us McAlisters, so I know you'll teach him what it's for and what it's not for."

I was a lot more interested in cars and girls than in guns, but I knew that for Uncle Stan, who had no children of his own, this was an important thing. "Thank you very much, Uncle Stan," I said. "Is it okay if I look at it?"

"Hell, no, it's not okay, son," he said sharply. "I know you just drank two beers, but any amount of alcohol don't mix with guns. You've got a lot to teach this young one still, Johnny."

"I'll teach him," Dad said. "Living in the city, he didn't grow up around guns the way we did."

"I'll learn, Uncle Stan, I'm sorry," I said, not wanting to anger the old man.

"I know you will, John," he said. ""I'm sorry I snapped at you. It's just that it's about the only thing I have worthwhile to give anybody, and I don't want to sit here and think it might be misused. I'd rather melt it down than have that happen. You just remember it's not something to use lightly, even if you're shooting cans."

"I will," I said. "Did you ever have to use it, I mean while you were sheriff?"

"Uncle Stan might not want to get back into all that," Dad said.

Uncle Stan sat there for a minute, pulling on his Bud, and then said, "You're right, Johnny. I don't want to, but maybe I should. I think he ought to know." Then he told us this story.

"I carried that revolver for twenty years, and didn't use it for nothing but blowing big holes in the ceilings of roadhouses to get everyone's attention when there was a bar fight going on. Then one Sunday morning back in the sixties, I was just setting down to breakfast with your Aunt Sarah, God rest her, when the phone rang. It was a lady who lived two streets over. She said she had heard gun shots in the house next door. I knew the man who lived in that house worked out on the river for three week stretches, and I and just about everybody else in town knew his wife entertained the barber while he was gone.

"I strapped on the pistol in that box there and hurried over, dreading what I was going to find. I didn't have a deputy then, and even if I had I couldn't of waited on him. I had the gun out of the holster and my foot on the first step of the porch when the husband pushed the screen open and half stepped out, his left shoulder holding the door open. He had a spray of bright red spots across one cheek, and there was a heavy odor of blood and gunpowder blowing past him in the draft that was coming through the door. I had known this man for years, but I barely recognized him, his face was so dark and twisted up. But I was mainly looking at the pump shotgun he held pointed straight down.

"He wasn't no more than eight feet away, and I kept the Smith up and pointed right at his chest. I don't think he even saw me at first, he had just decided to come out on the porch right as I was getting there. His name was Fred, and I started saying it over and over, real soft. My voice was cracking and sweat was dripping into my eyes, and I felt like I was going to crap my pants, but I kept saying it. When he finally looked at me, I said, 'Put the gun down, Fred, put it down.'

"His face relaxed, and he said, 'Hello, Stan, it didn't take you long to get here. What now?' His voice sounded better than mine. I told him again to put the gun down.

"He looked at the gun in his hand like he had forgotten it was there, and then looked back up at me. 'I'll get the chair, won't I?' he asked.

"I told him it would be second degree murder, maybe even voluntary manslaughter, and that he would be out in five or six years.

"'You sure about that, Stan?' he asked. 'You're not just trying to get me to put this old pump gun down, are you?'

"I told him that I'd arrested half a dozen men for the same thing, and the most they ever got was ten years.

"'Then do you want to do it or should I do it myself?' he asked.

"I started to ask what he meant, but the muzzle of the shotgun was coming up and before I could even think of where he might be going to point it my finger tightened and he went flying back through the door, the middle blown out of his chest."

Uncle Stan pulled another beer out of its ring, and took a long pull. He looked at me with those blue eyes, and said, "John, I thought about that morning hundreds of times, wondering what I could have done different. After about a year I finally accepted that the answer was nothing. I made my peace with it. But the point is, once you pull that trigger, you can't get the bullet back."

At that moment, the telephone rang, bringing me out of the past. I picked it up, and Henry Jackson asked, "Have you found our man Thomas yet?"

"No," I said, "have you?"

"I'm not looking for him. That's your job. Write this address down."

He gave me an address I didn't recognize. "Where's that?" I asked. "I've never heard of it."

"It's over by the defense depot," he said. "That's not your 'hood, huh?"

"No," I said, "and I bet it's not yours, either."

"You got that right."

"Is this a business address?" I asked.

"That's what I have been led to believe."

"Thanks for your help," I said.

"You can thank me by getting my nine thousand back. But you didn't hear this from me, you understand?"

"I got it."

"Don't disappoint me on this confidentiality thing, okay?" he said.

"Mr. Discretion, that's me," I replied.

"Hey, I'm not jacking around here," he said.

"Look, I can't think of any reason I'd tell where I got this from, so relax."

"You relax," he said, and hung up.

I pulled out a city map and looked up the address he had given me. It was just west of the old defense depot, in what could only be described as a challenged neighborhood. The depot itself had been closed down in the early nineties in a wave of base closings. It covered something like a hundred cyclone fence enclosed acres and was dotted with warehouses and bunkers that had been used to store various types of supplies for the military. Nobody had figured out what to do with it now, but it was a safe bet that it wouldn't be turned into upscale housing.

I folded the map and decided I would take a daytime reconnaissance that afternoon. I locked Uncle Stan's pistol up in the desk, put on my work out clothes, and ran over to the Y. Nobody shot me. I worked out for two hours, weights and stair machine, and walked back home. Again, nobody shot me. I took a long, hot shower, opened and ate a can of tuna, and lay down for a nap. I planned to be out late, and I wanted to be alert.

The phone rang about three, pulling me out of a dream in which Uncle Stan and another man with receding hair and glasses stood a few feet apart, blazing away at each other with no apparent ill effect. I grabbed the phone without sitting up, and mumbled hello.

"John, is that you, boy?" a familiar voice said.

"Yeah, hey, it's me. How you doing, Tommy?" I asked as I sat up and swung my legs off the side of the bed.

"You're not drunk already, are you, John?" the voice laughed.

"No, no, I was just lying down for a minute and I must have fallen asleep."

"Man, business must be pretty slow if you're sleeping in the middle of the day," he said. "Or are you lying down with someone?"

"I wish," I said. "I was up late last night and I probably will be again tonight."

"What's her name?" he asked.

"Nobody. I'm working."

"How's Mary?" he asked.

"She's fine. She's been back in Europe since the day after we came down to Dude's."

"She's a good one, John. I'd hang on to her," he said.

"I'm doing my best," I said. I wracked my sleep-fogged brain, and came up with the name. "How's Lacey?"

"Oh, she's off the team," he said. "Hey, uh, listen, you've never been out to my new home, have you? I know you ain't. I been meaning to ask you, but you know how time gets away. Why don't you come on down for dinner, say about six o'clock? We'll put something on the grill and have a few drinks, talk about old times."

"Tommy, that sounds great, but I've got to work tonight. Give me a rain check, will you? By the way," I said, starting to wake up, "were you able to…"

Tommy's voice cut in on me loudly, "Dammit, John, everybody always has to work. It's going to be a perfect evenin' here and you're talking about working. Screw work for once and come have a good time."

"Tommy, I really appreciate it, man, but…"

"But nothing," he said emphatically. "Come on down for a while, and if you have to work later you can. I won't make you drink too much."

I really didn't want to spend the first part of the evening eating and drinking, but Tommy was so insistent that I was afraid I'd hurt his feelings if I said no. "Okay," I said, "it'll be fun, but I'm going to have to leave by nine."

"Hey, that's great," he said, with what sounded like genuine feeling in his voice. "Now get a piece of paper and I'll give you directions."

After I hung up, I realized that I hadn't asked him about Tuggle. There would be time enough tonight. I washed my face and brushed my teeth, and put on dark blue jeans, a black t-shirt, and lightweight high tech hiking shoes. I checked the load in the Smith, then put it in my black day pack along with an old Nikkormat 35mm with a telephoto lens and flash attachment. I added a couple of tools, a black polypropylene pullover and two flashlights, one big and one little. I also put in a small coil of 11 millimeter climbing rope. I wanted the revolver with me all the time, and I didn't want to have to come back downtown before my nighttime reconnaissance of Tuggle's warehouse. I put on my blue jean jacket, slung the pack over one shoulder, and headed for the truck.

I took the south loop of the interstate around town, and got off on the Airways exit. I turned off on a side street near the depot, into a neighborhood of paint-peeling cottages, bars and little stores, with here and there a non-descript commercial building. All of the buildings had security doors and bars on the windows, even the residences. Maybe especially the residences.

A few old black people sat on the porches of some of the houses, staring at my truck as it went by. It had been their neighborhood, and the houses and lawns their pride and joy. The neighborhood belonged to the predators now, the drug dealers, the pimps and the gangs. The police tried to control it, but mostly all they could do was react. So the old people, who couldn't afford to move and might not have even if they could, had drawn lines of defense around their own small homes. The social compact was broken here, and a 75-year-old great-grandmother was ready, willing and able to do what it took to protect her own, including blowing you back out her bedroom window with a 12 gauge.

I spotted the address Jackson had given me, a one-story tan brick building on a narrow lot about fifty feet wide. It was built flush with the sidewalk, and had no front door or windows or any kind of sign. The address was barely visible through the gang graffiti that covered the bricks. A cyclone wire gate, with double rolls of razor wire on the top and black rubber rollers on the bottom, guarded a drive that ran in on the right hand side of the structure. Two big padlocks, one at knee height and one at head height, secured the gate to metal brackets screwed into the brick wall. The drive was old and broken, with weeds and grass growing through the cracks. A fence as high as the gate ran down the side of the drive and across what part of the back of the lot I could see. It was also topped with razor wire. The limbs and leaves of trees and bushes from the neighboring lots grew through and over the fence. There was an ell on the building about twenty feet back, creating dead space that I couldn't see, but I could imagine loading space and bays, and somewhere a door into the front part of the building. There were no signs of activity.

The lot on the side next to the drive was occupied by a vacant house whose tenant had given up or died. It had a rotting front porch and all the windows were busted out. The lawn was overgrown with weeds and littered with empty bottles and other trash. Inside, there would be more trash, a clogged commode, used needles and condoms, and maybe a spaced out junkie or two. Until the city got around to condemning it and tearing it down, it would sit there as a reminder to the other residents of the ultimate futility of their struggle.

The far lot held a commercial building that was separated from the tan building only by an alley that might have been three feet wide. It was of similar construction, except it was made out of red brick and had a steel door in front, with lettering on it proclaiming it to be a plumbing supply business. It also had a drive, on the side away from the building I was calling Thomas's warehouse, with the same rolling wire gate. There were weeds and grass growing out of its cracked pavement, but not as many and not as tall as the ones next door. I could see the end of a van peeking around the corner of the building, and thought I could hear voices through the open window of my truck, but I didn't see anybody.

I cruised on down the street another hundred yards, then pulled through the lot of a heavily barred store to turn around. A hand-lettered sign visible through the bars advertised a special on hog tripe and pig's feet. A young black man with a beeper stuck on his belt detached himself from the front of the store as I pulled through and walked toward me, a questioning look on his face as he patted his front pocket. I shook my head and kept the truck moving, back out onto the street. I decided I was flattering myself to think that I might be taken for a cop.

I went back by Thomas's address without slowing, and didn't notice anything I hadn't seen before. I didn't want to linger in broad daylight, but I took a couple of minutes to make the block and drive down the parallel street. It was all residential, but if anything even more of the homes on this street looked abandoned. Here and there was a weed choked vacant lot where the city had knocked down the house, creating living space for rats and snakes, which were more desirable neighbors than the ones who congregated in the empty houses. Most of the streetlights were either blown out or were hanging off their poles. There were more people out on this street, enjoying the kind of day that could make even a ghetto look halfway decent. A few kids played in the street and on the sidewalks, and young men with scarves wrapped around their heads sat on the backs of cars, smoking and drinking out of beer cans and bottles in brown paper sacks. The men watched me intently, but they were too cool to show any emotion other than what came out of their eyes. I got the feeling that if it had been a dead end street they might have blocked off the road behind me, pulled me out of my truck when I had to stop, and burned me at the stake.

I slowed a little when I got behind Thomas's warehouse, and saw that I was in luck. The lot that joined his in the back was vacant, except for waist high weeds and piles of trash that had been dumped on it. I could see Thomas's fence and part of the tan brick building over the tops of the weeds, partly screened by scrub trees that grew along the fence line. The house right before I got to the lot was abandoned, but the next house was occupied by an enormous fat black man who was sitting in a chair on his porch with two Dobermans lying at his feet. He was still fighting the fight, and I didn't want him to mistake me for the enemy, so I kept right on going.

I headed back over to Airways, and then to the interstate, thinking about my job for the night. Cracking Thomas's warehouse was going to be a lot harder than getting into his home. It wasn't just the razor wire or the metal doors I knew I would find in back, it was the location. First, I had to get there. Anywhere I left my truck, I would either be seen and followed, or I would come back to where I had left it and it would be gone or, at best, missing all four tires, the battery and the radio. I needed some help.

As I mused on my upcoming breaking and entering, I headed the truck south on Interstate 55, down into Mississippi. After about fifty miles, I took the exit Tommy had mentioned and headed east on a state highway. Another ten miles and I headed back north on a secondary road, looking for the gravel road Tommy had indicated.

The day was wearing out. Cows grazed peacefully in green pastures just starting to yellow, and a soft, cool wind gently tossed the tops of the pine trees that lined the road. The light was subtly fading, adding gold accents to the varying shades of green, and muting the colors of changing leaves of the sumac and persimmon that grew along the fence lines. Tommy had been right. It was going to be a great evening in the country.

On my right, at the top of a hill, I turned into a gravel drive that ran between two brick columns. A black iron pole ran between the columns, and a wooden plank hung off it from two chains. Burned into the plank were the words "La Paz."

There was no gate at the entrance, just a cattle guard. As I wound my way down the gravel road, I could see why. There were black Angus cattle scattered over thick, green pasture everywhere I looked, wandering up and down the short hills, grazing, or just standing around, chewing their cuds and thinking cow thoughts. The road was spotted with cow pats, old and new, and I slowed down once to wait for a group of young heifers to amble out of my way. I wasn't much of a hand at estimating livestock numbers, but I knew I had seen at least a thousand head by the time the road entered a stand of pines, passed over another cattle guard and through a fence.

I came out of the other side of the pine grove into more pasture, with a man-made lake that covered a couple of hundred acres sprawled across the middle of it. I could see an earthen dam at the far end, and more black cattle grazed on the far side of fences that ran right down into the lake on both sides. Tommy's house was on the near side of the fences, in a bovine-free island in the middle of the huge pasture.

The house was perched above the lake. It was made out of fieldstone, and looked like a long one-story ranch, but with a sharply pitched roof covered with split cedar shingles rising up a good twenty feet. It was surrounded by large oaks and hickories in front and going down both sides of the hill toward the lake. The gravel drive circled in front of the house and ran under a covered portico. The portico was supported by fieldstone columns and covered by an offset roof with the same shingles. I pulled under it, next to a green Ford pickup with Mississippi plates, and killed the engine. As soon as I did, one side of the double door into the house opened and Tommy's bodyguard stepped out.

He was wearing the same outfit I had seen him in at Dude's, complete with the rodeo belt and, I presumed, the Glock behind it. He had a big chew in his cheek, but no cigarette. Maybe Tommy didn't let him smoke inside. Thinking about his Glock made me think about the Smith & Wesson in the pack behind the seat, but I decided it would just be inviting trouble. I didn't want him going through my truck, though, so I rolled up my window and locked the door after I got out.

"You afraid I'm going to steal that old piece of shit?" he asked.

"No, not you, I thought one of those cows might make a break for it, try to avoid ending up on somebody's plate."

By way of comment, he spit a stream of brown juice, wiped his mouth with the back of his hand, and said, "Come on in. Tommy's expecting you." He held the door open, and I edged past him, watching him with the total concentration you afford a water moccasin that has dropped into the front of your boat from an overhanging limb, waiting to see if he's going in the water or crawling back to your end. A funky odor of sweat, tobacco smoke, chewing tobacco breath and cheap cologne hung around him. I hoped he wasn't going to be one of the dinner guests.

I stepped past Smoky into a space about fifteen feet long and ten feet wide. It was floored with different colors of slate, and the walls were made of the same fieldstone that covered the outside of the house. A long hall ran off to the left, with several doors visible, all opening toward the back of the house. But the focus of the entrance was the huge, acrophobic space that flowed above, below and in front of the landing

There was a thin, waist-high rail, supported by two or three equally thin posts, at the edge of the slate. I walked up to the rail and looked over. At least thirty feet below, there was a big circular room, floored in the same slate, with a raised fire platform in the middle. A beaten copper cone hovered over the platform, and a copper chimney ran from its top to the ceiling fifty feet above. The far wall was glass, uninterrupted from floor to ceiling except by vertical columns and one cross beam halfway up. The glass wrapped part way around on both sides, the tops of the walls angling to meet the ceiling. The effect was like walking up unexpectedly to the edge of a canyon and stopping just before you went over the edge.

Outside the glass, the burnt gold of the hickory leaves and the reds and yellows of the oaks framed the green-blue water of the lake and the deep green of the pasture. A slate-covered porch, surrounded by a knee-high fieldstone wall, wrapped around the outside of the room. Directly opposite me on the far side of the porch, stone steps led down to a slate covered walk that ran to the lake. I could see a gazebo and a boat dock at the end of the walk.

I jumped and my hands tightened reflexively on the rail when I heard Smoky right behind me saying, "It's a good drop, ain't it?"

"Yeah," I said, and turned around. I had taken my eyes off the water moccasin, I thought, and he had crawled back to my end of the boat.

He was standing closer than he needed to, well within my personal space, enveloping me in his funk. I realized that his smell was almost the same sweetish, rotten fruit on a hot day odor of a poisonous snake. He grinned at me with yellow teeth, letting me see that he could have flipped me over the rail and smiled as I hit the slate.

"Go on down the stairs and to your right," he said. "Tommy's in the kitchen."

I found Tommy standing at the sink, pulling a huge long tenderloin out of a dark marinade with a pair of tongs. He looked up as I came in, and gave me the big smile. "Hey, John," he said, wiping his hands on the apron he had tied around him. "I'm glad you made it." He gave me a bear hug, and then held me back away from him, his hands on my biceps. "Boy, you ain't eating enough. We're going to start fixing that right now. But first let's get you a drink. What'll it be?"

I saw an open bottle of Blackjack on the counter, and an ice tea glass beside it full of ice and red liquor. "I'll have what the cook's having," I said. "A fall evening just seems to call out for a drink of good whiskey. But give me about half as much and put some water in it."

"Now you're talking," he said. He got a glass out of the cabinet, filled it up with a handful of ice from a bucket sitting by the bottle, and poured it three fourths full of whiskey. He ran a little water in it from the sink faucet, and handed it to me. Then he picked up his glass, and said, "Here's to good times with old friends."

"To old friends," I said, clinking my glass against his. I took a sip of my whiskey, and Tommy took a big swallow of his.

"Tommy, this place is incredible," I said. "How long have you lived here?"

"In this house, since the spring, when it was finished. While they were building it, I lived in a trailer back in that grove of pines."

"How did you decide on this style?" I asked, gesturing vaguely to include not only the kitchen but the whole house.

"You remember Clay Morrison back in high school?" he asked. "Guy couple of years older than us who lived out by me?"

I remembered Clay. He was the one who had run his TransAm into the log and come back to school with the limp and the drool. "Yeah, I remember Clay," I said.

"Well," Tommy said, "his daddy had a house a lot like this. I remember watching them build it next to our old place. When they got it done, I told myself I was going to have a house like that when I grew up. I kept my promise."

"Like I said, it's incredible." I didn't add that I had been expecting some sort of grandiose but tacky place.

"John, I'm proud that you like it. You got better taste than a lot of my friends."

"Does your friend with the Glock live here?" I asked.

"Carl? No, I like my privacy too much. Carl stays down at the barn. I mean, it ain't just a barn. I keep most of my cars and trucks down there, and he's got a real nice apartment built into it."

Tommy led the way out onto the patio, and then down the walk to the boat dock. We stood on the end of the dock, sipping our whiskey and watching cows in the distance wander to and from the lake.

"It's a great ranch, Tommy. And I like the name. It means peace in Spanish, right?" I asked.

"Yeah, John, that's right. Trust you to know that. Most people come in here got no idea what it means. Fellow came in the other day with salt blocks for the cattle was calling me Mr. La Paz, thought it was my name.

"How big is this place, Tommy?" I asked.

"I got right at four thousand acres," he said. "We graze anywhere from two thousand to two thousand five hundred head at a time, depending on what the market is doing and how many calves we got. See that grass?" he asked, pointing out toward the pasture at the expanses of green. "That's a special variety that we plant. It makes the cattle leaner, and we get more per pound for the beef. People used to like marbling, but it's lean that sells now."

"It's a big operation," I said. "You must do pretty well with it." I didn't want to pry into Tommy's finances, but I knew he liked to have his success recognized.

"Oh, we break even, I guess," he said with a smile. "But it's like Dude's, just a sideline, kind of a hobby."

For about the hundredth time in the last five years, I almost asked Tommy what it was he did for real, and why he needed someone like Carl around. I think Tommy was half way expecting the question, because he was watching me expectantly. But I just smiled back at him, and said, "Tommy, I'm proud of you. You've come a long way."

"Thanks, man, that means a lot coming from you," he said. "Now let's go see about some supper."

We walked back up to the patio, and Tommy settled me into the type of wooden lawn chair you see advertised in specialty catalogs for hundreds of dollars. He fired up a gas grill, lit a couple of citronella candles against the mosquitoes, and went into the house. He came back a minute later carrying a tray with the Jack Daniels, a full ice bucket, a pitcher of water and a couple of glasses. He picked up the half full glass he had left on the patio, drained it in a long swallow, and threw the ice over the side onto the grass. "I'm going to check the potatoes and get the steak," he said. "Make us a couple of fresh ones, won't you?"

Tommy went back inside and I made him a new drink. It was easy. Fill the glass with ice, and then pour whiskey to the rim. I was still working on my first.

He came back a minute later, carrying the tenderloin in a big mixing bowl. He had wrapped it in bacon that was stuck in place with toothpicks. He lifted it out, and placed it sizzling onto the grill. The smell was great.

"Tommy, that's a good-looking piece of meat," I said. "Is it from one of your former residents here?"

"Yessir, a nice steer, we butchered him yesterday. I ain't goin' to serve you no supermarket beef when we got the best in the world walkin' all around us."

He picked up his drink, took a big slug, and settled back into a chair. "You still on that first drink, son?" he asked.

"Yeah, I told you I got to work later tonight," I replied.

"Well, if you won't drink with me at least you ain't got no excuse for not eating. How do you like your steak?"

"Medium rare is fine for me," I answered.

"Good," he said. "That's how I like mine, too. Some cattlemen won't eat it any way but well done, 'cause they've seen cattle full of worms and stuff. But that never bothered me."

"I appreciate you sharing that fact with me right before we eat, Tommy," I said. "Am I going to get mad cow disease, too?"

"Oh, hell, no, John. You was always too damned squeamish. All my beef is USDA inspected, even what we use here on the place. I bet that Mary girl you had with you down at Dude's would eat this right up, no questions asked."

"You're right, Tommy, she would," I said. I had a sudden overwhelming urge to have Mary with me in this golden evening, sipping whiskey and watching the bats whirl over the lake in the twilight. She would sit there, holding my hand, drinking in the sights, sounds, and smells of the day as a chaser for the sour mash, alive in and content with the present. "She surely would, no questions asked."

I looked over, and saw Tommy smiling at me. "I believe you like that girl," he said.

"Yeah, I believe you're right," I said, smiling back at him. "What happened with Lacey?" I asked.

"Oh, well, we're not friends anymore. She took off with some biker. I knew she was trash all along, but she was fun for a while."

"I'm sorry," I said.

"Oh, hell, don't be sorry," he said, with a grin. "I was getting tired of her, too. I'd a whole lot rather they run off than I have to run them off. I do hate to see them cry."

"I always knew you were a sensitive kind of guy," I said.

"That's me, Mr. Sensitive," he laughed back. "But you know, one day I'd like to find somebody to marry and live out here with me, maybe have some kids."

"Why not?" I said. "There's plenty of women would like to marry you. Just don't drink yourself to death first."

Tommy grunted at my comment, heaved himself up out of his chair, opened the cover of the grill, and turned the tenderloin. The bacon popped and spit as he rolled the uncooked part next to the flames. A big cloud of aromatic smoke rolled off the grill and across the patio, making my mouth water.

"I don't know about plenty, but I guess there's one somewhere around could stand living with me as long as this place was part of the deal," he said.

"Don't sell yourself short, Tommy," I said. "The house is nice, but you can get a girl without it."

"You're a good friend, John," Tommy said. "I'm going in to get the rest of the stuff. I'll be back in a minute. Don't you want another drink?"

"Thanks, Tommy, I might take a beer if you've got one."

"Hell, yes, I've got one," he said, heading back into the house.

The light was gone completely now, and the stars were coming out over the pasture. A cool breeze blew up from the lake, bearing the odor of water, fish, grass and cows. I drained the last of my whiskey, and lay back in the chair, trying to live in the moment, without thought for the future or past. I couldn't quite make it.

Tommy bustled back out the door, and laid plates, napkins and silverware on a built-in picnic table on one side of the patio. He handed me a beer, and then went over to the grill. He took out the sizzling tenderloin with the tongs and laid it on a plate that he put on the middle of the table. He disappeared back into the house, and came out a minute later with a plate of baked potatoes still wrapped in foil, a huge bowl full of tossed salad, and a bottle of salad dressing tucked under his arm. "Come on and sit down, John," he said, grabbing his drink.

We sat down at the table, Tommy tucked his head down, and mumbled quickly, "God is great, God is good, and we thank Him for our food, Amen."

"Amen," I echoed.

Tommy reached out for the plate of meat, and began slicing it with diagonal cuts at least two inches thick. He reached his hand out for my plate, and forked two slices onto it. It was a month's ration of red meat, but I knew it would hurt his feelings if I didn't eat it. He put two slices on his own plate, and then passed the potatoes and salad. We ate for a while, not saying anything. The beef was moist and tender, with the best flavor I had ever had. "Tommy," I said eventually, "that's the best piece of beef I ever stuck in my mouth. Never mind the house, I'll marry you for your cooking."

"It is good, ain't it?" he said. "Let me get you another piece or two."

"Lord, no, Tommy," I said. "I can't eat another bite."

"You only had two pieces," he said. "Don't you like it?"

"Well, maybe one more little piece," I said, when I saw the disappointed look on his face.

Tommy gave me another full size slice, and put two more on his plate. At least half of the tenderloin was still on the platter. It wasn't easy, but I got that piece down, too, and then pushed my chair back with a groan.

"You sure you got enough?" Tommy asked, helping himself to another piece and a potato.

"Positive," I said. "You want me to take some of this stuff back in the kitchen while you finish up?"

"No," Tommy said around bites. "Carl will get it after a while."

"He a butler or a bodyguard?"

"Carl gets the job done, whatever it may be," Tommy answered.

Tommy cleaned his plate, then offered me ice cream and pecan pie for dessert. I declined, and he suggested we take a walk down to the boat dock. He stuck his arm inside the door and hit a light switch, turning on dim yellow lights set into ground fixtures all along the path to the lake and running out to the end of the dock. We walked the slate path to the dock, then down to the end where there were a couple of deck chairs.

It was cooler out over the lake, with a breeze blowing up out of the south and slapping little waves against the side of the dock. The wind smelled like the pines along the side of the lake. I was sipping at the last of my beer, and Tommy was working on a fresh whiskey, this one without ice. The stars looked about fifty times brighter than they do in the city, with the river of the Milky Way splashed across the middle of the sky. Tommy had been right for sure. It was a great evening.

Tommy talked some more about his ranch, the vagaries of the cattle market, and scientific details on breeding and nutrition I was surprised he knew. He talked about it much like a banker or a doctor might talk about golf, something that was interesting and fun, but wasn't really serious. When the ranch talk ran out, we swapped a few high school stories, and then I took a quick look at my watch. It was almost ten, an hour past when I had planned to leave.

"You got to run?" Tommy asked.

"Yeah, it's about that time," I said. It was time to ask Tommy if he knew anything about Tuggle, and then hit the road.

"What kind of work you got goin' tonight?" Tommy asked. "You trying to catch someone with his hand in the cookie jar?"

"No, not tonight," I said. "I've just got some investigating to do that won't stand the light of day."

"You're not still working on that thing with the black fellow, are you?" he asked.

"Yeah. In fact, I wanted to ask you if you've turned up anything on that for me."

Tommy looked back over his shoulder before he answered. "John, you ought not to waste your time on some nigger crack dealer. That's just stupid."

"I thought you promised Mary you wouldn't use that word anymore," I said.

"I promised her I'd try not to. Old habits die hard. But my English ain't the point here. I hate to see a friend waste his time."

"Well, it's my time, and I'm not really doing it for Tuggle. My best client asked me to do it, so I'm doing it."

"You mean that rich society divorce lawyer?" he asked.

"I guess you could call her that," I said.

"A woman like that wouldn't spit on either one of us if we was on fire," Tommy said. "You don't owe her no favors." I noticed Tommy's grammar was getting worse the more whiskey he drank.

"Maybe you're misjudging her, Tommy. The fact she's rich doesn't make her a bad person. Hell, you're pretty rich yourself, it looks to me."

"I may have a little money, but I ain't society," he said, and spit into the lake.

I had thought Tommy was just kidding, but I realized as I looked at him in the starlight that he was really angry. I sat there for another minute, waiting for him to tell me if he knew anything about Tuggle, but he just stared out over the lake, like he was thinking. I figured the whiskey had maybe finally caught up with him. "Tommy," I said, "I guess I'd better head on out. I sure do appreciate the evening."

Tommy looked over at me as I stood up, then glanced back over his shoulder. "Sit back down for just a minute, John," he said, almost in a whisper. I eased back down in my chair as Tommy hitched his closer to mine.

He fixed his eyes on mine, stuck out his fat jaw, and said "John, you done me a big favor a few years back. You give me some real good advice. I didn't follow that advice, and I damn near lost my best chance to hit a homer in this life. Now I'm going to give you some good advice. Drop this thing. Drop it like a hot fucking potato."

"Why, Tommy?" I asked. "You can't just tell me to drop it and not give me a reason."

"Hush," he whispered vehemently. "You know how sound travels over water. Now look here, you thickheaded sonofabitch," he said softly, grabbing my knee in a painful grip and breathing whiskey fumes into my face, "did you tell me why you were warning me off that land swindler? No, because you couldn't. Same thing here. Don't be stupid like I was, okay?"

Before I could ask anything else, we heard a clatter of boots coming down the steps from the patio. We saw it was Carl as he came up to the shore end of the dock. "Business call, Tommy," he yelled, without coming onto the dock.

"Okay," Tommy called back. "I'll be with them in just a minute." Tommy gave my knee a last squeeze, and whispered, "Like I said, don't be stupid."

We got up and walked back to the shore, and Tommy took the portable phone from Carl. "This is Tommy," he said. "Hang on one minute and I'll be with you." He covered the mouthpiece with one hand, and said, "John, I'm sorry, but I got to take this call. I sure am glad you came out to see me. Old friends are the best friends. You mind if Carl shows you out?"

"No, Tommy, that's fine," I said. "I appreciate you having me. Come see me up in town soon."

"I'll do it," he said, smiling. "See you later. Don't get none on you. But if you do, come by and let me smell it."

I was trying to figure that one out as I followed Carl inside. Behind me, I could hear Tommy starting in on his conversation. Carl led me through the house and out to my truck. In the porch light, I noticed a dark streak across my windshield in front of the driver's seat that could only be tobacco juice. It also spotted the hood of the white truck.

"Carl," I said, as I walked over and unlocked the door, "I'm an old friend of Tommy's, you know. There's really no reason for animosity between us."

Carl just stared at me for a minute. I figured he was trying to puzzle out what animosity meant. Then he leaned over and spit more juice on the passenger side front tire. "Don't take it personal," he said. "I treat you the same as I treat any other no good low life bastard who comes sucking around Tommy for a favor."

I opened the truck door, shrugged out of my jacket, and tossed it in on the seat. I'd had a couple of drinks, and more food at one time since I could remember. I had work to do, and nothing to prove. And he had a gun under his belt buckle. I had no business fighting him. But those were fighting words if I had ever heard them. So I walked out from under the portico into the drive, out of the light, and turned around and waited for him.

"So how's this work," he asked, still standing in the light, "I whip your ass, you complain to Tommy, and I'm out of a job?"

"I could go inside right now and get Tommy and show him my truck. Tommy and I go way back. That right there is enough to cost you your job," I said, pointing at the pickup. "But this is between you and me. Tommy doesn't need to know, unless you have to explain why your face looks like ground chuck."

Carl smiled, and walked toward me out of the light. He didn't adopt any fighting posture, just came strolling up with a smile on his face. It would have been cooler just to stand there and wait for him, but I dropped into a crouch and put both hands up in loose fists. I thought he might take his boots off, like Billy Jack in the movie, but he left them on.

When he was about four feet away, he shifted from first to turbo in a tenth of a second, unleashing a flurry of jabs that I dodged or took on my forearms, giving ground all the way. It was pretty much what I had expected, given how quick Tommy had said he was, so I wasn't surprised. He was fast, but he was a chain smoker, so he wanted to get it over with before he got too winded. I could already hear his breath rasping as he blew big gasps of corpse-smelling air out of his mouth. I figured he would try something new any second. I didn't have to wait long.

I was watching his hands closely, not just to dodge or catch his punches, but for a move to the belt buckle and the Glock. If he went for that, I was going to have to be in on him fast, unless I wanted to try dodging high velocity hollow points or blocking them with my forearms. Because I was watching his hands, and because I had to stay close to do something about his hands if he went for the pistol, he almost got me. He threw a last hard left jab, then his right boot came up in a high kick that missed my chin by a hair, the corner of the hard heel scraping the end of my nose as it went past.

The boot hurt like hell, and it would have hurt a lot worse if the pointy toe had caught me under the chin. But it would have been better for him if he had taken them off. When his right foot missed me and swung on up into the air, the slick leather sole of his left plant boot slipped on the gravel of the drive, and he fell flat on his back, his legs sprawled wide. The breath came out of him in a gasp, and I made sure he didn't get it back anytime soon. I made a little hop up into the air, and came down with all my weight focused on one knee right into the middle of his stomach. It was one hundred ninety pounds, plus a couple of pounds of Tommy's tenderloin, and it felt like my knee went all the way to his spine. His eyes bulged, and he involuntarily tried to curl up, which was hard to do because my left hand was on his throat pinning him down as my right fished under his belt buckle and pulled out the Glock.

Once I had the pistol, I got off him and backed up a couple of paces to suck wind. He managed to curl over on his left side, both hands holding his abdomen, and lay there making choking sounds till he got his breath back with one big gasp. He immediately rolled over onto his knees, his hands still over his stomach, his forehead in the dust and gravel supporting him, and began retching. He brought up a big reddish-brown wad, and for a second I was afraid I had killed him. A hard blow to the body in the right place can do it. I took a closer look, and was relieved to see that the wad was only his chew.

He came up on his hands, saliva dripping in strands from his mouth and mucus running out of his nose. It damn near made me want to throw up, too. I popped the clip out of the Glock, shucked out the rounds into the gravel with the end of my thumb, then worked the slide to eject the round in the chamber. I gave the shells a couple of kicks, scattering them around, and then looked back over at Carl. He was tough, I had to give him that. He was sitting back on his heels, wiping his face off with his hands. I swear if I had given him another five minutes he might have come after me again.

"Carl," I said, "I'm going to leave your piece up on the doorstep, because you might need it to protect Tommy. But if you do such a piss poor job defending him as you did for yourself, I'll come back and whip your ass again."

He turned his eyes to me, and gasped out, "How, how did you know I had the gun? How'd you know where it was?"

"You're a bodyguard, right? So you got a gun." I was lying, but I didn't want to jeopardize the employer/employee relationship. "I figured it had to be under that rodeo buckle or in your boots. I found it on my first try."

He tried to push himself up. It must have hurt, though, because he gave a gasp and leaned forward on his hands again. "If you knew I had a gun, why'd you fight me?" he gritted out.

"Because I figured you had too much pride to use it, and it would have been kind of hard to explain to Tommy if you had. So I took that chance. Besides, I needed a good fight. You ought to understand that."

"You were lucky," he said.

"I made my luck," I said. "You were the lucky one. I could have busted the hell out of you while you were lying there holding your gut."

"Why didn't you?" he asked.

"Because I didn't need to. Now smoke a cigarette, it'll make you feel better."

I left him in the gravel, struggling to get up, and laid the gun and the empty clip by the front door. I got in the truck and backed it up around half the circle to get headed back in the right direction. Running over him then with a pickup wouldn't have been the sporting thing to do.

11 ———————————————

Hundreds of pairs of green cow eyes reflected in my headlights as I drove through Tommy's pasture. I rolled both windows down, letting the cool night air wash over my battered forearms. A drop of blood welled up from the scrape on my nose and dripped down onto my shirt before I could catch it. I pulled a bandanna out of my pocket and held it up to my nose, squeezing hard to try to stop the bleeding. I had acid indigestion from my little workout so soon after eating, and a sour taste in the back of my throat. But the truth was that I felt great. I had felt helpless, nervous and scared since last night when I got shot at, and the same way for most of the day. I knew I was still subject to being shot, but my little tussle with Carl had done a lot for my self-confidence. It didn't make much sense, but it sure did make me feel better.

By the time I hit the interstate to go back north, my nose had stopped bleeding and my stomach had settled down, but my forearms were starting to ache. Carl packed a pretty good punch for a chain smoker. Still, I figured I probably felt better than he did.

My mind wandered over the comment Tommy made right before I left. I tried to give it some serious thought, but couldn't manage it. I considered whether I should bag the inspection of Thomas's warehouse, given the active day I had had, but decided I might as well get it over with. I was juiced from my fight, and knew I wouldn't be able to sleep if I tried. And I had come up with a transportation plan.

An hour later, I walked through the open door of Ajax Bond, and found Henry Jackson alone, reading a casebook on corporate taxation. He was standing behind the tall counter, and had the book open in front of him. I walked right up to him and read upside down the title of the book printed on the top of the open page before he noticed me. He looked up with a start, and then grunted.

"Man, you got to make some noise when you come in here," he said.

"I did," I said. "You were just so engrossed in that fascinating reading that you didn't hear me."

"Did you take this shit?" he asked, waving at the book.

"No, I wanted to be a litigator. I didn't figure I'd need corporate tax."

"You were smart. This stuff doesn't make any sense at all."

"You act like you're surprised," I said.

"No, I'm just confused."

"No shit. The real secret is, it doesn't have to make sense. There are a few basic precepts in tax law, but most of it is based on politics. This year one special interest group wins, next year another one wins. So for the most part, there's no rhyme or reason to it. The bottom line is, don't try to understand it, just memorize it," I said.

"Yeah?"

"Yeah. Unless you plan to be a tax lawyer, just memorize what you need to get through the exam and to spot issues. When you start practicing, you'll pass off tax issues to somebody in your firm's tax department."

"I don't know, it seems like I should understand it as much as I can. I mean, I'm paying to learn this stuff."

"I admire your attitude," I said. "Maybe I would have been more like that in school if I had been paying for it instead of my father. But I'll tell you, memorize it first, then try to understand it. Don't let your search for truth get in the way of making a good grade on the exam."

He shrugged and closed the book. "What's wrong with your nose?"

I put my finger up to the tip of my nose and felt blood starting to ooze again.

"Here," he said, handing me a box of tissues, "don't go bleeding on my floor. You already got it on your shirt."

I took a couple of tissues and held them hard against my nose. "I got into an argument with a cowboy boot," I said nasally.

"The boot do that to your arms?" he asked.

I looked at my forearms for the first time since Carl had hammered on them. Both of them were already bruised black and blue from the elbow to the hand, and were scraped red in several places. No wonder they hurt. "No," I said, "he did that with his fists. But at least he didn't do it to my face."

"You're supposed to tell me he looks a lot worse than you do," he said with a grin.

"He doesn't look worse, but he feels a whole lot worse," I grinned back.

"Why?" he asked. "Does he feel bad about beating on you?"

"No, he may feel bad that he didn't kill me, but the rest of his bad feelings are purely physical."

He went over to the coffeepot and filled his cup. "Too late for you?" he asked, gesturing with an empty cup.

"No, it's going to be a long night. I'd love a cup."

"Come on back and fix it like you want it," he said, pouring my cup. I went through the hinged half door that separated the public space from the work space. The coffee was in a white enamel mug, and looked like blue black ink. I decided it would be socially unacceptable to take a sip before I determined what it needed, kind of like locking the pickup in Carl's face, so I dumped in a couple of spoons of artificial creamer, a pack of sweetener, and stirred. I was afraid I would just pull back the handle of the spoon.

I took the first cautious sip. I had made the right decision with the creamer and sweetener. I figured that if I drank the whole cup I would be awake for a week, like a methamphetamine addict blowing his paycheck on a binge. "That's good coffee," I lied.

"You really like it?" Jackson asked. "I think it's better than the fancy stuff you get at these coffee bars. All I do is double shot it, throw in a couple of pinches of salt, and let it perk for a good long while."

"I can tell," I said with a smile, taking another sip.

He walked over to one of the desks, opened a drawer, and came back with a bottle of generic ibuprofen. "You better take two of these now, before your arms stiffen up on you."

"Thanks," I said. He didn't offer any water, and I didn't see a sink, so I popped a couple in my mouth and tried to wash them down with the scalding coffee. I could only hope that all the red meat in my stomach would absorb the acid that the coffee and pain killer were bound to generate.

"So, did you find the warehouse?" Jackson asked, taking his coffee over to one of the desks and sitting down. I slumped down in the old swivel chair at the other desk and cautiously laid my arms on top of it. They hadn't hurt unbearably in the truck with the cool wind blowing over them, but they were starting to ache like a cracked tooth in the warm air of the bail bond office. The psychological effect of seeing what they looked like hadn't helped, either. Still, I told myself, I felt better overall than I would have if I had walked away from Carl's challenge. "Yeah, I found it," I said. "It's in a lovely neighborhood."

"I bet. That's not what I'd call a honky-friendly area."

"I don't think it's a people-friendly area in general, but a person of the European persuasion may get a little extra special treatment."

"You can count on that," he said with a big grin. "I'd rather be a brother at a KKK meeting than a white dude in that neighborhood after dark."

"You seem to be enjoying that image," I grinned back. "Allow me to suggest a few places out in the country where you might prefer not to find your bad self after the sun goes down."

"I know that's right," he said. "But don't worry. I'm a city boy, day and night."

"Well, city boy, I need your help."

"Haven't I already helped you enough?" he asked.

"And I appreciate it," I said. "But here's my problem. I want to take a look inside that warehouse, see if I can find anything that can help us come up with our man Thomas. I can't do it in the daytime, and there's nowhere I can park my truck at night where it won't be stripped when I get back. So I need a ride."

"From me?" he asked, pointing at his big chest.

"Why not?" I said. "You stand to gain nine thousand if we get him back, and it would only take a couple hours of your time. You drive past the lot behind the warehouse, slow down, I hop out of the bed of the pickup, you cruise back by in an hour and I hop back in. It's easy. I've done it plenty of times before when I couldn't leave my truck parked near where I was going."

"Why don't you get whoever drove you then to drive you now?" he asked.

"I don't have anybody now I can call, especially at this time of night. And I feel like getting this done and over with."

"You mean I'm the only chump available?"

"No, it's just that you've got an interest in this thing, too, and I knew you'd be up late."

"I'm up, but I'm working," he said.

"You got a big crowd, I see," I said.

"Don't be a smartass. The right person walks in, I make money. I'm closed, they go down the street, I miss the business."

"Can't you make an exception this one night?" I asked.

He didn't answer my question, but said, "I'm curious. Who usually plays taxi driver for you?"

"Well, believe it or not, I usually can get whoever I'm going out with to do it. But the only girl I'm seeing now doesn't live here."

He laughed and said, "I hope you aren't asking me out on a date."

"No, you're not my type," I said. "Too tall. But I'm telling you, there's a certain kind of woman out there who gets a real kick out of doing stuff like that. It's like television or the movies, and she's in them. And it's a cheap date."

He shook his head over the foibles of white folks. "It's not my idea of excitement. Besides, like I told you, I'm already going out on a limb giving you what I have."

"Henry, how is anybody going to know?" I asked. "You drive down a dark street in my truck, not even in your own vehicle, how will anybody know it's you? Even if all your best customers live on that street? And I'm not a cop. I just want to find him for his mother."

"Yeah, I've been thinking about that. If you don't turn him in, I don't get my money. So what's my incentive to help you?"

"You mean other than Christian charity?"

"Yeah, other than that," he said.

"Henry, you know as well as I do the man is probably dead. Hell, I'm surprised his body hasn't turned up yet. If we can prove that he's dead, you'll get your money back. If he's not dead and I find him, I don't know about the cops." I was remembering Steiner's comment about my legal obligations to share information with the police. "I've just been telling myself I'd cross that bridge when I come to it," I said. I thought for a minute and said, "How about this. If I find him alive, I tell you where he is, if you swear you won't tell the cops. Then you can decide whether you want to go to him and ask for the money."

"What kind of fool do I look like?" he said with a scowl. "I can think of at least five different laws I'd be breaking if I did that, including insurance fraud and extortion, and I'm just a law student. I'm sure the D.A. could think of some more."

"I didn't say you had to do it, I said you could decide for yourself. Don't get pissed at me," I said.

"Yeah, but if I don't do it, and I know where he is, I'm probably guilty of some other violation," he shot back.

I smiled at him and said, "You're going to be a good lawyer. You're right, it was a bad idea. It's been a long day, and I'm getting out of a habit you're just getting into."

"What habit?" he asked.

"Thinking like a lawyer," I responded. "Look, if I find him alive, I'll keep it to myself, not put you in any legal dilemmas. But if he's dead, which he probably is, you'll get your nine thousand back. What have you got to lose except a couple of hours sleep?"

He took a deep breath through his nostrils, and let it out in a sigh. He looked up at a clock on the wall. It was 12:05 a.m. "Why do I think I'm going to regret this?" he asked, shaking his head. Then he said, "I'll do it, but I don't want to be seen leaving here with you. You leave now, and I'll close at one and meet you."

"Man, that's great, I really appreciate it."

"You ought to," he said. He looked like a man who wasn't satisfied he'd made the right decision, and who might still change his mind.

Jackson rejected a suggestion that we meet at my parking garage, saying he didn't want to leave his car in my neighborhood. Despite my hurt feelings, I agreed to meet at his house on Mud Island. He said his neighbors weren't his clients, so he didn't mind their seeing him in my company.

I drove Poplar the two blocks to Front Street, then turned right and went under the convention center and past the Pyramid. There was no concert or basketball game at the arena tonight, and the wide, empty, moonlit spaces around the structure could have almost been Egyptian desert. It was always an eerie-looking sight to come upon as you drove in over the river from Arkansas, but it was even stranger up close and lonely late at night.

I turned back left and went over the bridge across the Wolf River to Mud Island. The island is really a peninsula between the Wolf, a small tributary that flows out of Mississippi and through western Tennessee, and into the big river. It used to have a small airstrip and not much else on it. When Dad first moved to the city, he would drive his car out to the island, walk along the edge of the Wolf, and jump shoot a limit of mallards in sight of downtown. Now, the end of the island has an open-air auditorium and a museum which are reached from downtown by a monorail that runs over the Wolf. The upper end contains a planned community of apartments and houses, some of them very expensive. Personally, I'm not convinced the island is safe from a hundred-year flood, but more and more people are building there.

I followed the directions Jackson had given me and pulled up in front of a narrow, two-story house on the typical small island lot. It had houses crowding it close on both sides, but I didn't figure Henry had a lot of time for a yard. There was a small front porch with a white rail around it and a rocker sitting on it. I couldn't see Henry spending a lot of time there, either. Still, it was a nice house, and plenty big enough for one person. It was certainly larger than my place.

I cut the engine and the lights, and leaned back in the seat. I had been too jazzed up from my fight with Carl to think much about what Tommy had told me right before I left his place, but I was starting to wonder about it now. Maybe he had just been trying to get me to quit wasting time, like he had said at first, but I remembered the look in his eyes and his comparison of my advice to him about the swindler, and knew there had to be more to it. But what? I knew Tommy was still connected with lots of law enforcement sources, and that he was probably connected with outlaw sources, if he wasn't one himself. But what could he have found out about a missing fence that would cause him to give me such an adamant warning? Maybe someone else was moving in on the business and had killed Thomas to get him out of the way. They might have quietly tapped him and slid his corpse into the river with concrete blocks strapped to it. I had been wondering why his body hadn't been found if a dealer had killed him, but maybe a dealer hadn't killed him. It didn't seem like there would be enough profit in Thomas's business, at least on a local level, for the mob to be interested in it, but I didn't know.

I started to feel a tingle of fear, thinking about the guys in the alley last night who had shot at me. Maybe they were pros, but if so they weren't very good. Three guys were a lot to send to pop one small time private investigator, but even so all they had managed to do was shoot off one of their team's big toe and kill a Buick. The thought made me laugh and feel a little better, but I still rolled up the windows of the truck and pulled the pack with the .357 up onto the seat beside me. I settled down to wait on Henry, checking the rear view mirror occasionally to make sure nobody was sneaking up on me.

I didn't have long to wait, but the time seemed to go slowly. The adrenaline from my fight with Carl was gone, and the events of the last two days were starting to catch up with me. I was regretting my decision to take on the warehouse tonight. The best approach seemed to be a hot shower and bed, with a fresh start in the morning to try to analyze what I had already learned. But when I thought about it, I realized I hadn't learned a hell of a lot to analyze. I was awake, sort of, and I had a ride. I might as well go ahead and get it over with.

Fatigue and the late night spookies were about to get me thinking the other way again when Jackson pulled up in a black Lexus, worked the automatic garage door opener from inside his car, and pulled into the garage. He came back out the front door a minute later, carrying two big Styrofoam cups. He set one cup on top of the cab, and I leaned over and unlocked the door. He opened it, handed me a cup, picked the other cup off the cab, and got in.

It was more of the same coffee, and I took a sip, grateful to have something hot and strong, even if it tasted like roofing tar. "Thanks," I said. "It's been a long day. That hits the spot."

"It is good coffee, isn't it?" he said. Someday, somebody was going to tell him the truth about his coffee, but not me.

"That's a nice car you got," I said, as I headed back off the island. "And a nice house. What do you want to be a lawyer for? There's not as much money in it as you'd think from watching television."

"I don't watch television, except sports," he said.

"You know what I mean. Lots of people think all lawyers are filthy rich."

"I'm not doing it just for the money. It's something I always intended to do. I don't want to be a bail bondsman all my life. I want to have a profession."

"I can't argue with that," I said. "It just seems like you got a pretty good thing going now."

"The money is pretty good," he said, "but I'm ready to try something else. I've got no kids, no wife to support or answer to, so why not? And I'll tell you something else. I have two sisters and a brother. One sister is a school teacher, the other is an accountant, and my brother is a dentist. I make more money than any of them, but when we get together with my mother for the holidays, or go to a family reunion, they're the ones who get all the respect. I tell you, I'm a little bit tired of that."

"I can see that. My mother still doesn't understand why I quit being a lawyer, but I think my Dad does. People do look at you differently depending on what you do, that's a fact."

"You got that right. And not just what you do, but what you look like. I ought to be used to that, being black."

"Well, obviously I can't speak to that. But I know enough to tell you to be what you want, not what other people want. If you want to be a lawyer, that's cool. But it's a lot of work and bullshit to put up with just to satisfy other people's expectations."

"I guess I'm going to give it a try, see how I like it," he said.

"I hope it's everything you ever wanted," I said. "If it's not, you got something lucrative to fall back on."

"Why did you quit?" he asked. "If you don't mind me asking?"

"I don't mind, but I'm not sure I can tell you. I was going through some other changes, getting a divorce that probably made me question my career, though I didn't do it consciously. And I'm not sure I had the proper temperament in the first place to be a trial lawyer. If you're a litigator, it's one adversarial situation after another. It can get to you after a while if you don't thrive on controversy. I might have been a better corporate lawyer."

"You like being a PI?" he asked.

"Yeah, I do. It's still other people's problems, and I still work pretty hard, but it's more on my schedule, and I spend a lot more time outdoors. There's enough thinking involved to keep it interesting, but it also involves a good bit of physical activity."

"Like tonight with the cowboy boot?" he asked with a chuckle.

"Usually not quite that exciting, but it can be."

"Well, let's hope nothing exciting happens the rest of the night," he said.

"I'm with you on that," I said.

I didn't feel like the hassle of getting on the interstate, so I drove my way through the city toward Thomas's warehouse. I worked steadily on Henry's coffee, needing the jump for the rest of the night's plan. When we got close, I pulled off the road in front of a factory's wire fence. I killed the engine and the lights, and opened up the pack that had been lying on the seat between us. I eased the polypropylene jacket past my forearms and over my torso, and checked the film in the camera. Then I popped the glove compartment open, and put the Smith in it.

"Whoa, now, whoa," Henry said. "You expect me to drive around with that in the glove box?"

"What's the big deal?" I asked." You've got your Beretta, don't you?"

"Yeah, and I've got a permit for it. I don't want to be caught driving around in some white guy's truck with a fucking concealed cannon in it."

"You worry too much, Henry," I said. "After you drop me off, don't drive around the neighborhood. Go straight to a twenty-four hour coffee shop and wait there until it's time to pick me up."

"Why don't you just take that thing with you?" he asked. "You might need it."

"Yeah, I might need it, but the odds are probably better I get caught, and if I'm carrying a pistol when I am, it's going to be a lot more serious, carry permit or not."

"So you're going to leave it with me, let me get caught with it," he said.

"All you're going to do is drive a truck. What are you going to get caught for doing that?" I asked.

"You never been black, you never will be, you never will understand," he said.

"I can't argue with that," I said. "The chances of me turning into a brother aren't real good."

He shook his head and laughed. "All right, let's do it," he said.

"Okay," I said, "it's one thirty. You cruise down the street behind Thomas's place, and when you get to the vacant lot behind it you slow down to about five miles per hour and pull over to the left side of the road. Don't stop, and don't hit the brakes. I don't want the brake lights to show. I'll jump out and go through the vacant lot to the warehouse. It shouldn't take me more than an hour, so come back by at two thirty, do the same thing, and I'll jump into the back of the truck. If I'm not there, come back by at fifteen minute intervals and I'll make one of them sooner or later. If you see blue lights, it means I blew it, so just take the truck on home with you and I'll call you for a bond."

"Let's get it over with," he said.

I put the pack on, got out of the cab and walked around to the other side between it and the fence.

"What are you doing now?" Henry called through the passenger window.

"What do you think?" I asked. "Getting rid of some of your coffee. That's one thing I learned from my grandfather—pee when you can."

I climbed in the back of the truck and lay down on the left side of the bed. I reached up and rapped on the window, and Henry cranked up the truck and slowly drove off.

The mixture of Henry's coffee, the cool night air and anticipation of the upcoming job had got my adrenaline going again. I eased over on my right side with my head cushioned on my arm, the bright street lights and security lights from the depot and the warehouses and factories sweeping over me and blocking any view of the stars. Henry took a left, then a right, then another left, and the overhead lights faded out. I knew we were on the street behind Thomas's place. I was hoping there wouldn't be many people out this late. I heard a snatch of conversation between two people on the sidewalk just after we got on the street, then nothing else. As the truck slowed and veered to the left, I got up so I was sitting on the edge of the bed, facing outward, my legs dangling off the side, hanging onto the edge with both hands. I took a quick look around. There was nobody to see me, and no street light pole for me to crash into. As the truck came up to the curb, barely moving, I pushed off with my hands and feet, and landed on all fours in the weeds on the other side of the sidewalk. The truck kept on going without a stop or a brake light, slowly moving back over to the right side of the road.

I crawled a few feet further into the weeds, then stopped and listened. The only sounds I could hear were crickets, the distant hum of traffic, and faint voices that seemed to come through the broken windows of the abandoned house on the side of the lot. I turned back around toward the street, and raised up on my knees, which put my head just above the level of the weeds. There was nobody on the street, and most of the houses, including the one with the Dobermans, were dark. There was a burst of wild sounding laughter from the abandoned house, but it quickly died out. There were more quiet voices, and then the flare of a lighter or match as somebody lit up a rock. I doubted they were on high security alert, but they probably had at least one gun that they wouldn't hesitate to fire blindly out a window in my direction if they heard me and thought I was sneaking up on them.

I picked my way carefully through the weeds, shuffling my feet so I wouldn't step on anything loud and crunchy. The lot was only about sixty feet wide, and some noise was inevitable, so I tried to work my way over toward the house with the dogs so my sounds wouldn't be as likely to reach the crackheads. I was counting on the Dobermans sleeping inside.

I soon reached the back of the lot near the corner with the adjacent lot. Now I had to figure where the best place was to cross. Here, the fence ran behind the back wall of the warehouse, with only two or three inches of clearance between the wire and the cinder blocks. I wasn't sure why they had felt they had to have a fence here, instead of just relying on the concrete wall for security. Anyway, there was no point in cutting a hole here, so I walked carefully over to where the wall ended at the edge of the driveway. Even through the thick screen of weeds and bushes, I could still see that the drive and loading area were bathed in bright white light from fixtures along the roofline. They were probably on light sensors and came on every night. Even if Thomas was dead and nobody was maintaining the place, lights like that would last till the electricity was cut off.

What I saw through the fence and vegetation was pretty much what I had expected. In the space that hadn't been visible from the street there was a loading dock reached by a set of concrete steps. On the dock, there was a wide roll down metal door and a regular metal door beside it. The dock stopped short about halfway along the building. In the half toward me and the fence, there was another wide metal door that came all the way down to the pavement, allowing access for a vehicle to drive right into the building. None of the doors looked like it was going to be easy to get through.

It would be simple to cut a hole in the fence here and slip through, but I didn't like that light. There probably wouldn't be anyone to see me, and I might have to get in it eventually anyway, if the two doors were the only way in, but my instincts told me to delay it as long as possible.

I slipped back down the border toward the house with the Dobermans, and stopped when I was a few feet from the corner. I pulled a pair of wire cutters out of the pack, stuck them in my back pocket, and put the pack back on. I found one of the thick metal posts that the fence was attached to, and started up the fence. It was tight and strong here at the post, and I was able to move quickly and quietly to the top. I pulled the cutters out of my pocket with my right hand, while I clung to the cross bar at the top with my left. I started to search slowly in the dark for the razor wire with the spread open jaws of the wire cutters, then stopped, wondering if it was electrified. They hadn't been in front, and they probably weren't here, but if I was wrong there was going to be a flash of blue light as I did a double backflip off the fence. I took a deep breath, and went on feeling. I found the first strand on the third or fourth try. It wasn't hot. I kept the cutters on it with my right hand, and leaned as far back as I could on my left arm while I snipped it. I didn't know how much spring it had in it, and I didn't want it whipping across my throat. It separated with a surprisingly loud snap, and I felt rather than saw one end fly up into the air, then settle back down on my side of the fence. I'd have to be careful not to get tangled up in it on the way down.

I felt around till I found the second strand, leaned back, and snipped it. This one didn't fly up, but out toward me, the end whipping across my cheekbone and scratching it. I wasn't having a lot of luck with my face tonight, but I was lucky that it was the end of the wire and not one of the razor sharp protrusions fixed on it that had hit me. I was also lucky that it hadn't been two inches higher and slashed across my eye.

I ran my right arm over the top of the fence, and cautiously raised it till I was sure that all of the razor wire was cut and out of the way. Then I climbed the rest of the way up the woven wire and leaned across it on the concrete wall of the warehouse as I worked my feet up till they were on the top crossbar. By standing on my tiptoes, I could barely reach my fingertips over the edge of the roof, but not enough to pull my weight up on. I looked around, but there was no convenient utility pole or tree to scramble up. It was a damned awkward situation, because the wall was so close to the fence that if I bent down too far, my butt sticking out in the back would overbalance me, since I couldn't go more than three inches forward before I hit the wall. But I knew from experience that if I stood here too long thinking about it, my muscles would start to cramp and shake. So I took a deep breath, crouched down about six inches, and went for it. The fingertips of both hands curled easily over the far side of the short wall surrounding the roof, and I pulled myself up and onto the roof. It hadn't been as hard as I thought, but it was a good example why I was never going to be able to buy disability insurance.

I stood quiet for a minute, looking all around, back the way I had come to make sure no one had heard me, and then forward at the roof I was standing on. Everything was quiet in the vacant lot I had come through and in the houses on both sides. In front of me, there was nothing but flat, gravel-covered roof. The lights that shone on the loading area didn't shed much light upward, but the roof was faintly illuminated by street lights.

I felt something warm and wet on my face, and wiped it off with the back of my hand. It was blood from the scratch on my cheekbone, and I could feel it well back up as soon as I had wiped it away. I had another leak, this one running faster than the hole in the end of my nose. There wasn't much I could do about it at this point, though, so I decided to ignore it and just drip. I hoped the DNA I was spreading around wouldn't come back to haunt me.

I walked around the corner of the ell of the building, and looked down on the loading area while standing behind one of the security lights. It was as I had seen it from the other side of the fence, concrete and metal, starkly bright in the artificial light. But I could also see that both of the rolling doors were held by massive padlocks secured through a metal ring welded onto the bottom of the door and another ring set into the concrete. If they were really serious about security, there would be similar locks inside, inaccessible from out here and secured by someone who left through the regular door. I hadn't brought a bolt cutter big enough to cut through the lock hasps, so I would have to spend time trying to pick the locks, with a good chance that I would find the doors still impregnable once I had done it.

The regular door didn't look much more promising. It had not one but two deadbolts, and a knob lock. Worse, it had two padlocks securing it, one at knee height and another at chest height. That looked like at least thirty minutes of standing in the glaring light, trying to work the locks open with a pick. Not very promising.

I considered my options. I could leave, and come back another time with bigger bolt cutters. That wouldn't help any with the rolling doors, though, if they were also secured from inside, and while it would cut down on the need for lock picking on the regular door, it wouldn't eliminate it. Plus, I didn't want to come back again unless I had to. It was a hassle getting a ride, and there were too many things that could go wrong. Another trip would just raise the odds against me. Ground-level entry looked problematic, so I began to reconnoiter the roof.

Near the back corner closest to the loading area, there was a bulky shadow that I assumed to be an HVAC system. I walked over and felt around on it with my hands. It wasn't the usual rectangle, but more of a rounded hump with one flat side pointed away from the street. I could feel that the flat side was open. I pulled out my penlight and risked a quick look. There was a big fan inside the opening, at least four feet across. It was perpendicular to the roof, but the space behind it curved downward to a wide mesh metal screen that lay parallel with the roof. It was no HVAC, just a simple fan that could probably be turned one way to bring fresh air in from the roof or turned the other way to act as an exhaust fan. It was set up in this hump so that rain wouldn't blow directly down the vent. In the winter, they would close the vent off completely. The screen, with its inch square holes, was to keep out leaves and other debris that the fan might suck in.

I leaned into the space till my head was touching one of the blades of the fan, and shone my light as far down as I could. It went through the screen, so they hadn't blocked it off for the winter yet. But other than that, I couldn't see anything in the beam. I pulled slightly on one of the fan blades. It was aluminum and bent easily.

I pulled my head back out and sat down to think. I wiped the self-replenished streak of blood off my cheek with my shoulder, and checked the time. It was one fifty, just twenty minutes after we had started out with me in the back of the pickup. I was making good time, but I still wasn't in the warehouse. The doors were going to take too damn long, even if I could finally get past them. I had already considered whether any part of the warehouse would be wired for security, but I figured that Thomas wouldn't want the cops snooping around every time a rat chewed through a wire. He could have it hooked up just to his house, but that would be expensive and I hadn't seen any sign of that when I had played houseguest. I wondered whether the fan could be on a temperature sensor or automatic timer. If it were on a temperature sensor, it would probably have to be hotter than it was to kick it in. If it were on a timer, it would probably be set to come on in the day. I decided it was the fan or not at all, at least tonight.

I took the pack off and opened it up. I got out the rope, tied one end around the vent cover, and put the rest of the coil just inside the vent. I put on a pair of light cotton gloves, and reached in and carefully bent one of the fan blades all the way back toward me. I took it slow, but it hardly made any noise at all. I bent another blade back, making a space big enough for me to crawl through. I thought for a second, decided I might be wrong about the sensor or timer, and bent the other blade back, too. Better safe than sorry. Then I reached back out, got the pack, and set it on the coil of rope. I wasn't sure whether there would be room to wear it past the fan, but I wanted to have it handy.

I wriggled past the bent fan blades and the fan motor to the screen that lay about a foot behind them. I shone the light down through the mesh and around. Directly below was a concrete floor, maybe fifteen feet down. I pulled the beam up to the screen itself, and was relieved to see that it was held in place only by large wing nuts. Of course, they were on the other side of the screen, but the mesh was large enough for me to get my fingers through and turn them. Before I did, though, I reached back and got the coil of rope, tied the end through the screen's middle, and wrapped the rope around my body to hold it tight. Then I carefully unscrewed the nuts, placing them in the zippered breast pocket of my pullover as they came loose. When the last one was off, I lowered the screen to the floor, and then let the rest of the rope slack down over it. I pulled the pack in, and managed to shrug it on in the tight space, pulling on the rope to make sure it was tight. There wasn't enough room for me to turn around and go feet first, so I eased my chest out over the hole and reached down and grasped the rope with both hands, thumbs on top. I worked my way upside down till my stomach, then hips, were over the edge and angled down. I spread my legs, and eased down further, the blood rushing to my head. When all that was left in the hole were my feet, hooked over the edge on each side, I pulled them off and swung down, holding hard to the rope so the centrifugal force wouldn't pull me off. When I had stopped swinging, I slid the remaining few feet to the concrete floor.

I looked at my watch again. It was a little after two. There was no way I would be back out on the street for the first rendezvous, and I was going to have to hustle to make the second bus.

It was pitch black inside the warehouse, the only light being the faint glow from the airshaft above. I pulled the pack off, got out the big flashlight, and switched it on. I was standing just behind the big metal door that could be lifted to let vehicles inside the building. Sure enough, it was secured with a padlock on the inside. Just beside me, toward the front of the warehouse, there was a ramp that rose up to the loading dock that I had seen from the outside. I shone the light on that door and saw that it had the same internal padlock. The floor on the other side of the ramp and behind it was at the same level as where I stood. There was nothing on my side of the ramp but concrete floor and walls, but on the other side I could see stacks of boxes.

I walked around the back end of the ramp and stopped at the first stack. They were four feet square cardboard. Somebody had taken a red marker and written things on them like "Hilfiger jeans, men and women, all sizes," "Starter jackets, Raiders and Cowboys," and "Puma shoes, 8 1/2 through 12, basketball." I pulled the knife blade out on my multi-tool, and opened the box marked "Starter Jackets." Sure enough, it was full of logo jackets, each one wrapped in its own cellophane wrapper. Henry's tip had been good; I was in the Designer's warehouse.

I wandered around the stacks, noting the various written notations, all in the same red marker. In one corner toward the street, I came across an old wooden desk. There was nothing on the top except a couple of ballpoint pens and some red markers, but in one of the side drawers I found a stack of manila folders, each containing several sheets of paper. I didn't stop to read them, just stuck them all in the pack.

The top of the desk, the boxes, the floor, everything was dusty, but it looked and felt like natural dust, not fingerprint dust. There were no marks on the dust on the desk, or footprints in the dust on the floor. It didn't look like the cops or anyone else had been here in a good while.

I went over to the regular door I had seen from the roof. All its locks were secure.

I worked my way through the stacks over to the other front corner and came up against a wall of boxes that started at the front of the warehouse. I followed the box wall for about twenty feet till it cornered and ran at a ninety-degree angle to the side wall. The boxes were stacked three deep here, about twice as high as I was tall. I shone the flashlight as best I could through the crack between two stacks. I couldn't be sure, but it looked like the light went further than if there had been more boxes on the other side. I put the light down with its beam shining on the corner, and slowly eased one stack out. Then I picked the light back up and shone it into the gap I had made.

Sure enough, there was space, not more boxes, behind the wall. Inside the space was a long, white Ford van. I walked around the van, and shone the light everywhere, but there was nothing else to see. The license plate was a Tennessee commercial vehicle tag with an inspection sticker that wouldn't expire for several more months. I wrote the tag number down, then went around to the front and looked in the driver's side window. The door had an old style button lock that looked like it was up, but I hesitated to try it. There was no small red blinking light to indicate an activated alarm, and if the van had been setting here any amount of time the battery would be dead. Plus, most alarm systems didn't activate unless the doors were locked. On the other hand, if I did trip an alarm, it was going to be hell getting out of the warehouse in anything like a hurry.

The van didn't have any windows except those in front, so I went around and shone the light through the windshield. There was a curtain just behind the two front seats, blocking off the view of the back. It was probably a good precautionary measure if you were routinely hauling stolen merchandise around. It looked like it was going to be leave with whatever it was I had gotten from the desk, and hope it was something good, or take a chance on the van door. I thought for a minute, then realized that if the warehouse wasn't on a security system because Thomas didn't want the cops snooping around, the van wouldn't be either. That's what logic dictated, but my tired brain wasn't getting to logic very fast. I hoped Thomas or whoever had parked the van here had been thinking better then than I was now.

The door opened easily and with a minimum of noise, no alarm or flashing lights. I shone the light around the inside of the cab. It was pretty clean, except for some light-colored mud on the floor mats in front of both seats. There were no butts in the ashtray, and no empty soda cans lying around. I looked in the glove box, but didn't see anything but a flashlight, the operating manual, and what looked like the registration. I left the flashlight and manual, and stuck the registration in a pocket. There was nothing over the sun visors, and nothing under the seats.

I pulled the curtain back, hoping I would find something, but there was nothing but two poles on each side that could have been used to support hangers, and empty space. I stepped back into the space, and shone the light all around. Nothing. Someone had done a pretty good job of hiding this van, but I couldn't figure out why.

I went back up front, and popped the latch that opened the hood. I got out of the van, eased up the hood, and looked inside. It was an engine, all right. I'm no mechanic, but everything that I could see looked pretty normal. I eased the hood back down, but didn't shut it because of the noise it would have made closing.

Then I got down on my hands and knees and looked under the van. Again, everything looked normal. I knew the truth was that there could be a fortune in crack stowed somewhere in the van, but I didn't have the expertise or time to look for it. I went around to the back of the van and looked under there, too, but all I saw was a muffler and an axle. As I began to raise back up, though, I noticed something sticking out from the bottom of the back bumper. I put the light on it, then pulled on it with my fingers. It was a piece of mud-encrusted grass or weed. I started to throw it down, then took a closer look at it. The mud was a light gray color, and the vegetation seemed familiar when I looked at it closer. I stuck it in my pocket.

I shut the van door quietly, and looked at my watch. It was two thirty six, and I was late for my first pickup, and probably wasn't going to make the second. Time to go.

I slid the boxes back in place, and then went around to where I had left the rope hanging. I thought about the camera, but figured there wasn't any value in a picture of anything I had seen. I scrambled up the rope, and worked my way awkwardly up into the space behind the fan. There wasn't room to turn around, so I went on out past the fan, took the pack off, then wriggled back in. My face had quit bleeding sometime while I was in the warehouse, but I must have scraped it again as I went past the fan, and blood dripped off it onto the floor as I raised the screen and secured it with the wing nuts. I untied the rope, then went backwards past the fan and out into the cool night air. I bent the fan blades back as best I could, untied the rope from around the fan cover, and coiled it into the pack. Other than some blood, footprints in the dust and the open hood of the van, there was nothing to show that I had been in.

I still had to get off the roof, but it felt like the hard part was done. I was more than tired; I was weary and exhausted, physically and mentally. I felt like a climber who has invested all his energy into reaching the summit, and now has to muster the concentration and strength to get back down the mountain.

I looked at my watch. It was two fifty. I had missed the second pickup, and tired or not, it was time to boogie.

I took the gloves off, stuck them in my pockets, and put the pack back on. I walked to the edge of the roof, and looked over and listened. I was hoping that the crackheads had left or passed out in the last hour, and that the Dobermans didn't have to be let out for an early pee break. I couldn't hear or see a thing, so I sat down on the edge of the roof, twisted around and hooked my hands over the wall, and let myself down as far as I could. I hung for a couple of seconds, trying to touch the fence with my toes, and then gave up and slid down the wall.

But just then, all hell broke loose. The fence was just a few inches below my feet, but when I hit it my left foot slipped off and I went flying back and out in a backwards somersault. My feet, then my back and my head hit the ground in a grinding thump that seemed to shake all of my internal organs and knocked the breath out of me. There was a sharp crack as the flashlight in the pack dug hard into my ribs. I wasn't unconscious, but I had that sick, desperate feeling of not being able to breathe, and even as I lay there trying to get my wind I thought of how Carl must have felt after my knee crashed through his vitals.

At that moment, my breath came back in a gasp, but just as I felt a sense of relief I heard somebody from the abandoned house yell, "Who the fuck is that?" As I started to get up and run, there was a series of explosions from the house, and bullets zipped through the grass and slammed into the fence on the other side of the lot as somebody emptied a clip out of one of the broken windows. I was down flat on my stomach with the first shot, but some of the fifteen or sixteen copper-coated lead slugs came dangerously close.

There was a momentary respite in the sound as the gun emptied, but it was almost immediately broken by a series of howls and barks as the Dobermans woke up. I had an armed crackhead on one side of me and two crazed attack dogs on the other. It was not a place to linger, and I was back up immediately and on the move. I hadn't taken two steps when something slashed across the outside of my left calf, cutting through my pants and deep into the flesh. It was the damn razor wire that had coiled down off the fence, but I kept going, stifling a curse. I could assess the damage later.

I was almost to the front of the lot, though it was hard to run fast through the tall, thick weeds. There were no more shots from the crack house on the right. He was either a slow reloader or he just had one clip. Just let Henry be there, I was thinking, when the door opened on my left and the harsh, staccato barking of the Dobermans rang out clear as they rushed into their front yard.

I froze and watched the dogs mill around, looking for their prey. They had stopped barking, but were whining and growling loudly. I could see their owner standing on the porch with a long gun of some kind in his hands, peering my way. I heard voices in the crack house, and he must have heard them, too, because he shouldered his gun, pointed it my way, and yelled, "Take that, you lowlife drugheads." I was still on my way to the ground when it boomed over my head, and a hail of buckshot hit the other house.

The dogs were barking now and a second shot blew out over my head. I slithered on my belly the last couple of yards to the front of the lot and cautiously looked out. To the left, I could see the dogs standing on the sidewalk not thirty feet from me, yammering their fool heads off. They were making so much noise themselves they hadn't heard me moving through the grass. I couldn't see their owner from ground level, but I knew he was still standing on his porch with a loaded shotgun.

I quickly turned my head and spotted my white truck coming down the street from the right. There was no time to think, and as the truck veered over my way I leaped out of the weeds, crossed the sidewalk and fringe of grass in two steps, and vaulted into the truck bed as it came abreast. I had seen the dogs out of the corner of my eye, charging toward me with their mouths open, and had caught a glimpse of a stunned-looking Henry through the driver's window.

"Go, go!" I was yelling, even before I hit the bottom of the truck bed, and then "Police, police, don't shoot!" hoping it would make the guy with the shotgun hesitate. Henry punched the truck, but he had been going so slow and the dogs were moving so fast that one of them sailed over the edge of the bed, his front paws landing right on my chest. He lost his balance in the rapidly accelerating truck, and I managed to get one hand around his collar, grabbed a loose roll of skin in the other and chunked him over the side. He hit, rolled, got up, and began chasing the truck, barking like the most pissed off dog in the world. He was one tough son of a bitch.

I was waiting for the shotgun to boom our way as I dived back down behind the tailgate, but what I heard instead was the semiautomatic pistol from the crack house. It fired four or five rounds in less than two seconds, then the shotgun started back up with its bass roar. No pellets struck the truck, so he must have been responding to the crack house assault.

Henry took the first corner on two wheels, but then slowed down to a reasonable pace. He wasn't going out of the neighborhood the way we had come, but through the back streets. I lay on my side, sucking air and trying to get my shit together. Through the open window, I could hear Henry cussing and talking to himself, but he kept the truck moving. In a minute, I heard the sound of sirens, and Henry's monologue increased in intensity and volume. His speed didn't change, though, and he kept stopping at stop signs and red lights. Even in this neighborhood, the level of the fire fight we had just escaped was going to bring the police quickly, but I hoped it would take them a long time to get any kind of statement that implicated anyone other than the guys with the guns.

I lost track of direction until we got on the interstate loop. I watched the mercury lights whip by overhead, and lay shivering in the cold air. I stuck my finger through the gap the razor wire had cut in my pants, and felt the deep gash in my calf muscle. It was at least two inches long, and a half inch deep. Stitches time. My forearms ached and my face was burning where it had been scratched. I felt the back of my tender head where it had hit the ground. I tried to think what to say if we got pulled over by a patrol car that was looking for a white pickup driven by an African-American male, with a bloody white guy in the back, and came up with a big nothing.

It wasn't long before I could tell we were off the interstate and on Riverside, with the bluff rising up on the right side. We went past Cybill's house, and then by my apartment. I realized I didn't want anything more than to be in my own place, take a hot shower, put on some bandages, and sleep for twenty-four hours.

Henry turned up to Front, and then turned west over the Wolf onto Mud Island. We wound our way through the residential streets and pulled up in front of his house. He got out of the truck, and walked along the side of the bed. As he did, he whispered out of the side of his mouth, "Stay down."

I lay in the truck and heard him open the door to his place. There was a muffled sound of a car engine starting, then the garage door going up. I heard him backing up his Lexus and saw the headlights as he pulled it in behind the truck. He got out, and I heard the small beep as he locked the doors with a remote entry device. He walked back by the truck bed, got in the cab, and pulled into the garage. I waited till the door was down, and then slowly sat up. Henry got out of the cab, shut the door, and flipped on a light switch.

He walked over, put both hands on the top rail of the truck bed, and stood looking at me, shaking his head. "You are a mess," he said slowly. "Why in the fuck I was ever fool enough to get mixed up with you is a mystery."

"Thanks for doing it," I said. "I'm sorry about that excitement at the end. I would have waved you off if there was any way I could have."

"Waved me off?" he asked. "Then what would you have done?"

"I don't know. Tried to get home somehow, tried to keep away from the cops."

"I heard some shooting in the neighborhood when I was making the block, but I couldn't tell where it came from. When I started pulling up to the curb I heard those dogs and saw the fat guy on the porch with the shotgun, then at the same time I saw you jump out of the weeds and in back, and those damn dogs started for us. Did he bite you?" he asked, pointing at my leg.

I looked and saw that my whole pants leg, from the cut down, and the boot on that foot, were covered in blood. There was a small pool of blood in the bed of the truck below my leg. "No, that was the razor wire, not the dog," I said.

"What about your face?"

"Same wire, different time."

"Razor wire, big mean fucking dogs, a fat guy with a shotgun, and I heard someone popping a nine as we pulled away. If they'd had a searchlight, I might just as well been busting you out of prison."

"Well, they missed with the shotgun, the nine and the dogs. The only thing they got me with was the razor wire, but it's nasty stuff." I tried to stand up, and felt a shooting pain in my upper back where I had landed on the flashlight after my effort off the three-meter board. The camera was probably a wreck, but I reminded myself that if the ground had been hard or if I had landed on concrete, I would have fractured my skull or at least knocked myself out and been lying there like an idiot for the cops to find.

"You going to be okay?" he asked, as I sat back down heavily.

"Yeah, I think so. Mostly I just need to sleep." The weariness I had felt on the roof of the warehouse was nothing to the waves of fatigue that were washing across me now. I felt like asking Henry to bring me a pillow and a blanket, and just lying there in my own blood and turning off the world. "Do me a favor, would you," I said, "and drop the tailgate."

I slid out on it, dangling my legs over the end. With the extra blood flowing into my leg from this position, the ooze from the razor cut turned into a steady drip, but I went ahead and put my weight on my feet. I held onto the tailgate a moment, then took a couple of steps. My head was all right, and I was mostly just stiff from my various exertions and beatings, and from riding in the cold wind in the back of the truck after sweating. I turned around to shut the tailgate, but Henry was already lifting it up.

"Henry," I said, "I owe you big time. I can't tell you how much I appreciate what you did. If you hadn't come back, I might have been killed, and if I hadn't been killed I would have been arrested. I'll shake your hand sometime when mine isn't covered with blood."

"No doubt about it, man, you do owe me. But you know what," he said, "I got a kick out of it." He grinned, "I'm not saying I'd want to do it again, you understand, but it made for a change from going to class or working the counter at the bond company."

"Well, shit, Henry, if I'd known you'd like it so much, I'd have let you go in the warehouse and I'd have driven the truck."

"I got enough kicks being your wheelman," Henry said. "But hey, why didn't the fat guy take a shot at us? He could have blown me away."

"You're not kidding. That's what I was worried about, but I didn't know anything to do about it but jump in the back of the truck and yell for you to go. I doubt I fooled him with that stuff about the cops, but he might have been so surprised to see a white guy flying out of the weeds that he fell for it. Could be he thought the cops were having a firefight with the crack house. But I really think it was the dog."

"The dog?"

"Yeah, the one that jumped in the truck. I think he was afraid of hitting the dog, and by the time I threw him out we were on the far edge of shotgun range. Then the crack house opened back up and he really had something to shoot at."

"Well, thank God he was sentimental about that devil dog. Did you find anything in the warehouse?"

I suddenly felt sick, and put my forehead against the cold metal edge of the truck bed. I thought for a minute I was going to puke up whatever was left of Tommy's tenderloin, but I forced it back down.

"You okay, man?" I heard him ask.

"Yeah, I think so." I carefully stood up, and wiped a hand across my mouth. "I'm not sure if anything I found in there will help us, but it's definitely the place. I'll tell you about it when my mind is working better. Now I better roll while I'm still on my feet."

"You think you better drive?" he asked.

"I can make it," I replied.

"Maybe," he said, "but by now the cops have talked to the fat guy, and he's told them about a white pickup involved in a drive by."

"What if the crackhead with the nine killed the fat guy? He was a big target," I said.

"If anybody was killed, I doubt it was him," Henry said. "He looked like a survivor. He's probably a life member of the NRA."

"Well, they'll be looking for a white pickup driven by a black guy."

"Yeah, with a crazy white man in the back. You're going to pass at least two patrol cars between here and your place, and you're going to be about the only vehicle on the street at this time of night. They're not going to have anything to do but check you out. And you know what they're going to see when they do? A man who looks like he's been in a razor fight, or who set out to butcher a hog, but the hog got the knife away and turned it on him. They're going to be impressed by that pool of blood in the back, too, and that three fifty seven in the glove box."

"So, you want to lend me your Lexus?" I asked.

He snorted, "Nobody but me drives that car. It cost too many late nights with junkies and whores. Besides, you'd bleed on it. I got an extra room. Spend what's left of the night here, then clean up and go home in the morning."

I followed him into the house and up the stairs. He showed me the spare bedroom, and the bathroom attached to it, and left. I dropped my torn and bloody clothes in a pile, took a quick but scary look at myself in the mirror over the sink, and got in the shower. I let the water run as hot as I could stand it, and soaped from head to toe, wincing as the soap stung my cuts. I toweled off, and drank several handfuls of water from the tap. I went out into the bedroom. Henry had left a t-shirt and some gym shorts on the bed. On the nightstand beside it was a glass of water, two ibuprofen tablets, and some gauze and white tape. I put the clothes on, swallowed the pills, and sat down on the bed and bandaged my leg. There was a knock on the door, and he came in carrying a pair of blue jeans and my Smith.

"You can wear these home tomorrow," he said, throwing the pants on a chair, "and I didn't think you'd want to leave this in the truck." He laid the big pistol on top of the jeans.

"What can I say, man, except thanks again. You're going to a lot of trouble for someone you barely know."

"Seems I'm getting to know you better, whether I want to or not," he said. "I got class at eight tomorrow morning, this morning, in three and half fucking hours," he said, looking at his watch. "I'll call you about seven."

12 _____

It had been early Wednesday morning when I had the warehouse adventure, and early Thursday morning I woke up to the first hard cold rain of the fall. I had spent the day before getting my leg sewed up, taking the pain pills my doctor had prescribed, catching up on my sleep, cleaning up my truck, and generally avoiding any kind of trouble. I had a huge bruise on the upper right side of my back, but the x-ray showed no broken rib. I told the doctor I had lost my balance while crossing a barbed wire fence on a fishing trip. It was partly true.

I got up, still sleepy but tired of being in bed. I cripped into the kitchen and got the coffee going, then took a long, hot shower. I shaved, put on old jeans, a t-shirt and a sweater, and got the first cup. I opened the door to the balcony, pulled an easy chair up close to it, and sat and watched the rain. It was rolling across from the northwest, soaking the Arkansas farmland, disappearing into the river, and coating Riverside Drive and the cobblestones that lined the bank by the boat landing with a translucent film. It pattered on my balcony, and stray drops and mist blew through the door and fell on my face and hands.

I knew from experience that even without a pain pill and fatigue hangover, I was perfectly capable of sitting here for hours on a day like this, doing little but reading and letting my mind drift. When I was practicing law, the weather had meant nothing to me. Baking summer heat or winter ice and snow, I was in the same climate controlled office six days a week, barely taking time to even look out the window. Now, I had more leisure time to spend outdoors, and my work took me outside much more frequently, and even affected whether I could do my work. I had gotten back into the rhythm of the weather, and had allowed myself to feel its natural effects on body and soul. Like a wild animal, I could obey my instincts and curl up in my den and wait for the sun.

I finished my coffee and took a couple of ibuprofen, trying to keep the aches at a manageable level without the narcotics. I had just poured a second cup and was making my way back to the chair when the phone rang. I looked at it for three more rings, then went ahead and picked it up. It was Amanda, sounding typically rushed and distracted. No weather rhythm for her.

"John, I'm still in this damn trial, but I wanted to take a minute and check in on your investigation for Lucy. How's it going?" I could hear her talking to her secretary while she waited for me to answer.

"Amanda," I asked, "have you noticed that it's raining?"

"Yeah, what's your point?"

"Nothing. Frankly, I don't know how it's going. I've been a busy beaver, but I haven't sat back yet to figure out whether I've accomplished anything. I'm sort of working on the analysis part now."

"What have you been busy doing?" she asked. I could hear her secretary say something to her, and heard Amanda mutter back.

"Amanda," I said, "if you weren't trying to do five things at once you'd remember you regretted it the last time you asked me that question."

"So I'd regret it if I asked you now?"

"Definitely," I answered.

"Well, keep trying to find him, okay? This is important to me."

"Believe me, I'm putting my blood and sweat into it," I said.

"This case is going into closing argument this afternoon, so I'll have more time to talk with you soon," she said.

"Great," I said, and started to wish her luck, but she had already hung up.

I had been prepared for a relaxing morning of rain-watching, but Amanda's call had gotten my juices going and made me feel guilty that I hadn't accomplished anything the day before. My pack was still lying on the floor where I had thrown it yesterday. I had taken the pistol out and cleaned it before I started on the pain pills, but I hadn't unpacked anything else. I got the rope and flashlight out and put them up, and then examined the camera. I couldn't see any evidence of damage, but I resolved to shoot and have developed the roll of film in it before I relied on it again.

I then laid the folders from the warehouse out on the kitchen table. Each one had a neatly typed label stuck on it, and as I began to go through them it quickly became apparent that Thomas had been running his business under a façade of legitimacy. One folder contained the articles of organization for a limited liability company named Tuggle Enterprises, LLC. Another held his business license. He had listed his principal activity as "retail." There was even a set of financial books, with general notations on expenses and revenue. There were "cost of goods" entries, but no specific listings. Another folder contained his personal federal income tax returns: he showed income of almost $500,000 in 2001, and over $550,000 in 2002. Thomas had obviously heard the old adage that pigs get fat and hogs get slaughtered, and had decided to play it halfway straight, paying the federal government its cut of his illegal activities. They had finally caught up with Al Capone on income tax charges, and Thomas wasn't taking that chance.

The last folder contained the payroll record for one employee of Tuggle Enterprises, Hayes Gifford. Gifford had made $1000 a week in 2002, and was paid $1100 a week through the first week of August 2003, when the records stopped. Even with social security and tax withholdings, he had made a good net income. I didn't recognize the address listed for him, and got out my city map and looked it up. It was in the north part of town, but still in the interstate loop. It was obviously not prime real estate, but I didn't have any reference point to tell just how bad its location was. I got the phone book out and looked him up.

I flipped through the contents of the folders again, then put them away in a file cabinet. It didn't seem like a lot for the effort and pain I had endured. Then I remembered the only other thing I had found, and went over and pulled my jacket out of the washing machine. I unzipped the chest pocket, and pulled out the piece of mud encrusted vegetation I had gotten off the bottom of the van. The grayish-white mud looked like the same stuff that was on the floorboards, which only made sense. I pulled open a drawer and took out a plastic bag, and dumped out the mud I had found on the floor of Thomas's garage. It looked like the same stuff, but I was no mud expert. I broke the mud away from the piece of vegetation, and took a closer look at it. It was a stalk, with a seed pod on the end. I cracked the seed pod open, and looked at the contents. It was a soybean, which didn't seem to mean a whole lot, except that the van had been somewhere outside the city limits in a field. The mud in Thomas's garage might be from the same place, or it might have been from his front yard.

I shut the balcony doors, put on socks and my boots, and poured the rest of the coffee in the pot into a thermos. I put the thermos in the backpack, checked the load in the Smith, and clipped it on my belt. I put my binoculars in the pack, and then decided to add the camera. Maybe it would work. I put on a waxed cotton baseball hat with the logo of a flyrod manufacturer whose products I couldn't afford, slipped on a waterproof parka, and headed out the door. It was a good day for thinking, but I decided I might as well try to do it on the move.

I headed out the north end of downtown and around the curve of the interstate circle around town. Interstate 40 runs from the Pacific Ocean to the Atlantic Ocean in a 3000-mile shot, broken only by a five-mile long gap in Memphis. It crosses the Appalachian Mountains, the Great Plains, the Rocky Mountains and the western desert in one long stretch of concrete and blacktop, except when it comes to the 170 acres of first growth forest in Overton Park, in the heart of Memphis. Then it takes a detour around the city, sparing trees that were alive when the Spaniards built the first fort on the Chickasaw Bluff in the 1700s. It took years of litigation, and hundreds of hours of donated legal time by dedicated lawyers, but that one small green spot escaped the bulldozer.

I got off on Jackson, and headed back into the city, looking for Gifford's address. I turned off Jackson almost immediately onto a side street that wound through a neighborhood that looked a lot like the one where Thomas's warehouse was located, except there were a few Hispanic faces here and there. Between gaps in the houses on the north side of the street, I could see a stretch of woods, mostly willows, with an occasional grassy area. The houses on this side backed up to the floodplain of the Wolf River, and as I looked through one gap I caught a glimpse of the Wolf's muddy brown water.

I was counting the addresses off, but it was hard to see. I had the wipers on against the streaming rain, and the defroster on high, but the windshield and the passenger side window were still mostly opaque. I was going slow, but that didn't look suspicious because of the weather. When the numbers started getting close, I rubbed the inside of the windows with a bandanna and dropped another five miles per hour. As I did, I saw the door of a green pickup slam shut in a driveway a few houses down. It was starting to back out as I went past, and I had a glimpse of the driver's face looking back over his right shoulder. It wasn't much of a look, but I had seen that face before. I confirmed the address as I went on by, and watched the truck in the rearview mirror. It backed out, and went the way I had come. I turned into a driveway, waited for the count of five, and then went after it.

I made up some of the distance between us, then settled in about seventy-five yards back. I had turned my lights off when I had pulled into the driveway, and left them off now despite the heavy rain. He came to the stop sign at Jackson, and hit his left blinker. I took my foot off the accelerator, and started coasting up behind him, but he spotted a break in the traffic almost immediately and turned onto the main street. I pulled up to the stop sign, waited for my own break, and then followed him out onto Jackson. With the weather and my stop, he was pretty far ahead of me, but I saw him work his way across the lanes and head up the ramp to I-40 west, back around the way I had just come. At this rate, I figured I'd probably follow him back to my apartment.

The speed limit on this stretch of the interstate is 55, but most people go at least 65. The driver of the green truck was an exception, though, keeping his vehicle right at the posted limit. I hung back a good hundred yards, fighting the spray from the big semis that roared past me. I watched carefully, ready to follow him off an exit, but he stayed in the middle lane all the way around the loop and headed across the bridge into Arkansas. He turned north at the junction of I-55 and I-40, heading up toward St. Louis. He got off at the first exit, though, on U.S. 64, and went west at the same steady pace. There wasn't as much traffic here, so I hung back even further, and welcomed a car that pulled out of a roadside store between us.

The rain was still coming down, hard and cold, and my feet were getting numb despite the defroster that was turned all the way to warm. Sitting in one position in the truck was starting to make my wounds act up. The stitches in my calf burned and pulled, my back throbbed like someone was hitting it with a ball peen hammer, and the deep scratch on my cheek ached. My forearms felt tight and swollen where Carl had battered them. It was too soon for any more ibuprofen, so I'd have to make the best of it.

We went through spreading suburbia on the outskirts of Marion, Arkansas, past a sprawling boxcar-switching yard on the south side of the highway, and then we were into the fields. They stretched away to the horizon on every side, broken here and there by small groves of trees surrounding shacks or graveyards. The cotton and soybeans had been picked, and the fruitless black stalks of the plants stuck up in a tangle over the land. The heads of the rice had been cut off at the same height in every field; where the stubble hadn't been burned off, it stood straight and golden brown in geometric patterns that looked like alien hieroglyphics laid down between the dikes. It was some of the most productive soil in the world, but it looked menopausal now, maybe because of the contrast to the bursting plant life and fecund, sexual smell of the earth in the growing season.

The highway skirted several small towns, and at one of them the intervening car pulled off. Less than an hour after leaving the interstate, we came to Parkin, right on the St. Francis River. It is home to several hundred souls, but to the highway traveler it looks mainly like a collection of gas stations. I maintained my hundred yards back, halfway hoping that the green truck would pull into one of them, so I could pull into another for something to eat. But he rolled right on through town, across the arched bridge over the river and back into the farmland. I took a quick look at the river as I went across. It hadn't been raining long enough to put it in flood stage, but it was already high and browner than usual.

A couple of miles past the bridge, I saw the brake lights and then the left blinker come on. I immediately took my foot off the accelerator, and began to think fast. Decision time. On the interstate, there had been so many cars that I was just one more motorist. If he had noticed me get off at the Marion exit onto 64, well, so did lots of other people, especially in pickups. But pulling off behind him onto a secondary road would be pushing it. Even if he wasn't up to any funny business, he would certainly notice me, and he might start thinking about a white truck that he had seen on his street back in town. I hit the accelerator, and went on past the road at 60 miles an hour.

As I drove past, I was glad I had made the decision to keep going. A sign proclaimed it to be a state highway, but it was narrow and gravel, and the green truck had only gone about fifty yards down it. I would have stuck out like a sore thumb if I had pulled in behind him. The question was what to do now. I could end the chase at this point, but I didn't really know anything. The other choice was to give him some time, and then head down the road and see if I could spot him parked somewhere. If he saw me then, or on his way back out, he might recognize me, but more likely than not I would be just another white truck, time having erased any connection to a truck that had followed him down the highway. As much as I wanted to go home, I decided to give him some time and then drive down the road.

I was hungry, and I doubted he would be coming back out the way he had gone in real soon, so I turned around and headed back into Parkin. I pulled into one of the gas stations, filled up the truck, and went inside. I paid for the gas, a sausage biscuit and a cup of coffee, did some mild flirting with the cashier who was cute in a rode hard sort of way, and sat down at one of the plastic booths to eat. It was pretty crowded, since there wasn't much to do in the fields with all the rain, and younger men who would usually have been working sat at the tables with older men who probably came here every day. Half of them were smoking, so I hurried through the biscuit and went to the bathroom to take a leak. I did my business, resisting the urge to stock up on flavored condoms and sexual novelties from the vending machines. I came out and headed for the truck.

It had been thirty minutes since I had watched the green truck pull off the highway, enough time for my image in his rearview mirror to fade. I headed across the St. Francis River and down the highway, and pulled off onto the gravel road. There were deep ditches on both sides at least fifteen feet deep, and rapidly filling with brown water as the rain ran out of the fields. Every now and then there was a bridge made out of pilings and planks that crossed the ditches, offering access onto field roads. With the rain these roads were deep gumbo mud that even a tractor could get stuck in, so I didn't bother to look for tracks.

After about a mile, I crossed through a thin stand of trees that grew along a fence-line, and spotted the first human habitation. It was a house trailer situated close to the road, with patches of rust down its sides. Three unpainted wooden steps led up to a door with a porthole in it. The yard would be baked hardpan in dry weather, but in the rain was nothing but a big mud puddle. Two wet, sad-looking dogs gazed at me from under the trailer, but didn't bother to come running out to chase me. Smart dogs. There was a full-size satellite dish in the side of the yard, and an old pickup pulled close to the stairs. But it wasn't the one I was looking for, so I kept on going.

Another mile down the road, on the left, or east side, a good gravel road intersected with the highway. The road crossed the ditch on a plank bridge with a waist high rail, and then ran in a straight shot through bean fields toward a line of trees a half mile away. The trees ran out of sight to the south. I realized that they probably bordered the St. Francis, which had taken a turn back to the west here. At the end of the road, back up against the trees, I could see a couple of large grain bins and a big metal equipment shed with some kind of vehicle parked in front of it. I pulled over to the side of the road, got out my binoculars, and rolled the window down halfway. I rested the armored, waterproof 8 X 50s on the top of the window and focused. The big glasses pulled the complex in so it looked to be barely more than a hundred yards away. Even with the rain, things were startlingly clear. I do love good optics.

In the foreground, I could see the grain bins visible from the road. They were at least forty feet high with pipes and tubes running out of their tops through which the grain would be loaded and unloaded. To the left of them was a big metal shed at least a hundred feet long on the side toward me and a good twenty feet tall. It was probably full of farm machinery and the tools needed to fix the machinery. And parked in front of it was a green Chevy pick-up, the same model driven by the man who had been in the photo with Lucy that I had lifted out of Thomas's house.

The rain was blowing in on me, but I took another minute to scan the scene. With the glasses I could see that the building complex wasn't quite back against the trees, and that the road ran on past it for another hundred yards. Indistinct among the trees, I could see a house. It faced my way, and had a porch that ran along its entire front. It didn't seem to be painted, but neither did it look old or trashy. I looked back left and right, but couldn't see anything else but field. I focused in on the truck again, and confirmed it was the same model and color I had been following. Then I rolled up the window, dried off the binocular lenses, and tried to figure out what to do next.

Obviously, there was more than one green Chevy truck in eastern Arkansas, so there was no guarantee that this one was Gifford's. I could wait and watch with the binoculars till he came out of the equipment shed, and hope he didn't notice me sitting out here. He might not in the rain, but I knew that people who spent much time in open spaces got in the habit of looking far. I didn't want him to see me sitting out here and starting up and driving away. I dropped the gearshift into drive, and headed up the road.

I passed another trailer and an abandoned sharecropper shack within the next mile, but didn't see any green pickups. Before I came to any more turnoffs, the gravel road dead-ended into a paved state highway. It was a lot busier road, even in the rain, and five or six cars and trucks passed during the minute I sat at the stop sign and planned my next move. I knew Gifford could have used the gravel road as a shortcut to this road, and that he could have gone east or west, and for all I knew was still traveling. But I had a feeling that was his truck back there, and I decided to go with my instincts and make that assumption. Besides, I wasn't going to find him on this busy road, and it was too damn wet, cold and light to hide my truck and try to sneak up the fence line and wait in the trees to make sure it was him. I headed west, turned right at the first road that took me back to 64, and then drove back to Memphis in the unending rain.

13 _____

It was just noon as I crossed across the bridge into Memphis, ready for more ibuprofen and some lunch. I parked on Monroe on the steep hill between Front and Riverside, just down from the library that would be full of winos looking for a dry haven, and set the brake. I almost put the pistol in the glove box, then decided better safe than sorry and clipped it to my belt under the parka. I wasn't going far, but I had to assume whoever had taken a shot at me was still out there and might want to finish the job. I pulled up the hood on the parka, zipped it, and stepped out into the rain.

I walked up the bluff, crossed Front, and went across Monroe into the Little Tea Shop. It was red beans and rice day and despite the rain it was crowded. I found a two top against the wall, and gave the waitress my order: red beans and rice, corn sticks, slaw and broccoli with cheese sauce. Green vegetables are good for you. I unzipped the parka, but left it on to cover the sidearm.

I looked around the room at the usual collection of lawyers, bankers, brokers and businessmen, and waved at a couple of my former law partners who were sitting a few tables away. They waved back, but I was glad to see they weren't coming over to chat. I knew from experience that the conversation would be brief and awkward, mostly because there wouldn't be much to say.

I sat at the table, trying to mull over in my mind what I had found out about Thomas. He was undoubtedly a fence, a good one who made more money than most of the highly educated and privileged people who sat around me.

They might not run in the same circles as Thomas, but they would be glad to represent him in court or handle his checking or brokerage account.

His arrest on drug-dealing charges didn't make a whole lot of sense, but the police did make mistakes, and they would probably be inclined to believe he was into drugs given his record of other charges. Maybe Thomas was into drugs, I thought. Not low-level dealing, but higher up in the distribution chain. He had the necessary business mind and organizational skills, and a handy warehouse. I hadn't seen any drugs in it, but there were a lot of boxes I hadn't opened. The thought had just crossed my mind that the police could easily make the leap from receiving stolen goods to drug dealing, but maybe the opposite was true. If the police were fixated on Thomas as a fence, it could be that they never considered him in any other category, at least till they got the tip he was making money on crack.

The waitress soon brought my food, with an admonition that the corn sticks were just out of the oven and too hot to touch. I put a few drops of hot sauce on the red beans and rice, and dug in. I had needed a real meal just as much as I had needed all the sleep I'd had the day and night before, and by the time I was through I felt a lot better. My leg and back still hurt, but overall my sense of well-being was much better.

I pushed my plate back and munched on the last corn stick as my mind turned back to my case. Where did Gifford fit into all of this? He had been Thomas's employee, and was obviously a friend, if not more, of Lucy's. From the abandoned look of the warehouse, it didn't seem like he was carrying on the business by himself. Assuming that was his truck I had seen, he did have business at a soybean farm in Arkansas. I had found a soybean stuck in the mud on the bottom of the van in Thomas's warehouse, so maybe the van had been at the same place. Or maybe it had been at one of another 100,000 soybean fields within a hundred-mile radius of town. The equipment shed the green truck was parked in front of could have been full of designer clothes and shoes, or drugs, or both.

What, if anything, did the guy shooting at me in the alley have to do with any of this? The stolen goods business looked to be a small operation, so unless someone else was trying to move in on it, I couldn't see why three white guys would wait for me in an alley to discuss why I was looking into it. On the other hand, if Thomas were a drug distributor, anybody looking into his business would have been at risk. It was seeming less and less likely that the shots had been fired as part of a botched robbery attempt. I gave an involuntary shiver, and looked around the room. No one seemed to be paying any attention to me, much less looking like they wanted to kill me.

I thought back to Tommy's whispered but emphatic warning for me to drop this investigation, and wondered what he might know. I had long suspected he was pretty casual about stepping over the legal line when it suited him, but I had never considered the possibility that he would deal drugs. Maybe, I hoped, he didn't, but maybe he knew people who did. If he did, the fact that he had only told me to stop the investigation, and not to immediately pack my bags for South America, might mean it wasn't too late to get off the shit list. But getting off the shit list would mean dropping the investigation, and I didn't feel inclined to do that. I had something to prove to Amanda, and maybe to myself.

I paid my check, and stood outside under the awning watching the rain fall and looking at cars parked on Monroe to see if a hit man was inside any of them. I thought about what I should do next. In a way I wanted to go back to the apartment, but I knew if I did it would be hard to get back out. I had had a halfway productive morning, and I didn't want to stop now. I decided to track down Amanda and ask if she had remembered where she had seen Gifford.

I buttoned up the parka instead of zipping it so I would have better access to the .357, and left the hood down for better visibility. My concentration on the possibility that someone might want to kill me had diminished with the activity and fatigue of the last couple of days, but my thoughts in the restaurant had brought that risk back into focus. But I still felt funny going around armed.

I walked down the mall between the trolley tracks that glistened in the rain. There wasn't much pedestrian traffic, just a few people hurrying under umbrellas back to offices after lunch. I turned off the mall, and made my way to the civil courthouse that covers a whole city block. I walked up the concrete steps at the southwest corner and past the stern-visaged statue of Justice, through the double doors and into the foyer. I took off my cap and shook the rain from it, then got out my wallet and showed the guard my PI license and carry permit. Then I took off the parka, unclipped the Smith, handed it to him and got a receipt. I thought it was better to show him the license and the permit before I showed him the gun.

I didn't know what courtroom Amanda was in, or even whether it was circuit or chancery court. I made my way around the hall, looking at the posted sheet outside each courtroom that told what proceedings were on for that day. Lawyers stood out in the halls, striking deals and settling cases, or conferring with clients on the long benches that stood on each side of the halls. I had no nostalgia, and realized I didn't miss it at all.

Just around the first corner, I saw Amanda in earnest conversation with a lawyer I didn't recognize. He was middle-aged, slightly overweight, and expensively dressed. His client, who looked a lot like his lawyer, sat behind him on the bench, listening intently to the conversation. The client looked familiar, but I couldn't place him. Amanda's client, who looked a lot like her, only redheaded, sat on the bench on the opposite side of the hall, also listening intently. I kept walking, and sat down on a bench a little further up the hall. I could hear scraps of the two lawyers' conversation, and watched Amanda gesticulating as she made her points. I heard the male lawyer say "bullshit" and start to turn away, but Amanda grabbed him by the coat sleeve and turned him back around. The volume of her voice went up, and I heard her say, "It's a good offer and you know it. You're just grandstanding for your client. How's he going to feel when the jury starts feeding his nuts into the blender one at a time?"

The other lawyer jerked his sleeve out of her grasp, and spat out, "Who's grandstanding for a client now, bitch. Don't tell me how to practice law." He turned around, took his client by the arm, and walked him into the courtroom. So much for courtesy at the bar. Amanda turned around, smiled reassuringly at the redhead, and said, "Come on, let's go kick his ass." As they walked into the courtroom, Amanda looked over and saw me. She gave me a quick puzzled look, then turned back to the task at hand.

I waited a minute, and then slipped into the back bench of the courtroom. Amanda had been right this morning; the case was going to the jury. They filed in from a back door as I took my seat, five men and seven women, three of the men black, two of them white, all but one of the women white. I couldn't help wondering what thoughts and strategies had gone into the jury selection. Even the most liberal lawyer puts aside political correctness and colorblindness when picking a jury, taking into consideration race, religion, sex, occupation and economic status in an effort to find a panel that will see things her way. From what Amanda had said, these jurors had been at it a long time, and were probably relieved that their ordeal was almost over.

The judge walked in as soon as the jury was seated, and we all stood up. She was a woman I had known slightly when I practiced, with legal abilities I hadn't thought much of. But she was well connected politically, and when an older judge had died on the bench, she had been appointed as his replacement. Despite expectations to the contrary, she had turned out to be a good jurist. She thanked the jury briefly for their service, explained the closing argument process, and then asked Amanda if she was ready.

Amanda stood up and walked over to stand a few feet in front of the jury box. She quietly but forcefully recounted the facts of the marriage, the verbal and physical abuse by the husband, the wife's initial discovery of his infidelity, his promise to reform, and his continued cheating. She then reviewed his list of assets, stock holdings and options, annual salary, limited partnership and limited liability company interests, hunting club and country club memberships, pension plan, and fancy automobiles. She recalled the testimony of the accountant who had estimated his net worth at $12 million, and calmly asked for a lump sum alimony award of $6 million, and $5,000 per month child support for each of the minor children, plus educational payments. I looked at my watch, and saw that her presentation hadn't taken quite thirty minutes. I couldn't tell what the jury thought of the substance of her argument, but I knew they liked the length.

Amanda sat down with a quick smile at her client, and grasped her hand briefly. Her opponent got up, walked over to the jury, and began his argument. He knew he was nailed to the floor on the cause of the divorce, so he was attacking Amanda's assessment of his man's assets. He explained the complicated nature of his client's business in a pompous voice, suggesting that it was beyond Ms. Baker's ability to understand. He had a stack of graphs and charts that he had used as trial exhibits, and he proceeded to put them up on an easel one by one and go through them ad nauseam, with the purpose of showing that his man was worth a lot less than his wife suggested. He lost me on the second chart, which dealt with the depreciation of real estate owned by limited partnerships, and I could tell the jury was also doing the big snore. At first I thought he was oblivious to his effect on the jury, but I soon realized that he was trying to confuse them, and make them think that maybe they really couldn't understand the complexity.

After an hour and a half of this, at about three thirty, the judge interrupted him, and called for a recess. The jury filed out, and the judge called the two lawyers up to her and said, "Mr. Brown, you've had three weeks to go through this. This is closing argument, not a rehash of every fact. Let's get on with it, shall we?"

"Your honor, with all due respect, I'm afraid that this information takes a while to present. I'm going just as fast as I can."

"Mr. Brown," the judge said, looking at the clock on the wall, "we're going to reconvene at three forty-five. You'll have until four thirty to finish your argument. If you go one minute over, I'm calling a halt to it in front of the jury."

Brown started to open his mouth, thought better of it, and said, "Yes, your honor."

The judge got up and went back into her chambers, and the two lawyers and their clients headed out into the hall. Amanda gave me another brief look as she went by, then turned back to her client. I went out into the hall and followed the two men into the bathroom. I stood in a stall while they went to a urinal on the other side of the bathroom, and listened as the lawyer and client pissed and discussed the argument. "I've been watching them," the client said, "and I think it's starting to sink in with the men. When they get back to the jury room, they'll convince the women I'm not worth as much as that bitch is saying."

"I hope so," the lawyer said. "Basically, we're admitting liability and just arguing damages. That's always a risky proposition."

"Maybe so, but she literally caught me with my pants down more than once, so I might as well admit it. What was the point in contesting the authenticity of the pictures? Hell, it was obviously me. I think I looked pretty good in them. I think I'll get a copy when this is over. Anyway, maybe the jury'll think I'm honest on this money thing if I'm up front about the infidelity."

"Maybe," the lawyer said. "But do you want me to ask Amanda if her settlement offer still stands, or make her a counterproposal?"

"Settle it? Shit no, we've come this far, and I'm feeling lucky. Let's see what happens. If the jury comes in at less than three million, we'll go to Tunica on me, shoot craps all night long."

"You're the boss," I heard Brown say. They went back out the door without washing their hands.

Brown took up his argument where he had left off, droning through the rest of his exhibits until four twenty, then spending his last ten minutes summing up the overvaluation his client's wife had put on his assets. He stopped right at four thirty, thanked the jury in advance for their reasoned, impartial decision, implying anyone would be a fool not to believe him, and suggested award figures far below those Amanda had requested. He took his charts and graphs back to the defense table with him, giving Amanda a friendly-seeming smile on the way.

"Ms. Baker, do you wish to make concluding remarks?" the judge asked. I could see a couple of the jury members sit back with a barely stifled groan. Some of them had forgotten that Amanda, as plaintiff, was going to get the last bite at the apple. They were ready to go back to the jury room, make a decision, and go home. Amanda must have known it, too, and I thought she might decline any further comments, but she said, "Your honor, if I may have four or five minutes, I believe I can conclude." The jury looked relieved by her statement, but as if they weren't sure they believed she could be so brief.

Amanda reached under her table and took out a stack of posters, joined together by a spiral binder at the top. It was the same kind of set up Brown had had for his graphs and charts, and as she walked up to the jury box and placed them on the easel there was at least one audible sigh from the jury box.

The judge looked sharply at the jury, and I saw Brown smirk, but Amanda didn't say anything. She flipped the cover back over the easel, exposing the second poster, to which was taped a blown up black and white photograph of what had to be her client and the defendant on their wedding day, walking down the aisle of a church, arm in arm. The next picture was of the same young redhead, cuddling a newborn baby in one arm in a hospital bed. The third picture was of the defendant in a tuxedo at a dinner table, surrounded by wine bottles and similarly dressed men and holding a plaque that proclaimed him broker of the year. The fourth picture featured the same woman and a different baby. The fifth picture showed the defendant behind the wheel of a Mercedes, the sixth, according to the caption at the bottom, showed him duck hunting in Argentina, the seventh featured him behind the wheel of a boat that looked to be at least thirty feet long, and the eighth showed him standing beside a black Bentley, a big grin on his face. The ninth and tenth photos were of our man playing footsie with a hot looking young blonde at a table in an outdoor café. The caption at the bottom read "Cozumel, February 2000." Photos eleven through twenty were outtakes from a video, featuring him with the same blonde in an enclosed patio off a beach house, in the full daylight. Eleven had his hand inside her bikini top, and by the time we got to twenty, which showed his head down between her spread thighs, we had gone through most of the widely recognized variations.

Amanda spent no more than five seconds on each picture, giving the jury an eyeful but not lingering. They were all marked as trial exhibits, so there was no objection Brown could make. The jury had seen them all before, but not one after the other, and not in the starkly contrasting sequence of family man and father versus rich playboy and cheat. Amanda flipped over the last picture, which showed the defendant and the redhead, with a small boy and girl, dressed up and ready for church. The caption read, "Easter, 2000."

"Ladies and gentlemen," Amanda said, "six million in alimony, five thousand per month per child for support, and he's getting off easy. Thank you. Your honor, that's all I have, thank you, too," she said, picking up her posters and heading back to the plaintiff's table. It was the shortest concluding rebuttal you would ever hear, and probably the most effective. Once again, a picture was worth a thousand words.

It was almost five, and the judge asked the jury if they would like to start deliberations, or come back the next day. The jurors unanimously voted to get it over with. I could see Brown almost piss in his pants. If they wanted to get started today, he knew they weren't intending to pay much attention to his charts and graphs, but were instead focused on exhibits eleven through twenty of Amanda's closing. The judge spent five minutes instructing the jury, then dismissed them to begin deliberations. Before she was out the door to her own chambers, Brown was involved in a feverish discussion with his client. Amanda and her client got up and walked out together without looking back. I started to follow them, but before I could reach the door Brown rushed past me into the hall. I caught the door on the back swing, and stepped outside the courtroom. Amanda and her client were on their way to the ladies room, but Brown yelled "Amanda, wait a minute!"

She and her client turned around right outside the door of the restroom and waited. I hung back a little, but I could hear him say "We'll do five million and the child support. Is it a deal?"

Amanda looked at her client, who shook her head. "No deal, Frank, let's see what the jury has to say."

"Come on, Amanda, you're kidding me, right? Five fucking million dollars? You're insane. Mrs. Talbot, any lawyer would tell you to jump on that offer."

"Mr. Brown," the sweet-faced redhead said, "you can tell my husband to stick his thumbs up his ass and walk around on his elbows." She then turned and disappeared into the restroom.

"What's that noise?" Amanda said, cocking her head and putting a hand behind her ear.

"I don't hear anything," Brown said.

"Come on, Frank," she said with a bright smile, "can't you hear that high-pitched whine? It sounds like the jury just turned the blender on high." With that she hurried into the ladies' room, leaving him speechless. He stood there for a few seconds, almost raised his hand once to knock on the door, then walked slowly back to the courtroom.

I sat on the bench and waited. When Amanda and her client came out, they looked like they had been snorting cocaine, but it was the elation that comes after a hard fought trial when you are as near certain as possible that the jury is coming back your way. I got up and kissed Amanda on the cheek, and told her she had done a hell of a job. She smiled, thanked me and introduced me to the soon not to be Mrs. Talbot. Amanda didn't mention that I had shot exhibits nine through twenty; maybe she thought it would be too embarrassing.

When I mentioned that I needed to talk with her, she said, "It's five fifteen now. I don't think the judge will ask the jury to go past seven at the latest. You can stay here with us or wait for me in the bar in my office building."

This was her moment, and I didn't want to distract from it. "I'll wait at the bar," I said. "Good luck."

Before I could turn around and walk away, the courtroom deputy stuck his head out the door. "Ms. Baker? Jury's coming back in."

14 _____

Deciding not to wait around, I got my gun from the security guard, pulled on the parka and put on the cap, and stepped out into the dusk. It was still raining hard, and the wind was gusting out of the northwest. It was cold, and getting colder. The weather would probably blow itself out by the next day, leaving a sparkling blue sky and nippy temperatures, but many of the leaves would be gone from the trees and winter would be on its way. I headed up Washington Avenue to the mall, and then cut down to Amanda's office. I went into the ground floor lobby, and took the escalator up to the second floor.

There was a pretty good crowd in the bar, mostly brokers and lawyers who wanted to get an early start on the weekend, or who needed a couple of drinks in them before they could go home and face their wives or husbands. I found a table in a corner where I could watch the door for Amanda, and took off my cap. The other customers still had their coats and ties on, like they were trying to impress each other with their tailoring, and I saw the waiter trying to figure out my jeans and boots while he took my order for a draft Harp's. "That's five dollars, sir," he said, not moving. It took me a moment, but I realized he wasn't going to get the beer until I paid for it in advance. Maybe he thought I was a well-groomed homeless person who had wandered in off the street. If I hadn't agreed to meet Amanda there, and if the idea of a draft didn't seem so good all of a sudden, I would have gotten up and left. Instead, I got out my wallet, took out a pile of bills, and handed him a five. He brought the beer back in a minute, gold-colored in a thick, frosted glass, and set it down in front of me on a cardboard coaster.

He was young, probably in college, and seemed harmless enough. Maybe he would have to pay for the drink himself if I didn't. I pulled out my wallet, and handed him a twenty. "Let me know when I've drunk that up, and I'll give you another," I said. "And let me give you a little piece of advice. You see these guys around here with the six hundred dollar suits and the seventy five dollar ties? They work for other people. There's some rich guy somewhere, maybe he made it himself, maybe he inherited it, who pays the fees and commissions for these guys. And as likely as not, that guy's not wearing a suit, because he doesn't have to. You understand what I'm saying?"

"Yessir, sure," he said. "I didn't mean any disrespect, it's just that we sometimes get people who wander in from the street…." His voice trailed off, as he realized that he was in fact saying that I might be a well-groomed homeless person.

I peeled off another twenty, and handed it to him. "Next time they do," I said, "let them drink that up."

I had just started the second draft when Amanda appeared, still shaking rain out of her hair with one hand. She was immediately greeted by two different groups, one at the bar and another at a table. She waved and said hello, but declined invitations to join them, and came straight over and sat down in the chair opposite mine before I could pull it out for her. Her face was glowing, and her eyes were bright.

"Six million?" I asked.

"Six million," she said with a wide smile. "The foreman told me afterwards they would have given me more if I had asked for it."

"Better not to be greedy," I said with a smile.

The waiter came back over, and asked Amanda for her order. She turned her happy eyes on him, and made him blush just by looking at him. "I'll take a double Sapphire martini on the rocks, with a twist," she said. He looked over at me. "You doing okay with your beer, sir?"

"Yes, I'm fine," I said.

When the waiter left, I said, "Amanda, that was masterful what you did with the photographs. You played that jury like a musician."

"Thank you," she said. "I couldn't have done it if you hadn't taken the shots."

"Hey, I got a free trip to Mexico for about an hour's work. That's not a bad deal, even if I did feel like I was shooting a porno movie."

The waiter brought her drink, and waited till she took the first sip to make sure it was okay. Now he thought he was the wine sommelier. "Sweetheart," she said to me while he stood there, "you were shooting a porno movie."

The waiter blinked, looked from her to me, and then said, "How are you doing with that draft, sir?"

"I'm still fine, thanks," I said.

"What gives with him?" Amanda asked, as he walked away.

"He thinks I'm an eccentric millionaire, and now he thinks he knows how I made my money," I said.

"You're a man of many talents," she said.

"Not me," I said. "This is your night. You're the one with the six million dollar verdict."

"I am, aren't I," she said with a smile, and knocked back a good inch of her martini. "Whew," she gasped, putting her hand on her throat, "that goes down like smooth fire. I never drink during a trial, even on the weekends, and that first one afterwards always tastes great."

"I'm surprised the former Mrs. Talbot is not celebrating with you," I said.

Amanda took another pull at her drink, and said quietly, "The former Mrs. Talbot is celebrating with her boyfriend of five years."

"Really?" I asked.

"Really," Amanda replied.

"And this didn't come out in discovery or in trial?" I asked.

"Never. Brown never asked. Can you believe that? He knew his client was a cheating slimeball, and my client seemed so innocent and motherly, he never asked. From what she told me, she was probably cheating on him before he started running around, but he was such a self-centered bastard that he never even suspected it. She thinks the second kid is probably not even his. I told her she would have to testify truthfully under oath, but the dumb son of a bitch never asked her. Can you fucking believe it?"

"So she gets six million plus custody of the kids, and ten thousand a month support, half of it for a kid that's probably not even his?"

"Yeah, but she does deserve half of what he has, regardless of what she did," she said, knocking back the rest of her drink. She was definitely making up for lost time.

"Maybe so," I said, "But the jury surer than hell wouldn't have given it to her if they had known."

"You're right about that," she said, looking around for our waiter, who was hustling over from the bar. "I'll take another one of these," she told him, pointing at the empty glass he was taking away. He looked over at me, saw my beer was still almost full, and headed back to the bar. "I've been waiting for the last two years for Frank Brown to ask that question, and he never did. Now it's too late. You can't begin to understand what a relief that is."

"I hope his malpractice insurance is paid up," I said.

"It better be. I told my client to keep her mouth shut about it, but she's the kind of vindictive bitch who won't be able to wait to tell the ex that he wasn't the only one getting some on the side."

"He can't get a new trial on that basis, can he?" I asked.

"Hell, no. He had plenty of time to ask the question. He just never did. You ought to know that, you practiced law."

"It's been a while," I said. "I thought maybe the rules had changed."

"No," Amanda said, taking the first sip of the fresh double the waiter had brought, "the rules are the same. Make a dumb mistake, and you'll get your ass handed to you on a platter."

"I guess that's what I miss about it," I said, smiling broadly.

"It's the same in the business you're in now, right?" she asked. "Like the time you stepped on the cat and the neurosurgeon took a shot at you. You've always got to be on your toes." Amanda had only been drinking for fifteen minutes, but her words were starting to sound a little mushy. Martinis can do that to you in the best of times, but even more so after weeks of stress, too little sleep and not enough food.

I signaled the waiter, and asked if he would bring us menus. I picked mine up and opened it, but hers lay on the table beside her. "How long are you going to nurse that beer?" she asked. "I thought this was a celebration."

"I had one before you got here," I said. "Besides, one of us is going to have to drive. You have fun, and I'll worry about that. Let's get some food. I'm starving."

"Men are always starving, for one thing or another," she said.

"Now, that sounds like a sexist comment, especially given what you've told me about Mrs. Talbot."

"Women starve, too," she said, "but for different things."

"You mean Mrs. Talbot's affair was about her need for love and companionship, like in all the movies, but her husband's was for nothing more than a roll in the hay?"

"Something like that," she said with a smile, "but let's please don't get in a gender battle tonight. I feel like being with a friend, not an adversary."

"You got it," I said, touching my glass to hers. I gestured the waiter over, and ordered some fried mushrooms and buffalo wings. Amanda said she didn't want anything, but I was hoping to get her to eat some of what came to the table. She started to order another martini, but I interrupted her and suggested a good bottle of wine, something appropriate for a celebration. I knew she was going to drink some kind of alcohol, but I thought she'd be better off with wine instead of more gin.

"Take your time and pick a good one," I said to our waiter, hoping he would get the message. "Now," I said to Amanda as he walked away, "one piece of business before we get back to celebrating. You remember the picture I showed you of Lucy and the man you thought you had seen before but couldn't place? His name is Hayes Gifford. Does that ring any bells?"

Her eyes turned inward, and I saw her try to concentrate, but the effort was too much. "It's kind of like the picture," she said. "It seems familiar, like something from a long time ago, but I can't place it. Do you have the photo with you? Maybe looking at it with the name in mind would help."

"No, I'm sorry, I don't. I can bring it by your office tomorrow."

"What's tomorrow?" she asked.

"Friday," I answered with a straight face.

"Then I'll have motions starting at nine a.m. I always do on Friday. But I can't remember what the fuck they're about. I'll have to get to the office by seven to go over the files. Why don't you get a copy made and leave it with my secretary."

"Amanda, you might prefer not to be in possession of that picture, remember?"

"That's right," she said. "You were a bad boy, weren't you?" she giggled.

Good grief, I thought, Amanda Baker, giggling? It was definitely time to shut off the booze. Just then our waiter, who had not gotten my message, brought an ice bucket over with a magnum of champagne sticking out of it. I started to say something about having meant a good, small bottle of red, but Amanda interrupted me, saying, "Champagne! I love champagne." The waiter beamed at her, twisted off the cork, and poured a small amount in her glass. After two martinis had washed over her taste buds, it could have been kerosene for all she could tell, but she tipped it back, smiled her approval, and held her glass out for more. The waiter filled her glass, then mine, glancing with disapproval at my still half-full beer. I asked him to hurry up with the appetizers.

By the time the food came, Amanda was working on her second full glass of champagne. I managed to get her to try a buffalo wing, but she smeared hot sauce across one cheek in the process, and then started gesturing at me with the chicken bone as she reenacted her direct examination of Mr. Talbot's lover. Other people in the bar were starting to look at us and smile and nudge their friends. I excused myself, got the waiter and paid the check. It was one hundred and fifty dollars. It must have been a hell of a bottle of wine, but I didn't think I could pick up the bottle and take the rest home with me.

When I got back to the table, Amanda was trying to recharge her glass and spilling booze all over the place, mostly on herself. I convinced her that we should leave by telling her we were going dancing. As we walked out, my hand tight on her arm for support, a man I recognized as a well-known divorce lawyer called out from a table we were passing, "Hey, Amanda, I heard you just kicked Frank Brown's ass in Judge Cauley's court. Couldn't happen to a nicer guy."

"You're right, Richard," she slurred back as I kept her moving, "and you're next, buddy."

His friends at the table gave a collective groan of dismay and approval at her rejoinder and Richard, trying to save face, said loudly, "Those are big words from a shit-faced rich girl who's about to get laid by a washed up peeping tom!"

His comment went past his circle of friends and to half the bar, and a hush fell over them all. Everyone was shocked by what he had said, even Richard, who sat there with a stunned look on his face as if he couldn't believe the words had come out of his mouth. The silence was spreading to the rest of the bar, as people looked around to see what was going on.

Amanda was now literally spitting as she tried to say something, and was trying to pull out of my grasp to get at him. I swung her around to me, looked into her eyes, and said, "Trust me on this one, partner. You're going to get in trouble if you say anything more."

I turned to Richard, and said calmly, "The truth is, buddy, she will kick your ass every time in the court room. If you've got another kind of ass-kicking in mind, we'll be outside on the east side of the building for the next five minutes. I've got seven thirty-five," I said, looking at my watch. I collected Amanda, steered her out the door and down the escalator. We stood outside under the porch, watching the rain and waiting for Richard.

Amanda had shaken off my hand by the time we got outside. "I didn't need you to protect me in there."

"You didn't need me to protect you from Richard, but if you had said what you wanted to you would have regretted it. There might even have been a bar investigation. I was protecting you from yourself. That's what friends do sometimes."

"Is that why you challenged him to a fight?"

"No, I've got to admit that was for me. And between the two of us, I hope he doesn't come out. I'm too beat up to want to fight even a fat cream puff like Richard."

"Well," she said in a nicer tone, "just don't do it again."

"I'm glad you're not going to be one of those mean drunks," I said. "And I promise I won't do it again, unless you have two double martinis and several glasses of wine on an empty stomach and a three week sleep deficit."

I took a close look at Amanda in the dim light, and saw that the adrenaline from her encounter had burned off some of the booze, but that she was still far from sober. She smiled at me, and I smiled back, and I belatedly realized she had mistaken my sobriety check for a let's kiss look. Before I knew it, she had closed her eyes and put her mouth on mine. Her lips parted immediately, and her tongue gently probed my mouth. I was too stunned to do anything but kiss her back, enveloped in a sweet cloud of gin and wine, perfume, wet hair and the smell of a woman who has worked hard all day.

She put her hands on my shoulders, disengaged her mouth from mine, and looked up at me unsteadily. I flattered myself it wasn't all the booze when she said in a husky voice, "That was thank you."

"At your service," I said. My voice wasn't rock steady, either.

I looked at my watch. It was seven forty-three, past Richard's deadline. "Let's go," I said. "It's cold out here." She had her arms wrapped around her, and was starting to shiver. I took my parka off and wrapped it around her. "Do you really want to go dancing?" she asked.

"No," I said. "I've just found that's a good line to get drunk girls out of a bar. Why don't you let me take you home, I mean, so you can go to sleep," I finished awkwardly.

"We can just call me a cab," she said. "I've got my cell phone in my purse."

"I'm not sure I'd trust the cabbie," I said.

"Do you trust yourself?" she asked with a grin. "I mean, with that big gun on your hip and all?"

I had forgotten about the pistol. "Maybe. I'll take that chance."

"Okay," she said. "Where's your car?"

"My pickup is a long way from here," I said.

"Good," she said. "Daddy would turn over in his grave if he saw me come home in a pickup. We'll take my car."

We went back into the building and through the enclosed walkway to the parking garage. I was glad we didn't see anyone from the bar. Her cream colored Infiniti Q45 was parked in a reserved space near the entrance. Everybody but me seemed to have a foreign luxury car these days. I'd have to see if Infiniti or Lexus was making a pickup. She handed me the keys, and I got her settled and buckled into the passenger seat.

It was still raining hard, and I almost didn't see the bum who wandered in front of me just as I was pulling out of the garage. I braked hard, and stopped a few inches from him. He smacked the hood with the flat of his hand, and began cursing so loud I could hear him over the rain and through the Japanese soundproofing. I pulled around him, hoping he was heading to the bar to drink up my twenty.

Amanda was asleep before we got out of downtown, her head lolled over on her left shoulder, a thin trickle of saliva running out of the corner of her mouth. There was a box of tissue in the console by the gear shift, and I took a few and wiped her face. She didn't budge. I drove all the way out Union to Hollywood, then cut over to Central and down to her house on Goodwyn. The big place was completely dark. I pulled up to the garage and found the garage door opener over the sun visor. I opened the door, pulled in, and closed it behind me. Amanda slept undisturbed.

I left the car lights on, got out, and found the door to the outside. It opened into the backyard, inside the locked iron gate. There were no lights on back there, either, but I felt my way down the slick brick walk to the back door, and inserted the key I had picked out before I had gotten out of the car. It worked, and I opened the door, switched on the outside lights, and propped the door open with the leg of one of the chairs from around the small table where Amanda had been drinking coffee a few days before. I took a quick look, but I couldn't find the switch for the inside light. By the time I got back to the garage I was soaked, except for the part of my head that was under my cap.

I shut the driver's door, then went around to Amanda's side and opened her door. I unbuckled her seatbelt, pulled the hood of the parka over her head, and turned off the car lights. Then I knelt on the garage floor, reached in, put one arm behind her back and one under her thighs, and eased her out. She couldn't have weighed more than 120 pounds, but it was a lot of weight to pick up from an awkward position. As I stood up, I felt my calf pull, and hoped I hadn't popped a stitch. I closed the car door with my butt, carried her out of the garage, slamming the door behind me with my foot, and walked up the path and onto the back porch.

I looked down at Amanda, cradled against my chest. She was sleeping through the whole process, even with the raindrops that had splattered down on her face. I walked through the sun porch and turned into a long hall. At the far end, I could see a dim light from what was probably the glass that framed the front door. Amanda needed to get a light timer. I went several steps till there was an open door on my left, but I smelled coffee and other kitchen smells, so I kept going. I felt my way down the hall to the first door on the right, pushed the partly open door back with my knee, and rubbed the back of my right shoulder on the wall until it hit the light switch. Amanda stirred and murmured in my arms as the light hit her face, but didn't wake up. I looked around the room, blinking in the sudden brightness.

There was an old, unmade dark wood bed against the far wall with a heavily brocaded canopy and skirt. I carried Amanda over and laid her in it, pulled off her shoes, shucked her out of my parka, and covered her up. I turned on the lamp beside the bed, and went over and turned off the overhead. I got some tissues and dried the rain off her face, then took a quick look around the room. It wasn't just the bed, but everything else in the room that made it look like it should have been on the opposite side of a rope in a museum. I don't know much about furniture, but it all seemed Victorian to me: dark heavy wood, brocaded fabric on the love seat against the wall that matched the bed, and a gold-framed portrait of some dour gentleman who looked like he would have benefited from a big bowl of prunes. The room was large, but there wasn't even a closet, just a big wardrobe made out of the same dark wood. The only signs that someone lived in the room were the few paperbacks on the nightstand, Amanda's toiletry items and makeup on the vanity, and the clothes I could see through the open doors of the wardrobe.

There was a half open door on the far side of the room. Behind it was the bathroom, also in period, with a heavy, claw-footed tub and commode with the tank up on the wall behind it.

I slipped out of the bedroom, went back to the kitchen, and groped around till I found the light switch. The kitchen was modern compared to the bedroom, maybe circa 1940. There was a black rotary dial telephone on one counter. I opened a few drawers, but didn't see a phone book. I dialed information, got the number of a cab company, and called. The man said thirty minutes. He didn't seem impressed by the address.

I went back down the hall, stuck my head in Amanda's room but didn't hear any sounds, and kept going. There were no more doors opening off the hall, but it was only a few steps till I came to the foyer and the front door. It was a big space, a white marble floor with dark, probably black, diamond patterns set in it. An unlit chandelier hung above it, suspended from a ceiling that was lost in the gloom. A grand staircase swept up from the foyer, but I couldn't see upward through the shadows for more than a few steps. Rooms opened off the foyer on each side. I peered in one, and then the other, and figured out that the white objects I saw were dust covers slung over the furniture. There was a heavy smell of dust and old upholstery coming from both rooms, and I imagined more of the same upstairs. Amanda was living in the three rooms in the back, and preserving the rest for posterity. It seemed like a damned strange way to live, and unhealthy, too. But who was I to judge? I didn't have a wife, two kids and a house in the suburbs with a Volvo station wagon in the garage myself.

I went back to the kitchen and scouted around till I found another key to the back door. I wanted to lock Amanda in when I left. It was still early for the cab, but I decided to wait by the road, even though it was raining. I felt weird being in her house with her asleep, or maybe I just felt weird being in her house.

I went to her bedroom to check on her for the last time. She was still sleeping, but she was making moaning sounds and rolled her head on the pillow. I walked over to the bathroom, turned on its light, and left the door ajar. Then I walked over to her bed and turned off the lamp on the nightstand.

When the switch clicked, she woke up. "Who is it?" she asked almost hysterically.

"It's me, John McAlister, I brought you home, remember? I was just turning out the light so you can sleep."

"Damn, you scared the shit out of me," she said in a calmer voice.

"Sorry, that seems to be my specialty," I said. "Are you all right now? Can I get you anything before I leave? Maybe a glass of ice water?"

"Yeah," she said thickly, "that would be great. My mouth feels like it's got all the cotton in Mississippi stuck in it."

I went back to the kitchen and opened the freezer. No icemaker, just old style metal ice trays. I cracked one open, barking my knuckles in the process, put some cubes in a glass, added water, and walked back to the bedroom. The bathroom door was closed, and she hadn't turned the lamp back on. I heard the old commode rumble, then the sound as she brushed her teeth. The door opened and she came out. She had left the bathroom light on, and before she closed the door I could see that she had put on a robe. I could tell, though, from her silhouette and from the back lighting, that it wasn't much of a robe, and that there wasn't anything underneath it.

The room was even blacker after the door shut, and I stood there trying not to leap to conclusions. Always a bad habit, I thought, especially for a lawyer or an investigator. "Can you see?" I asked. "I have your water over here by the bed. Do you want me to turn the light on?"

"I don't need to see," she said. "I've slept in this room for the last seventeen years."

As she talked, I sensed that was coming closer to me. Then I felt her hand on my arm, and I pressed the glass into it. She stood beside me, drinking deeply, then sighed. I heard the ice clink as she set the glass on the nightstand, then she turned and put her hands around my waist, one of them reaching awkwardly around the revolver on my belt. I felt that her face turned up to mine as she pressed her body against me and said, "John, you really don't have to go." Her breath smelled like gin and toothpaste.

"Sweetheart," I said, trying to fight down the stirring in my groin, "you've had a lot to drink. Why don't you get some sleep?"

"I'm not drunk anymore," she said. "You won't be taking advantage of me. I want you to stay." Her lips brushed mine, and I could feel her belly and breasts pressing against me. "You want to stay, too, I can feel it," she said with a little giggle.

So much for self-control, I thought. "Amanda," I said, taking her shoulders in my hands and slowly pushing her away, "you lie down and get some sleep, now."

"Okay," she said, taking my hand in hers, "I will, but you come, too."

She lay down on the bed, and tried to pull me after her. At that moment, I wasn't thinking very clearly, and I almost let her win the tug of war. But then I thought of Mary, who had never told me she didn't date other men, who maybe had a bunch of other boyfriends, and who I saw only a few days a month when I was lucky. I kneeled down on the floor beside the bed, my hand still in Amanda's, and said, "Baby, you're one of the most attractive, smartest, desirable women I have ever met. Every male nerve in my body is screaming to hop in that bed with you now. But I'm seeing someone else. I'm sorry if I sent you the wrong signal earlier tonight. I really am. But I can't sleep with you."

She was silent for so long that I had a brief hope she had passed out, then she said, "I'm sorry, John. I shouldn't have acted this way. I don't let my hair down very often, and sometimes I just get so damn lonely."

I rested my forehead on the edge of the bed, and she let go of my hand and put her fingers in my hair. "I meant it, you know. This time last year, you couldn't have chased me out of here with a ten gauge shotgun," I said.

"John," she said, "that's the sweetest thing anyone has said to me in a long time. But what else should I expect from a boy who drives a pickup? Now get out of here and let me sleep."

15 _____

I should have slept like a log that night, but aches of different kinds kept me tossing and turning till I finally gave it up at five a.m. and put the coffee on. I took a shower while it brewed, then dressed in jeans, a cotton chamois shirt, and my boots. I knew it was going to be the coldest day of the fall so far. I poured coffee into an insulated cup with a lid, put on a waist length down jacket, and stepped out onto my porch. The rain had blown through early in the morning, and the stars were out bright and hard. The actual temperature was only in the thirties, but it felt bitter cold because of the strong wind out of the northwest and the contrast to the mild Indian summer weather we had been enjoying. Headlights went back and forth in the distance over both bridges, but here in the city it was quiet except for the wind. I stood at the railing for half an hour, till I could see that the sun had come up behind me by the rays flying over my head into the western sky at the speed of light.

I came back in the apartment with most of the coffee drunk and a ravenous appetite. I had been too busy watching Amanda's booze intake the night before to eat much of the appetizers I had ordered, and too tired and frustrated to go anywhere but home when the taxi had dropped me at my truck. I looked in the refrigerator, but beer was my only choice. It looked like go out or stay here and starve.

I had written down Henry Jackson's home phone number two mornings ago while I waited in his kitchen for him to open up his garage and let me drive my truck out. I called it now, and he picked up on the third ring. "Jackson," he said loudly, sounding fully awake.

"Morning, Henry," I said. "This is John McAlister. I hope I didn't wake you up."

"No, I been up since five, riding my exercise bike and watching television. They got some interesting stuff on this time of day."

"You're kidding, right?"

"Not about exercising. But why are you calling so early? Why are you calling here at all? I don't remember giving you this number."

"I got it through trained detective work," I said. "The reason I was calling was to see if I could buy you breakfast. Have you got class this morning?"

"Yeah, but not until nine. Why do you want to buy me breakfast?"

"Because I'm starving, and I'd like to keep working on this damn Tuggle case. I thought maybe I could run a few ideas by you while we ate."

"If I go with you, you can charge it to the expense account, right?" he asked.

"I'll pay for it myself," I said. "Breakfast is cheap."

"I'm a cheap date, huh? I let you spend the night one time, and you start taking me for granted."

"Henry, you're the only person I know other than me who can bullshit at this time of the morning. Meet me at that new coffeehouse on Union by the ballpark in half an hour."

I hung up, got the Smith off the nightstand, checked the load, and stuck it in its holster. Despite everything, I had thoroughly dried and oiled the revolver when I had come in last night, and it was ready to go, not a speck of rust on it. I was getting tired of carrying it, both because I felt kind of silly going around armed and because its weight and bulk were a hassle. It was a hell of a weapon, but I had about decided I was going to find a lighter, more compact pistol if I didn't figure out soon whether I was still in danger or not. For now, though, it was worth all of its weight in gold, and I strapped it back on, feeling like Marshall Dillon.

I double locked the door behind me, then walked briskly to the coffee shop, keeping an eye on the cold, windy streets around me. I got there in five minutes and sat at a table by the window and watched the traffic slowly pick up toward rush hour. Henry walked in a few minutes later, wearing a red wool baseball cap and a knee-length black leather coat. He spotted me at the table and came over, rubbing his hands together. He sat down and said, "I hate winter. Winter sucks. You can tell it I said so."

"This is not winter. This is fall. Even when we get winter, it's not really winter. If you want winter, you ought to go up to Michigan where my ex-wife is from."

"No thank you. This is more than enough for me. What have they got to eat here?"

I waved our waitress over, and tried to ignore her lip ring while she told us about the coffee specials. I got some kind of East Indian/Colombian blend coffee, bagels and scrambled eggs. Henry ended up with the same thing, after she told him they didn't have any American coffee.

"Let me tell you what I'm wondering about our man Thomas, see what you think," I said.

"Okay, man, but I'm starting to wonder about you. When I first met you, I said you didn't give a shit about finding him, now I think maybe you're getting carried away with it a little. That stuff the other night was a little over the top, don't you think?"

"I thought you said you had fun," I said.

"Yeah, but I don't do it on a regular basis. I get the feeling you do. You keep doing that kind of shit, the odds will catch up with you."

Lip Ring brought the coffee in large cardboard cups with holder rings around them so you could pick them up without burning your hand. Henry didn't wait for his to cool, or even blow on it. He just picked it up and took a big slurp. "Tastes like black water," he said. "I told you these places don't make good coffee."

Mine was too hot for me, but I could tell by the color and the smell that an Arab would probably think it was strong enough. On the other side of the table, Henry was taking big swallows of his like he was downing a soft drink on a hot day.

"Thanks for your advice," I said. "I've always been a goal-oriented person. The goal may not always be worth attaining, but I usually take the most direct route to it."

"Well, from now on, I'm suggesting you detour around the fat guys with the shotguns and the razor wire."

"More good advice," I said.

"I mean, did you see that son of a bitch?" he said. "He must have weighed three hundred fifty pounds, standing there with that shotgun looking like a toothpick in his hands! I bet him and those two dogs can put away some groceries."

"See, you did have a good time," I said.

The waitress brought our food and filled Henry's cup. After I had eaten half my breakfast, I told him about the photograph of Lucy and Gifford, the payroll record on Gifford I had found in the warehouse, the soybean stuck under the van, and my tail of Gifford over to the farm in Arkansas. "The point is, Henry, I'm starting to wonder if Thomas wasn't a drug distributor. He had the setup, the know-how, maybe the fence business was just a red herring for what he was really doing."

"I understand your points," Henry said. "I just don't believe it. I've misjudged people in the past, but I can't accept that Thomas is anything more than a shifty salesman. I get to meet a lot of people who are in the drug business, and Thomas just doesn't fit in."

"So, what do you think Gifford is doing going over to Arkansas? You think he stores more stolen goods over there?" I asked.

"Was the warehouse full?" he asked.

"No, there was a lot of stuff in it, but plenty of room for more."

"Then why would he take stuff an hour's drive away in Arkansas? And there's not enough population density over there to make the quick sales you would want, so I'm doubting he would want to expand operations there."

"Maybe this is another operation," I said.

"You mean drugs. But why wouldn't he just keep drugs at the warehouse here?"

"I don't know," I said. "Maybe too much traffic would be noticed, even in that neighborhood."

"Hell, he could just stick it in a van with clothes and shoes, he wouldn't have to have semis arriving from Miami with loads of cocaine in them. And I doubt he's into drugs, but did you look in every place in that warehouse where he could be keeping them?".

I thought of the hundreds of boxes I had seen in the warehouse, and had to admit it was quite possible that some of them contained something other than designer clothes or shoes. "So, what do you think Gifford is doing over there?"

"Who the hell knows? Maybe he's got another job. Where did you say it was?"

"About three or four miles southwest of Parkin," I said. "Does that mean anything to you?"

"Across the St. Francis, off U.S. sixty-four?" he asked.

"Obviously it does mean something to you," I said.

"My mother's family is from near Wynne, west of there. I must have been through Parkin a hundred times when I was a kid going to visit my grandmother."

"I thought you said you were a city boy."

"I am, but my family comes from a long line of country folks. We were slaves over there till Lincoln supposedly set us free. Then we sharecropped till the new farm machinery put us out of the picking and chopping business. My mother grew up in a two room shack with no electricity or running water, and my grandmother lived there till she died. They would plant the cotton right up to the front porch, not waste any of the acreage."

"So what do you think Gifford is doing over there?" I asked.

"Most likely, he's working for a white man. There's not a lot of black farmers over there, especially with the kind of setup you say you saw."

"You know that kind of gray-white mud you get over there? I mean, when it dries on your shoes or tires?" I asked.

"Gumbo. Yeah, what's your point?"

"Well, the soybean I found under the van in the warehouse was covered up with that kind of mud, and I found a piece of mud like that in the garage at Thomas's house," I replied.

"There are a whole lot of places around here in less than an hour's drive where you can find mud and soybeans."

"I know that," I said. "It just seems like too much of a coincidence. I have a feeling that farm has something to do with Thomas's business."

"Why don't you check and see who owns it? You could do that in the county courthouse, couldn't you?"

"I believe I may," I said. "Or I may just go over there and poke around a little."

"You kind of like sticking your nose where it doesn't belong, don't you?" Henry asked.

"It's a habit that grows on you," I said, "especially when someone will pay you for doing it."

"Well, watch out for fat guys with shotguns and devil dogs," he said.

"I'll do my best," I said. "Are you sure you don't want to come?"

"I'm sure. I'll never get my law license if I get convicted of aiding and abetting a crazy white guy in a B and E. But you got my curiosity aroused. I'm going to ask a couple more people about Thomas, see if I can find anything out. Come by my business around twelve tonight, and I'll tell you what I know, and you can tell me what's in that equipment shed."

"You got a deal," I said. "I can get some more of that real coffee of yours instead of this black water."

I went back home and took a shower, worked the rest of the morning on other files, and then got ready for the rest of the day. I dressed in a first layer of polypropylene long underwear and wool socks, then added a pair of medium weight wool pants and the chamois shirt. I put on a heavier pair of boots, and stuck a pair of gloves and a wool stocking cap in the pack. I added the camera, the binoculars, water bottle and energy bars to the pack, and then threw in a fleece pullover. I put the Smith back on my belt, put the down jacket on, and locked up. I was headed over the river before I remembered that the camera might not work, but decided not to worry about it.

The wind was still strong out of the northwest, buffeting my truck as I crossed high above the river. The wind had blown out all the rain clouds, and would fade and die with the sunset. It would be a still, quiet night, with the first frost of autumn falling thick and turning the last green vestiges of summer to brown.

I headed west through the farm country on the increasingly familiar highway. I wanted to find out who owned the farm where I had seen Gifford, and I was trying to figure out how to do it. It was in Cross County, so I could head through Parkin and go to Wynne, the county seat, and see if I could find the owner by looking in the real property records in the courthouse. A lot of places, though, don't index real property by location, especially in rural areas, but by the names of grantor and grantee. I could look under the names Gifford and Tuggle, but I doubted either one owned the farm. The other way, of course, was to ask someone, but I didn't want my inquiries to get back to the owner. People in the country are suspicious of anyone who asks a lot of questions about a particular person or place, often assuming they are from some government agency up to no good. Even if they don't like the person involved, they are sure to tell him that some stranger was asking questions about him or his property. On the other hand, I had spent a lot of time learning how to ask questions in depositions in such a way that the deponent would be lulled into a false sense of security and give me information he hadn't intended to reveal.

I was in Parkin by three, and turned off onto the gravel road that led south a few minutes later. I slowed when I got to the trailer I had noticed on the last trip, and pulled into the mud and gravel that served as a combination front yard and driveway. I parked parallel to the road so my license plate didn't face the door, just in case whoever I talked to decided to memorize the numbers. The rain had left oil-slicked puddles everywhere, but the water was drying up fast in the cold wind.

The trailer looked even worse than it had when I had driven by the day before. Several windows were broken out and covered by thick, opaque plastic stuck on with curling duct tape. Briars and weeds grew around the three wooden steps leading up to the door and around and through the concrete blocks that supported the mobile home. No yard of the month award here. The aluminum sides actually shook in the strong wind, and I couldn't imagine that the cold air didn't blow inside. It was probably better now, though, even with the cold air, than in the storm season when it sat like tornado fodder in the middle of the weather patterns blowing up out of the southwest from Texas and Oklahoma.

The pickup I had noticed before was gone, but the dogs were out from under the trailer before I stopped, barking furiously and tearing around my truck in circles. They were medium-sized mutts, brown and gray with some hound and shepherd and who knows what else in their lineage. They looked like they were barking mostly for entertainment, but I got out of the truck cautiously in case they were serious. My limit on attack dogs in the truck with me is one a week. They kept yapping as I slowly stepped down, but they backed off. I figured they were mostly bark.

As I stepped around the front of the truck, the door of the trailer opened and a shrill female voice yelled out, "You goddamn dogs shut up!" A young white woman stepped out onto the top wooden step, and stood looking at me. A little boy about three held onto her leg, and she balanced a baby on one hip. She had greasy blond hair, and was wearing jeans and a black t-shirt with a picture of a race car driver on it. There was a blacker, wet circle on the shirt around each nipple; she had been feeding the baby when she had heard the dogs. She was short and stocky, and her face was so bloated that the flesh around her eyes must have limited her vision like blinders on a horse. She didn't say anything, just stood there looking at me.

"How you doin'?" I asked, putting a little more country into my voice than usual. I stopped where I was, afraid I would make her uncomfortable if I came closer. She still didn't say anything, so I raised my voice a little to be heard over the dogs, and said, "I'm looking for a fellow named Jimmy Rigby, black guy about my age. He was in the Army with me years ago, said he lived on a farm near Parkin. I was in the area, thought I'd try to look him up. Nobody in town heard of him, so I thought I'd drive around in the country for a while, stop at houses and see if anyone knew him."

It wasn't the best cover story in the world, but I thought it might go pretty much unnoticed. Lots of people, myself included, respect veterans, and think it's natural they might be looking for someone they served with. The fact that a white man would be looking for a black friend might seem a little odd out here, but it also tended to divert suspicion. If I said I was looking for a black man, then I probably wasn't a bill collector or policeman who was really looking for her husband. If she had been black, I would have said I was looking for a white guy.

"I never heard of him," she said. "Course, I don't know many coloreds. My husband might know of him. He works with a bunch of 'em on the highway crew. He'll be home in a hour or two if you want to come back by."

"Thanks," I said. "Hey," I added as an afterthought as she was turning to go back inside, "do you know who has the place up this way, with the grain bins? I could see a house back in the trees, but there was a cable across the road. You'd probably know it if Jimmy lived there, though, I guess."

"That's the old Baker place, least ways the farm is. That house is one of them duck clubs. Fellows come over from Memphis to hunt. I ain't never been in it, but my husband guides some over there. He says the inside is like one of them fancy places you see on television. There's some niggers, I mean coloreds, work over there, but I don't know their names. You can come back later and ask my man if you want to."

"I appreciate it," I said. "But I've got to get back home to Nashville tonight. Thanks anyway."

By the time I got back around to the other side of the truck and had climbed into the cab, she had taken the children back inside. I started up the pickup and headed down the road. I wasn't sure what she had thought of my story, but she had seemed to believe it. I had gotten a little nervous when she said her husband worked at the place, but I couldn't help that now. Even if he mentioned at the duck club that someone had asked about the place, they would have to be awfully suspicious to follow up on my inquiry. I hadn't learned much from her, but I hadn't needed to. A name was all I would need to find the owner in the records in the county courthouse. I would have to match up legal descriptions of property owned by anyone named Baker to the physical layout of the farm, but the fact the land was on the river would make that a lot easier. Even if the old place had a new owner, I would be able to find out who it was.

I cruised on past the farm without slowing down. I caught a glint of light coming out of the trees, maybe reflecting off a bumper, but I couldn't see anything else there or up by the grain bins. There was another farm road that ran into the main gravel road about a mile down. It had the standard wooden bridge across the ditch, but no locked cable. I slowed down and took a quick look at its surface, then kept going and circled back to 64, where I headed west toward Wynne. I didn't know when the courthouse closed, but I thought I might be able to get a quick look at the records this afternoon. Even if it was closed, I had to eat, and I wasn't sure I was up to another meal at a gas station.

The day was slipping away fast as I drove into the setting sun, its light turning the brown fields gold and yellow. I saw several small flights of ducks, blown down south by the storm and looking for safe water to rest on for the night. The big flights wouldn't come for another couple of weeks, about the time duck season started. But there were ducks in the air, big ducks, mallards mostly, not the local woodies that stayed all year round. It was a sign that the season was changing, a sign older and more meaningful than any date on a calendar.

By the time I got to Wynne and cruised around and found the courthouse, the sun was almost down and the doors were locked. I noted the hours posted on the door, and saw I could come back tomorrow at a decent hour and get the job done. Then I went looking for a place to eat. I hadn't eaten since my breakfast with Henry, so I was starving. I passed up a couple of places that looked like they still did most of their cooking in animal lard, and settled for a family steak place. I needed to start watching my diet, but not now. I had a long, cold night ahead, and I wanted to pack in all the fuel I could.

After a better than expected steak dinner, I paid the check and walked out into the parking lot. The wind and the sun had blown out together, and the stars shone out bright even through the artificial light of the town. A planet, Venus or Jupiter, I didn't know which, hung low and bright in the western sky. It was the kind of evening that makes you stop and fill your lungs with fresh air, and wonder why you have been spending so much time inside.

I headed back east on the highway, wondering if Amanda was going to believe my expense report. I turned before I got to the road that I had followed

Gifford onto, and came around the back way. I got on the gravel road at its south end, and watched the odometer as I headed north. After two miles, I cut off my headlights, and cruised slowly along in the starlight for another half mile till I found the farm road I had spotted that afternoon a mile south of the duck club. I pulled just off the road and stopped before I got to the bridge. I walked across it carefully, trying to test its strength, but it had looked fairly new in the daylight, and I wasn't really worried about it. If it could handle tractors and other heavy farm machinery, it would hold me and my truck. What did concern me, though, was the road on the other side of the bridge. Many roads that ran through fields were no more than unplanted strips of soil, and I knew from personal experience they could almost swallow a truck, especially after a rain like the one we had just had.

I stepped off the bridge and had a pleasant surprise. There was mud all right, but there was also a fair amount of gravel scrunching under my boots. I took the time to walk down the road a hundred yards, far enough to see that the gravel hadn't been just added for a short stretch to support big trucks with trailers that had to come into the field to pick up loads of beans or whatever was being grown in the field that year. Far off to the north, where I judged the grain bins to be, I could see a light, probably a mercury type that came on automatically when the sun went down. There was a fainter twinkle or two near it, probably lights at the duck club.

I went back to the bridge, and scuffed the mud off my boots onto its plank flooring. Then I got into the truck and slowly drove across the bridge and down the road. I left the headlights off, and was careful not to touch the brakes. I was a good mile from the duck club and the grain bins, but I didn't want any lights flaring out across the field. I rolled my window down so I could hear the sound of the tires on the road. As long as I could feel and hear gravel crunching, I felt pretty good about not getting stuck. The road went straight for a couple of hundred yards, then dog-legged to the right for a while before turning back toward the river. Right in this last turn, there was a low place with a shine of water in it. I didn't see it in time to stop the truck with the gears. I could either brake, flashing my taillights right at the grain bins, and stop and check how bad a hole it was, or I could take my chances.

I opted for the second choice, threw the truck into low, and stomped on the accelerator. The front tires actually flew halfway across the low place before they hit the water, but the hard acceleration kept them going through the water and up onto the road on the other side. The drive was in the back tires, though, and as they went into the water I could feel them begin to slip and spin. Then the back left tire dug in and got traction, and the truck shot out of the hole diagonally off the road and into the soybeans, taking out the first three rows for some twenty yards before I could wrestle it back onto the track.

Once I was back on the road and out of danger of getting stuck in the field, I took my foot off the accelerator and let the truck pull along at dead slow till I got my breath back. I had never touched the brake, but I knew I had made a fair amount of noise. On a cold, still night like this, the sound would have carried a long way. I listened intently for any indication that my little mishap had been noticed across the field, but didn't hear anything, and didn't see any lights except the ones I had already noticed. The only sounds I could hear were the soft crunch of the tires on gravel and ditch water hissing and boiling off the hot engine.

I gave the truck a little gas, and in a minute came to where the road ran into a similar track that was parallel to the river, right up against the trees that grew beside it. I made the turn to the left, took my foot off the accelerator, slipped the transmission into neutral, and waited for gravity to stop me. I killed the motor and sat quiet, listening and watching. I could hear the engine begin to cool, the distant sound of traffic, and a faint burbling of running water from the river, but nothing else. I could still see the bright light at the grain bins, but I couldn't see the other lights from this angle. I got the binoculars out of my pack, and scanned the road and the rows of harvested beans for thirty minutes, plenty long enough for anyone to walk down the road and investigate my presence. No one came, so I checked the contents of the pack by feel, crawled out of the window of the truck without opening the door so I wouldn't turn the dome light on, reached back through the window for the pack and the down jacket, and started slowly down the road.

I took a counted hundred steps, then kneeled and spent a minute with the binoculars. I repeated the same procedure eight more times, till I figured I had come half the distance to the duck club. There was a point of woods sticking out in front of me a short distance into the field, and I eased up to it and cautiously looked around. The road ran straight north again after it jogged around the woods, and at its end I could see the dark shadow of the grove of trees that was visible behind the grain bins from the main road. In the shadow, there were several lights, both outside and shining through windows. I sat down in the weeds, rested my elbows on my knees, and looked it over with the binoculars. With the magnification, I could see the house in the grove. It looked to be two stories, and made out of rough plank or maybe logs. A front porch running along its entire front was illuminated by one of the lights I had seen, and in the light's glow I could see at least two men. They were standing at the edge of the porch, and I could hear an occasional unintelligible scrap of conversation. There were two or three vehicles parked in front of the house, but I couldn't tell much about them because of the low light and the difficulty with depth perception caused by the eight-power magnification.

I stood up out of the weeds, crossed the road, and went five or six rows into the beans. The rows ran parallel to the road, and I started toward the house between two of them, walking slowly. The ground underfoot was soft but not too muddy, and the space between the rows was wide enough that I didn't scrape the barren stalks as I walked. In a wet growing season, the field would be covered with thigh high, lush vegetation, so thick that the individual rows would be obscured. Now, though, it was thinned out and quiet going, but I still stopped every hundred yards and listened and scanned the scene with the binoculars.

When I was about two hundred yards from the house, I knelt down for a final view through the glasses. As I focused in on them, the two men on the porch turned and went into the house. I could hear their voices as they went, but still couldn't make out what they were saying, and could only barely see them. As the last one went through the door, he stopped and yelled back over his shoulder, "We're going to eat, Hayes, come on up to the house."

So Gifford was here, but I still didn't know why. I turned the binoculars toward the grain bins, and saw a flare of light that quickly died, as if someone had opened and then immediately shut a door into a bright place. I skipped over the grove of trees between the bins and the house, and put the glasses back on the porch. In less than a minute, I saw a figure walk up the stairs and go into the house, slamming the screen door behind him. It was hard to get a good look at him, but he was black and looked like he could be Gifford.

I shrugged off the pack, sat down on the ground, and considered my options. Basically, I could leave, could go check out the grain bins and equipment shed now, or could wait and check them out later. I looked at my watch, and saw that it was only seven. I hadn't come this far to leave now, but I didn't think this was the best time to look into the equipment shed. Gifford had just gone in for dinner, or maybe to serve dinner to the white men who had been on the porch, but there was no guarantee he wouldn't get a plate and head back to the equipment shed. I could be at the shed in less than a minute, and could take a quick peek inside and be on my way in five more minutes. I would be a long way from the truck, though, if he came back unexpectedly, and once I got inside I might see that I needed more than five minutes. Besides, I might learn something just by sitting out here in the field and watching.

I decided to wait, but to wait a little closer. I unzipped the pack slowly, got my raincoat out, zipped up the pack, and put on first the raincoat and then the pack. After that I slowly crawled down the row of soybeans, going slowly and getting my hands and knees wet to match the wet spot on my ass I had gotten from sitting on the ground. I halved the distance to the house, and then took a careful look over the top of the beans without using the binoculars. I couldn't see anyone outside, but I thought I could hear the faint sound of voices. I couldn't tell if they were real or if the television was on in the house. I eased back down, took off the pack, and sat in the dirt. It was time to wait, and I can do it with the best of them.

I could hear the faint, intermittent murmur from the house, and distant traffic on the highway two or three miles away, but no other sound. I didn't need to watch the house all the time, because I knew that from this distance I would hear anyone come out onto the porch. It had been a long, busy day, and I was still tired and beat up from my fight with Carl and the night at the warehouse. The big meal I had eaten was keeping me warm, but it was also making me sleepy. I wished I had some coffee, but I hadn't thought to get any at the restaurant in Wynne. I pulled the hood of the parka up, and lay on my back, my head pillowed on the pack. Without the city lights to obscure it, the Milky Way was smeared across the heavens, and stars twinkled everywhere, making you wonder if they had a different sky over here. I shifted around in the dirt, trying to get comfortable. I knew I might fall asleep, but I also knew from past experience that it would be a light sleep, and that I would wake up at the first noise. There was no chance that anyone was going to stumble across me out in the middle of the bean field, so I figured I might as well rest until later. Besides, I was so tired all of a sudden that I didn't think I had any choice. I stuck my hands through the pocket slits in the raincoat, and into the pockets of the down jacket, and lay and watched the stars beam down their cold, distant light till my shutters closed by themselves and the only constellations I saw were the ones that drifted around the sky dome that was the inside of my skull.

I woke up to the slamming of the screen door on the porch of the duck club. I lay still for a few seconds, catching up with reality, then took a quick peek over the top of the beans. I could hear voices, and saw, even without the binoculars, three men on the porch. I put the glasses on them. One was Gifford. He was balancing something on one hand, but I couldn't figure out what it was. One of the others had his back to me, and I couldn't tell much about him, except that he was about medium height and looked white. The other man was facing me, but all I could tell was that he was white, about the same height as Gifford, who was taller than the third man, and had light-colored hair, blond or gray. They stood talking for a minute, and I saw the man with the light hair gesture toward the equipment shed a couple of times. The white guys went back into the house, and Gifford headed toward the shed. I traced him through the trees, losing him now and then, and then watched him walk up to the shed. He opened the door and went back in. There was the same flash of light, but I couldn't see anything inside during the second the door was open.

I turned around, held my sports watch down between my thighs, and checked the time. It was nine fifty. I was dressed warmly, but my pulse rate had dropped while I slept, and I started to shiver. I pulled the stocking cap out of the pack and put it on under the hood of the raincoat, cussing myself because I hadn't thought to do it before I went to sleep. I put on a pair of gloves, tucked my legs up under the coat, and sat there in a ball till I quit shaking. I wished again I hadn't forgotten the coffee. The night was still and cold, and you could actually see the frost crystals dropping through the air. The dried leaves on the bean plants beside me already had a light coating of ice, as did the front of my coat. By morning, the frost would be thick and white on the earth and everything on it that had lain unprotected from the sky.

I decided to get closer to the action. I hadn't heard or seen any sign of a dog, so I figured I was safe from detection by the sense of smell. I was confident no one would see me, but I didn't want to take a chance, so I started crawling on my hands and knees. I went first perpendicular to and away from the river, looking down the rows, till I saw I was even with the shed. Then I headed down the row toward it. I would go a few yards and stop and listen, then start back up. Just as I was starting to think I was about close enough, the door opened and threw a beam of light over the field. I sunk down flat on my belly, but the light shut off as quickly as it had come on. I heard a rattle as if a chain were being handled, then the sounds of footsteps on the road in front of me. The stocking cap was pulled low over my forehead, and my chin was stuck in the dirt, so I left my eyes open and stared down the row. All I got, though, was a half second glimpse of a figure that had to be Gifford as he walked past the end of the row.

I listened to his footsteps fade away, then a few seconds later heard the screen door slam. I waited what I estimated was ten minutes, then slowly eased myself up and looked over the top of the beans, first toward the house and then back at the equipment shed. Nothing. There were lights on in the house, and a very faint glow of light around the door of the shed, but no people in sight. I sat down in the dirt and looked at my watch. It wasn't quite eleven.

My crawl had warmed me up, so the first fifteen minutes weren't too bad. After they were up, I took a quick peek back at the house, and saw that the lights were still on. I settled in to wait some more. It wasn't a bad night to sit out in a bean field, watch the stars, smell and feel the richness of the planet, and receive the icy benediction of the season's first frost. Unless, of course, you were tired and sore as hell, in which case you might opt for your own bed. Oh well, I consoled myself, I was getting paid and I wasn't sitting behind a desk, and it was better now than in the summer when there would be mosquitoes and snakes.

By the end of the second fifteen minutes, I was starting to shiver again. When I looked back over the beans, though, I could see that someone had turned off the lights in the house, leaving only the porch light on. I shivered through another fifteen minutes, and took another look. The lights were still off, and by now they were probably sleeping. I decided to give it another quarter of an hour to make sure, even though I was freezing my butt off. Next time I would wear more clothes.

Ten minutes was all I could wait. I took a peek at the house, saw nothing, then began to crawl to the end of the row. I wanted to get the grove of trees between me and the house before I stood up. When I was almost to the end, I pulled the revolver out of its holster, and duck walked the last few feet to the end of the row. I didn't usually like to go around with it on my belt, much less in my hand, but something told me it wouldn't be a bad idea now. I took a last look around the beans and down the road, but all I could see was the diffused glow of the porch light through the trees. I slowly stood up, then walked quickly across the road to the corner of the shed.

I stood for a minute in the shadows around the corner from the door, but when I didn't hear or see anything I risked moving into the dim light that seeped around the edge of the door. There wasn't enough illumination to see how the door was fastened, so I carefully put my hand out and ran it down the edge of the door frame till I felt the chain I had heard rattle from the field. I followed it gently with my hand, and found that it ran through two semicircular pieces of metal, one screwed into the door frame and the other into the door. A reasonably sized padlock held the ends of the chain together. People were getting just too damned security conscious these days. Maybe they expected someone to come along and hot wire the tractor.

I left the door behind for the moment and walked down the side of the building, trailing my hand along the unbroken corrugated metal wall. I came to the corner, and turned and walked along the side that faced the state road. There was no break here, either, but when I turned the next corner I saw that the north side of the building was mostly open. I could steal a tractor if I wanted to, after all. There was no light inside, but I could dimly see large pieces of farm machinery that I couldn't identify. I moved in among them, and made a quick inspection by feel and the faint illumination from the stars.

There were the usual tools leaned up against the walls, and barrels of what I assumed were fertilizer or pesticides or herbicides. I felt around and discovered that the back corner closest to the river was walled off in concrete blocks into a space about fifteen by twenty. There was no door in either of its walls. I felt up as high as I could but didn't reach anything but more wall. The top was obviously covered, anyway, since the light that was visible from outside couldn't be seen in here. I started back out, and in the process hit my leg, right where the stitches were, on a sharp corner of one of the machines. The pain took my breath away, and when I got it back it was all I could do not to cuss out loud. I muttered several four letter words under my breath, but managed not to cry. I limped out, and sat down for a minute on the concrete apron in front of the open wall of the shed, holding my leg and waiting for the pain to go away. It seemed like it took a long time, and when I took my hand away it was damp. I had opened the wound back up enough for it to bleed through my long underwear and wool pants. More money at the doctor and the dry cleaners.

I got up and walked along the side closest to the duck club and the river. There was nothing here but two fuel tanks used to fill up the farm trucks and machinery. They were mounted on iron legs about ten feet off the ground so they could use gravity to drain the fuel out. They either leaked or a lot of gas and diesel got spilled, because there was a strong smell of petroleum around them.

I got back to the corner where I had started, and stood for a minute listening and thinking. It wouldn't take a lot of time to get the padlock open, but when I did the light inside was going to shine like it had when Gifford had opened the door. It would last for less than a second, but it would be bright, and if anyone at the house was up to go to the bathroom and was looking this way, I was cooked. I also knew there might be nothing interesting behind the door, or at least nothing that had to do with the disappearance of a fence in Memphis. On the other hand, they were sure being careful with whatever was in the room, especially since it was so close to the house and we were out in the middle of nowhere. Besides, I hadn't driven all the way over here and sat out in a field for several hours to go home empty-handed. I stuck the gun in its holster, got my lock picks out and went to work. In less than five minutes, I had the lock popped and the chain pulled through one of the metal rings. I held the ring on the door in my left hand, got the revolver back into my right, and pulled the door open quickly, more worried about the light than a squeak. I stepped across the threshold, and pulled the door closed behind me.

There wasn't much light inside, just a low watt bulb that stuck out of a socket set into the wall, but it seemed bright after all my time outside in the dark. I squinted and shaded my eyes with my left hand, and looked around. I was standing on a concrete floor, and the walls were nothing more than the inside of the metal outer walls on two sides, the inside of the concrete blocks on one side, and a floor-to-ceiling chain link fence on the back wall. The ceiling was plywood, supported by joists about ten feet over the floor. There was a cheap desk pushed up against the wall by the door, and an old metal folding chair beside it. On the desk, there was a coffee can with some pens and pencils in it, and a blank legal pad. A calendar was stuck to one of the wooden wall studs. It featured a picture of a slightly chubby young blonde with a bare midriff and blue jean shorts sitting in the cab of a cottonpicker, smiling out at the viewer. The caption under the picture proclaimed her Miss Farm Implement 1999. The place had the chemical smell you get in the garden section of the hardware store, with an overlay of dust and a strong odor of human sweat, like a poorly ventilated gym. It was dank and cold with the moisture of the last few days' rain and the cold that was now seeping in through the metal and concrete.

I tried the desk, but its drawers were locked. It wouldn't take long to get into them, but I wanted to look at whatever was behind the chain link fence first. I walked over and tried to peer in, but pesticide barrels were stacked up two high just inside the wire everywhere except in front of a head high gate located in the middle of the fence. It was made out of the same wire, with yet another padlocked chain securing it. The forty watt bulb didn't shed much light back here, so I pulled a penlight out of my pocket, switched it on, and shone it through the galvanized metal diamond outlines of the fence.

I turned it on the ceiling and wall behind it, then down on the floor to my right. Nothing but the concrete wall and the cement slab I was standing on. I shifted the beam of light to the left, and almost dropped the flash through the wire. In its spot, there were two feet, wearing some kind of fancy basketball shoes. The backs of the heels were on the floor, and the toes of each shoe stuck out at forty five degree angles. I shifted to the right, so I could shine the light further to the left, and saw the beginnings of legs encased in white nylon warm-up pants. I almost dropped the lights again when the right foot moved and a sleeper's sound between a groan and a sigh came out of the darkness behind the barrels. I switched the light off, and stood there with my heart thumping.

I tried to think, but it wasn't easy with the adrenaline rushing through me. The logical thing to do was obvious: get the hell out of there and call the sheriff. The odds were heavily against the feet inside belonging to Thomas. Why would Gifford, who made a good living working for Thomas, and who was close enough to him to be in a picture with his mother, have anything to do with him being locked up in an equipment shed in Cross County, Arkansas? It had to be somebody else, and who it was and why they were here was absolutely none of my business. I holstered the revolver, got the picks out, and started on the padlock.

It was easier and faster this time, maybe because I had just opened up the lock on the outside. I popped it open in a couple minutes, then carefully pulled it out of the links, and worked it out of the gate. I pulled the gate open, drew the .357, and switched the light back on. Both feet were now pointing straight; whoever it was had been awakened by the sounds I had made getting the gate open, though I had been as quiet as I could. As I watched, the feet pulled back out of sight. My heart was thumping even harder now, and my grip was slippery on Uncle Stan's Smith. I eased inside the gate, stood sideways behind the barrels, and stuck the flashlight out at the end of my arm, pointing toward where the owner of the feet would keep his head. There was a grunt, but no shot.

"Who are you?" I whispered, still standing behind the barrels.

At the sound of my voice, there was more grunting, but no words. It was unlikely he was sitting with a gun behind two doors padlocked on the outside, but you don't get old in my business by taking avoidable chances. I turned the light off, kneeled, stuck my hand up as high as I could, and turned the flash back on. I aimed it back toward the grunting, and bobbed it and my head out from around the barrels and instantly back in at the same time. It was insurance I didn't need.

I stood up and shone the light on the man in front of me. He was half lying, half sitting, with his arms pulled behind him. He was wearing a dirty white sweatshirt, and the hood was pulled up over his head. I thought at first that the sweatshirt was covering the lower part of his dark brown face, but I looked closer and saw that he had white adhesive tape across his mouth and chin. That explained the grunting. His eyes were wild, but he seemed to be looking at me with hope.

He gestured with his head and eyes back over his shoulder, and I cautiously stepped up beside him and looked. There was a big eyebolt set into the concrete floor, with the chain of a set of manacles running through the eye, and one of his hands in each of them. I put the gun away.

He didn't look like the Thomas in the picture, too dark for one thing, and I was sure of it after I pulled the hood off his head. His hair hung in long dreadlocks, and he had a gold nose stud through his left nostril. His bloodshot eyes searched mine with a questioning look. I reached around behind his neck, and felt the overlapping ends of the two pieces of tape around his face.

"I'm gonna rip this off," I whispered. "I know it'll hurt, but don't make any noise, okay?"

He gave me a nod, closed his eyes, and gritted his teeth. I pulled hard and fast, and the tape came around his neck and face and off his mouth and chin with a tearing sound. It had spots of blood and little curly black hairs stuck to it. He made a strangled noise in his throat, and then wiped the side of his face hard on his shoulder. The tape was still stuck on the right side of his face, but I thought I would let him deal with that himself later.

"Motherfucker, motherfucker," he mumbled thickly, over and over.

"Who are you?" I asked."

"Did Axe send you?" he asked me back in a clearer voice.

"No. Who are you?" I asked again.

"They sent you to get me, right?" he asked, staring at me hard.

"No," I said, "I'm looking for someone else. Tell me who you are. Maybe I can help you."

"Are you a cop?" he asked.

"FBI," I said. I thought it might get his attention more than saying I was a private investigator.

But I saw his eyes hood over, and for a minute I thought he wasn't going to say anything else. Then he said, "Shit, what do I care? Just get me the fuck out of here."

"Tell me who you are and what's going on, and I might," I answered.

"You going to leave me here with those crazy motherfuckers?" he asked, desperation in his voice.

"Not if you answer my question," I replied.

He sat back against the wall, and looked up at me. "My name's Bobby Anderson," he said. "Now get me the fuck out of here."

"What do they call you on the street, Bobby?" I asked.

"Man, I'm not out on no street," he said.

"You're a famous rap singer and I've never heard of you, right?"

"I'm a brother so I got to be hustlin' on the street or rappin'?" he asked. "You a racist or something?"

"I know a hustler when I see one, Bobby, black or white. And you got a mighty big mouth to be sitting out here sixty miles from your 'hood chained to a pole. You want to tell me what's going on, or you want me to kick you in the head and leave you here?"

He looked up at me sullenly, but common sense won an unexpected victory over bravado. "That white motherfucker, claims he's a cop, arrested me and brought me here yesterday. Stuck me in the goddamn trunk of his car, I don't even know where I am."

"Give me a little description," I said. "There's a lot of us white motherfuckers."

"Tall dude, yellow hair, dressed up real nice," he said.

Interesting, I thought, but I only said, "Okay, tell me more."

"Yesterday morning, about four, I'm sleeping by myself in my own place, I wake up with a gun stuck in my nose. This dude says get up, I'm under arrest. I say, shit, what for, you got nothing on me."

"You say this to a guy with a gun up your nose?"

"Shit, man, I'm used to cops," he said. Maybe he really was a rap star. "I say, show me your warrant, and he roll the hammer back on his piece, and stick it on up in my nose past my stud, makes tears come to my eyes. Get up, he says, and I get up. I'm sleepin' in these clothes, and he let me put my shoes on, then he cuffs me. When you ever see one cop come on a bust, right? So I'm wonderin' is he really a cop, or is this a hit, but the bottom line is I ain't go no choice but do what he say. So I do. He march me outside, pop open his trunk, and say get in. That is not a good sign, man. I'm trying to think of something to say, or whether I should yell out or try to run, and he say, in the trunk or die in two seconds. I can tell he's not fuckin' around, so I'm in the trunk in one second. He shuts it and we drive off."

He looked up at me to see if that was enough. "More," I said.

"I ride around in his trunk for what seems like an hour, maybe more, most of the time pretty smooth and steady, like we're on the freeway. Then we take a short ride over a bumpy road, and he stops and opens the trunk. He pulls me out and we're in the middle of nowhere, the sun's not even up, and I'm thinking, Bobby, my boy, you is fixin' to die. But he don't shoot me, he just walks me into this shack thing we're in, makes me sit down here, and puts these chains on before he takes off the cuffs."

"Tell me why somebody might want to shoot you, Bobby?" I asked.

"Come on, man, that can wait," he said. "Let's get the hell out of here."

"Now, Bobby," I said. "Or you can just keep hanging here." Despite the fact that he was obviously scared, he was doing his best to cover it up. He was a tough guy, and if I wanted any information, I knew I'd better get it while he was helpless.

"Well, I did some time for possession with intent to sell. I was innocent, but I had this dumbass public defender, he told me to plead it out, so I did. I was hanging out with some dudes that was dealing, but I wasn't. They had what you might call short life spans, lots of enemies. I been out of jail for a year, but I still see some of the same brothers, so I'm figurin' somebody may have confused me with one of them."

"Uh huh," I said. "I get it. You're not a dealer, but you know people who are. It was a case of mistaken identity when you got busted by the cops and put in jail, so you think it's a mistake now, except this is not where the cops would bring you."

"Man, you catch on fast. You are one smart white boy. Now let's get the fuck out of here," he said, pulling on the chains.

"We're getting there," I said. "But first tell me what's happened since you been here."

"Look, they could come back here any minute. Let's go and I'll tell you later, I promise," he said, the fear creeping back into his voice.

I was ready to go, too, but I wanted the information. "Tell it," I said. "Tell it fast, but tell it."

He must have decided it would be faster to tell it than to argue, so he started talking. "The white guy walks out, and a black guy walks in with a shotgun. Oh, shit, I'm thinkin', here we go, but he just tells me to keep my mouth shut, says he'll get me a bucket when I need to piss, and he'll bring me something to eat later. He goes out into that room out there, and I can hear him messing around. I call out to him a couple of times, trying to find out what's up, and he comes back in with the shotgun, says if I don't shut up he's going to tape my mouth. So I shut up."

"What's he look like?" I asked.

"About forty-five or fifty, tall, goatee and mustache, losing his hair. Dressed like a country nigger, lace up boots, khaki pants and shirt. Even without the shotgun, you'd think twice about messing with him."

Gifford for sure, I thought. "What was the rest of the day like?" I asked.

"Weird, man, weird," he said, shaking his head. "After a while someone else came in, said a few words I couldn't catch and left, then the black guy brings me in a sandwich and a bottle of water. He unlocks one of my hands so I can eat, and stands there watching me. I try to get him to talk, but all he says is shut up or I'll tape your mouth. After I eat, he brings in a bucket and puts it in front of me, and lets me loose long enough to piss in it. He keeps the twelve gauge on me the whole time, so I got no chance to do anything. Then he locks me back up, takes the bucket and the empty bottle, and goes back out into the other room."

"I got no idea what's happening, and that nigger won't tell me nothin', but they've fed me, and I ain't dead yet, so I'm startin' to feel a little better. I'm thinking this is maybe some kind of strange police deal, and they're going to keep me here till I get softened up and then start asking me to stool out my brothers. This I can handle, and the worst thing at the end of the road is more time at the penal farm. Then it starts getting really weird."

"I hear the door open, and then voices, and the white guy who brought me here comes in the room with the black guy. I start trying to talk to the white guy, but he says the same thing, shut up or I'll tape your mouth. He tells me I'll get a chance to talk, but not till I'm asked. He puts the cuffs on me, then undoes these chains and he and the black dude pull me up. It's show time, Bobby, I'm thinking, but they ain't going to all this trouble just to kill me."

"We walk into the other room, and there's another white guy sitting in a chair, looking at me. He's old, like in his seventies, white hair, and he says bring the prisoner in. He's got a high, old man's voice, but the other white man says yes sir, and they bring me in and sit me down on a stool. Is your name Bobby Anderson? he asks me, and I say yeah. The nigger reach over and knock me on the top of the head with the shotgun barrel, and goes, say yes sir. So I said it."

He had forgotten he was in a hurry to leave, and was getting into his story. Like a lot of guys in the business he claimed not to be in, he was a talker, a raconteur, a jive artist.

"The old man then says, Bobby Anderson, you're on trial for distribution of narcotics, in particular crack cocaine. Do you plead guilty or not guilty? What, I say, what kind of shit is this? This ain't no courtroom! Then the nigger reach over and rap me on the head again. He says, answer the man's question, then shut up."

"My head is hurting bad now, even though I got this stack of dreads on top of it, so I say innocent and shut up."

"Then the old dude says, the prosecution may proceed with its case, and the white guy who kidnapped me starts reading stuff off a clipboard. Man, he's got the names of half the brothers I know on it, and me right in the middle of it, saying I'm dealing rock, buying and selling, beating up folk for not paying me, all kinds of shit, everything but I'm mean to my momma."

"None of it's true, right?" I asked.

"None of it 'bout me," he said earnestly.

"Let's assume for the sake of argument that I believe you," I said. "What next?"

"The cop finishes up, and the old guy says, Mr. Anderson, you may now put on your defense. I look over at the nigger with the shotgun, make sure he's not going to hit me, and he gives me a nod. So I say what is this? This ain't no courtroom, you're not a judge, you got no right to hold me here. And then the old fucker holds up his hand, and says Mr. Anderson, this court does not recognize technical legal arguments. This court has moral jurs, uh, jurs . . ."

"Jurisdiction?" I said.

"That's right, moral jurisdiction, this court has moral jurisdiction over this matter. What the fuck does that mean?" he asked, but he really wasn't looking for an answer, and kept on talking. "He says, if you have something to say about the charges that the prosecution has brought, now is your chance. That is all you are allowed to talk about. So I start off by saying ain't none of that shit true. Then the old man say, Mr. Anderson, we do not tolerate profanity in this court. Then he look at the black dude and say, if the prisoner uses profanity again, act accordingly, which I know means rap this poor nigger on the head with the shotgun barrel. So I bullshit him for fifteen minutes or so on the stuff the cop laid out, trying to blame it on the other brothers, I mean they ain't here and it ain't nothing the cops don't know anyway, and I even try to tell them I'll turn on my friends and testify. I ain't going to do it, you understand, but I'm looking to get out of this shit anyway I can."

"When I'm through, the old dude acting like he the judge turn to the cop, and ask do he have anything to add. He says, it ain't nothing we ain't heard a dozen times before, your honor. I have nothing to add. Then the old man say to me, stand up, so I stood up. He says, based on the evidence presented to this court, the defendant is found guilty as charged. This court orders that you be executed at dawn tomorrow."

"I'm thinking maybe I didn't hear him right, so I start to open my mouth, and hear come the shotgun barrel again, whap on my head. Then the black dude stick the muzzle hard against my crotch and say, don't move. The old white guy is walking out the door, and the other one gets the tape and wraps it around my mouth and head. Then they chain me up again in here. The black dude been out there in that other room most of the time, and he let me piss a couple of times, but I ain't had this tape off till you come in. I been sitting here wondering do they mean it, they really going to do me, or are they just softening me up, get me to turn state's evidence."

I stood looking at him, thinking about his story. No doubt about it, things were pretty weird. I knew he was more than capable of lying, and that he probably was about his lack of involvement in drug dealing. But I couldn't believe he had come up with this story on the spur of the moment after I told him I was an FBI agent. I didn't want to interfere in a real law enforcement operation, even if it was way outside of the rules of the Constitution, but despite my growing conviction that the younger white guy was probably Steiner, I couldn't believe this was a sanctioned police activity.

I looked at my watch. It was 12:30 in the morning, past time to be out of here. Anderson saw me looking at the time. "Come on, man, let's go," he pleaded.

I wasn't crazy about letting him loose, especially if he was a dealer. There was a chance this was a legitimate deal, and that I would be in big trouble with the authorities. I didn't want to have to keep up with him and watch my back all the way through the soybean field and in the truck, either. If he believed I was an FBI agent, he would think he was going from one jail to another. But if they were really going to execute him at dawn, I wasn't sure there was enough time for me to get back to the truck, drive to the closest police station, tell my story, convince the cops I wasn't some kind of nut, and get them back out here before they dropped the hammer on him. I made up my mind, got the lock picks back out, and went to work on the manacles.

Once I got them off him, he stood up a little shakily, and rubbed his wrists and worked his shoulders back and forth. Then he pulled the tape off, cussing as it pulled on his skin and hair. He threw the tape down in disgust, and massaged the side of his face and his neck. I handed him the water bottle, and he drained it without taking it from his mouth.

"All right," I said, "follow me and don't say a word. We're going through a soybean field to my truck. It's a pretty good hike, so let's move fast."

"I'm with you, my man. Let's go."

We went out to the main room, and I stood for a minute inside the door, listening. There was no sound. I switched the light off so it wouldn't shine out the door when we opened it, pulled the .357, and stepped out into the night. Anderson came out behind me, way too conspicuous in his white sweats. The night was dead still, cold and black. The light inside had ruined my night vision. I knew I should have sat inside with the light off for a while to get my eyes used to the dark, but I hadn't wanted to spend the time doing it.

As I stepped up to the corner of the building, I caught a whiff of an odor that didn't belong. It wasn't fuel, or drying vegetation, or chemicals, or the smell of fallow earth. The idea light went off a half second too late for me to stop my stride past the corner, and even as the thought—aftershave—flashed in my head, there was a waft of air as something hard smashed into my head just above my ear.

16 ───────────────────────────

I woke up slowly, with the kind of throbbing headache I used to have when I was drinking too much right after my wife left me. I was lying on my right cheek against something hard and rough, and the left side of my head was killing me. I tried to open my eyes, but the left one was gummed up and wouldn't open. The right eye was staring at a concrete floor an inch away. I tried to raise my left hand up to my head, and found that it brought the right one with it. I tried to see why, but I was having trouble focusing my one working eye. Then I felt the handcuffs. I seemed to remember handcuffs, but I didn't think they belonged on me. I put my hands to the side of my head, and felt a big knot with an oozing split down the middle of it just above my ear. The hair was crusted with what had to be drying blood, and there was more crust across my face and cementing my eyelids. I rubbed some of it off my eye and managed to prop it open with my thumb and forefinger, but all I could see was more concrete floor. I was thinking about trying to stand up, when a voice nearby said, "He's awake. I thought he might be out for a lot longer. You must have gone easy with that shotgun butt, Hayes."

I was starting to piece it back together slowly, when I caught that scent of aftershave again. It brought the whole thing back in on me as if I had never checked out.

I struggled to sit up, but as soon as I made it I wished I hadn't. I felt a sharp, stabbing pain in my skull, the room did a flip, and bits of undigested steak rocketed out of my mouth. I kneeled on the floor and wretched, the pressure of each heave threatening to blow the side of my head off. My stomach finally relaxed, and I settled back on my haunches, trying to catch my breath.

The same voice said, "I take it back, Hayes, you must have given him a pretty good lick."

I got my eyes focused, and looked up to see Steiner standing beside Gifford. Steiner's face held a mixture of disgust and amusement, but Gifford's was flat and expressionless—the old Browning semiautomatic twelve gauge he held showed more emotion.

I was back in the shed, in the front part with the desk. Anderson wasn't in sight.

"Get the mop and bucket and clean that mess up, Hayes," Steiner said. Gifford handed him the shotgun, and went out the door.

"Remember me giving you some advice, McAlister?" Steiner said, walking over and sitting at the desk chair. He pointed the shotgun at my head, and said, "You should have taken it."

The muzzle looked like it was an inch across, and it was no more than five feet from my face. For a second I thought he had sent Gifford for a bucket to clean up more than my vomit, then I realized it wouldn't make much sense for him to blow my head off inside the building. He lowered the muzzle, and shook his head and laughed. Gifford came back in with a bucket and mop and started cleaning up my mess. I pushed myself up against the wall, and tried to collect my thoughts through the throbbing in my head and the lingering nausea.

"Where's your vehicle?" Steiner asked.

"I got dropped off," I said. It seemed like a good idea to suggest that there was somebody else out there.

"Why do I doubt that?" he asked with a smile.

"Don't know," I said with a shrug.

"Hayes, when you get through there, take the shotgun back and take a look around," Steiner said. He pulled my keys and wallet out of his pocket, and tossed the keys to Gifford.

Gifford finished up with the bucket, went out, came back in for the shotgun, then left again. Steiner took out the Chief's Special I had seen at the police station and laid it on the desk beside my .357.

"So," he said, "why don't you tell me how you got over here."

"I took the interstate to highway sixty-four, then turned left on the state highway past the river," I said.

"I've got a lot of time, and no restraints. Absolutely none. Do you understand what I'm saying?" he asked. He wasn't smiling now.

When I thought back over it, I couldn't think of any reason not to tell him. I had already told him I was working for Lucy. He might put her with Amanda, but nothing I was going to say would help him do that.

"Like I told you earlier," I said, "I'm trying to find Thomas Tuggle. I found out Gifford worked for him, so I followed him over here. That's it."

"And you're working for Tuggle's mother, right?" he asked.

"That's right," I said.

"Anderson said you told him you were an FBI agent," he said.

"Anderson should know better than to believe everything a white man tells him," I said. "By the way, where is he?"

"Back where he was," Steiner said, pointing at the wired off room at the back. "Now, how did you find out Hayes worked for Tuggle?"

"I went in Tuggle's warehouse, looked through his records," I said. Again, I couldn't see any harm in telling him.

"How did you know where his warehouse is?" he asked.

"Word on the street," I said. "Everybody knows the Designer. For a little money they'll tell where his place of business is." Don't mention Henry, don't mention Amanda.

"His mother pay you?" he asked.

"Yeah," I said. "I wouldn't have taken the case unless I'd gotten money up front. She didn't look real reliable."

"She was paying you with money obtained from criminal activities. That makes you a criminal, too," he said, pointing at me with the .38.

"Me a criminal?" I asked. "Where the hell do you get off calling me a criminal? You think it's legal to break my head and hold me here? It's assault, and kidnapping, and federal violation of my civil rights, and probably a whole lot more shit." I felt really bad, and I was getting tired of this whole thing. I told myself to calm down, that it wasn't going to do any good to lose my temper.

But Steiner just smiled at me and said, "Remember, I've got the badge and the gun. That makes me the good guy. Now tell me what Anderson said to you."

"He said a white guy claiming to be a cop arrested him and put him in his trunk and drove him over here," I replied.

"That's it?" he asked.

I stopped a minute like I was thinking, and said, "Yeah, pretty much. He promised me a thousand bucks if I let him go. It sounded like easy money. I didn't know you were involved. I just figured it was some kind of drug gang fight."

"So you were going to get yourself in the middle of a gang war?" he asked.

"Look, I was just trying to find Tuggle. But here I was, and all I had to do for a thousand was let him out of the cuffs and drive him back to Memphis. Why not?"

"My friend," he said with a shake of his head, "I'm afraid you're going to find out why not. I don't see any way around it."

I felt like Anderson must have when Steiner told him to get into the trunk. It was not a good sign, and it got worse.

"Didn't you get the message when you got shot at in your alley?" he asked.

"No," I said, "what message? I thought they were just trying to rob me." I had a firm feeling that knowledge was danger, and I wanted to stay ignorant.

"No," he said, "they were supposed to warn you off the Tuggle case. You were supposed to get beat up a little, but the guy with the gun lost his head when you ran at him."

My pulse was racing in my sore head, causing sharp spikes of pain every time my heart beat. I didn't want him to tell me these things.

He was watching me closely, and then he said, "Yeah, you know, don't you? I'm sorry, I don't really have anything against you."

"What the hell are you talking about?" I asked, trying to put believability in my voice.

"Don't waste our time," he said. "You stepped in the cow patty, and there's no way to get the shit off your shoe."

"Man, believe me, I don't know what you're talking about."

"Yeah, I think you do," he said. "But let me give you the details. You deserve it after all your hard work."

I didn't think knowing the details would be good for my health, but I didn't think it would do me much good to put my hands over my ears. Besides, I couldn't do it with the handcuffs on.

"I've been on the force for twelve years," he said. "Before that I was an MP in the Air Force. It's the kind of job I was born for. Other people break the law, I go out and get them, bring them to justice. I'm good at it."

"It's nice to see a man happy at his work," I said.

"That was the problem, though, you see, I wasn't happy," he said. "I had what you might call a fundamental dissatisfaction with my job." The tone of his voice was still light, but there was a serious look in his flat, green eyes.

I suppressed a remark about the police chaplain, and waited reluctantly for more.

"Here was my problem," he said, picking up his pistol and gesturing with it. His index finger was off the trigger, wrapped around the grip. "I couldn't do my job more than half-assed. On any given day, I could drive around the city and identify a hundred people that I knew were engaged in major criminal activity, and I couldn't arrest them. Scum I knew were ripping off other people's property, selling them drugs, even outright murdering them. And I couldn't do anything about it. Oh, I could get evidence on some of them, and I did, but it was just the tip of the iceberg. I even manufactured evidence on some of them, but I knew I'd get caught eventually and thrown off the force, or put in jail myself."

I didn't think this was the time for a lecture on criminal constitutional law, so I kept my mouth shut. Steiner's right hand, with the little gun in it, was hanging between his knees. I was about eight feet away from him, weakened by the blow to my head, and handcuffed. I thought about rushing him, but decided that there was at least a ninety percent probability that it would end with me catching a jacketed hollow point in the face. While I calculated, he went on in the same serious tone, almost as if he were trying to convince me of something.

"I'd lie awake at night, thinking how much better off this town would be if I could just move those hundred people out of the way. Oh, I knew they'd be replaced eventually, people are always going to break the law, but it would be a start, you know. I even did the math. If there are one million people in the Memphis area, one hundred criminals would be one one-hundredth of one percent of the total population. Think about it," he said, gesturing at me with the gun again. "Think about the benefit to the vast majority of the population that you could derive by getting rid of this core group of criminals."

I nodded my head like I was thinking about it, but he was really talking to himself. His eyes weren't flat anymore, but intense and full of light. "Then I met the judge, and we figured out how we could do it," he said.

"The judge?" I asked, despite myself.

"Yes," he said, "a real judge. His son was arrested for buying rock from a dealer. When I found out who his father was, a light went on in my head. I went to the judge and got him talking about his son. The son was almost forty years old, and had been on one kind of drug or another since he was a teenager. They're an old Memphis family, and the judge just can't accept the fact that his son's never going to amount to anything. He served on the criminal bench for three or four years back in the seventies, and that experience, plus what's he's gone through with his son, makes him think just about everything wrong with the world is caused by drugs. I think he's overstating his case, making excuses for his son, but there's no denying drugs are the engine that drive a lot of crime. I told him my theory, and my solution, and I could tell he was intrigued.

"He called me the next day, and had me come back out to his house. We sat at a patio table out by the pool and drank coffee, and he suggested the plan. He never said he was speaking hypothetically, or checked to see if I was wired. I don't think he cared.

"He told me he was in his seventies, almost beyond the point of making a difference in the world. He had money to leave his son, but he knew he would just squander it. The judge wanted to do something more, something lasting. So he told me to bring him the one hundred, that we would deal with them together."

He hadn't raised his voice, but he was speaking emphatically, with the strong light in his eyes. "And we're doing it," he said, "we're dealing with the problem. You wouldn't believe how good it feels, how fulfilling. I've never been happier in my life."

His face was shining now, like Amanda's after the jury came back with the six million dollar verdict. "Can you understand?" he asked. "I wish you could understand, really feel what I'm feeling," he said earnestly. "Because if you could, it would be okay, you coming here, I mean."

Somewhere, deep in that blood-gorged mass of gray tissue in his head, something had gotten crossed up. Maybe it was a matter of too much or too little natural secretions or hormones in a certain place, or a synapse that didn't fire right, or a nerve that hadn't developed like it was supposed to. Or maybe it was environmental, something he had seen or experienced at a critical stage of his development. Maybe the good news was that more people don't end up like him than actually do. But the bad news was that I was stuck with him in the wee hours of a frosty November morning, far from any help and totally in his power. And I knew. The involuntary shudder I gave wasn't caused by the cold.

Before I could start to tell him that I thought maybe I could understand, there was a crunch of gravel outside and Gifford walked into the shed. The light faded in Steiner's eyes, his tongue stuck far out of his mouth for a second, and his face gave a curious twist. Then he gave me a normal-appearing, cynical smile, and turned to Gifford.

"I found a white pickup down in the south field, right by the river," Gifford said. "I brought it up to the house, put it in the shed."

"Anything interesting in it?" Steiner asked.

"A flashlight, some tools, nothing else."

"Any sign of another person?"

"One set of tracks leaving the pickup. He could have dropped someone off earlier. I didn't follow the road back out to the highway."

"No need to," Steiner said. "He's alone."

"You sure?" Gifford asked.

"Sure enough," he said. "Did the judge wake up?"

"No," Gifford said. "I let him sleep. I didn't see no need to get him up."

"You're right," Steiner said. "No need at all. Do you feel up to watching these two the rest of the night?"

"I can do it," Gifford said. "I had me a good nap this afternoon."

"Okay," Steiner said. "I'm going to go back to the house, try to get a little sleep. The judge and I will come get you about five thirty. You want me to bring you some breakfast?"

"No," Gifford said. "I won't eat till afterward."

"All right," Steiner said. "Do you want me to leave this big pistol of his here with you?"

"No," Gifford said, "I like the shotgun. How much are we doing in the morning?"

"I don't know," Steiner replied, looking at me, "that's up to the judge."

"Okay," Gifford said.

"Goodnight, then," Steiner said to both of us, giving me a little wave and a stare with the flat green eyes that hid the flawed soul behind them.

17 ——————————————

A wave of colder air blew in the door as Steiner went out, causing both Gifford and me to shiver. He pulled an electric heater out of the space between the side of the desk and the wall, and switched it on. It rattled some on the concrete floor, but the waves of heat felt great. Gifford sat on the chair where Steiner had been, his booted feet stuck in front of the heater. The shotgun was across his lap, his right hand holding it by the pistol grip. There were several smears of my blood on his shirt where the butt plate had brushed him before he had thought to wipe it off.

I felt queasy and my head was banging, but I didn't have that desperate feeling of impending dissolution that comes with severe nausea. Steiner's story, and its implications for my future, were not calculated to induce cool, measured thinking, and I knew it was my only hope. So I took a deep breath, and asked, "What happened to Thomas?"

He instantly jerked his feet away from the heater and sat straight up in his chair.

"What happened to Thomas Tuggle?" I repeated.

"How do you know Thomas?" he asked.

"I'm a private investigator," I replied. "His mother, your friend, Lucy Tuggle, hired me to find him. Didn't Steiner tell you?"

His big chest was going up and down now as he breathed fast and hard, staring at me with wide eyes. "Lucy hired you? Does she know you're here?"

I had hit home, and I kept pushing it. "Sure," I said. "I told her I was coming over here to look for him."

"But does she know about me?" he asked. "Does she know I'm here?"

"Yeah," I said. "I followed you over here from your place off Jackson just yesterday. You've got a green Dodge pickup."

A sick, desperate look came over his face, like the tables had been turned and he was the one who had been slammed in the head with a shotgun butt. He stood up and walked around the room, muttering, "Oh, Jesus, sweet, sweet Jesus."

He dropped back into the chair as if his legs wouldn't support him, and stared at me, sweat beaded on his high forehead. "You're telling me the truth, right?"

I almost laughed at the notion that he could crack my head and handcuff me, and still expect me not to lie to him. But I didn't. I was playing this strictly for personal survival, and he didn't look like the kind to kid around with. So I just said, "Sure. Why would I lie?"

"Does he know about Lucy?" he asked, flinging a hand in the direction of the duck club.

"Steiner? Yes, he knows. I told him back in Memphis, when I went to the police station looking for the cops who arrested Thomas on the crack charge. Then I just told him a minute ago about following you over here yesterday."

"Why did you tell him?" he asked in an anguished voice.

"Why not? Besides, he gave me the distinct impression that I would regret it if I didn't."

"What do you mean, regret it?" he said. "He's going to kill you no matter what you say."

I had already come to this conclusion, but to hear it said right out loud caused a spurt of fear to wash through me. Gifford didn't notice, though; he was going through an agony of his own. The beads of sweat on his forehead were now running down his face, and his eyes had a faraway, hunted look. I couldn't tell whether the smell of fear that pervaded the atmosphere was from him or me. He reached down and yanked the heater's cord out of the wall socket, and sat staring at the wall, his mind trying to work behind his eyes. I was quiet, but my mind was working, too, although it wasn't getting anywhere fast.

The little heater ticked as it cooled, and the cold crept back in fast through the concrete floor and cinder block wall. It permeated the fear sweat on me, and I started to shiver again. Gifford seemed oblivious to the cold, his eyes staring at nothing a few feet above my head. He seemed totally unaware of the shotgun in his hand, its muzzle pointed at the floor. I was sitting with my feet stretched out, and I slowly pulled them back so the heels were touching my butt. I got my palms flat on the floor, and eased away from the wall behind me. Even in Gifford's distracted state, I knew there wasn't much chance of getting past the shotgun. And if I did, I wasn't sure what I could do with Gifford. He was bigger than I was, obviously fit, and not weakened by a concussion. Bad as my chances were, though, I didn't see them getting much better. I took a couple of quiet, deep breaths, tensed my muscles, and started to count to three.

I was on two when Gifford suddenly shifted his gaze to me. I thought at first that he had sensed I was about to jump him, but the hand holding the shotgun never moved. I slowly relaxed back against the wall. Bad odds had become impossible odds. I would bide my time.

"I've gone down the broad and crooked road, and there ain't no way to get off it," Gifford said, as much to himself as to me. "There just ain't no way." His voice was hopeless, and as bitter as a vinegar martini.

He stared through me for what seemed like a minute, and I thought he was through talking. But then the focus came back to his eyes, and he said, "You see, I've been working for the judge all my life. Not like a full-time job, but whenever his family needed something done, in the yard or around the house, or over here at the farm, they could call me. And I expected them to, wouldn't of had it any other way. They paid me good, too. My daddy did the same thing for the judge's old man."

I gave a little nod, and kept listening. I wasn't sure where this was going, but I had a pretty good idea. First Steiner, and now Gifford, were using me as a priest, a psychiatrist, a lawyer. They wanted to talk with someone outside of their trio, and they couldn't. Not unless they knew that person couldn't talk about it later, no matter what. And I was that person. It was better than the priest-penitent privilege, the attorney-client privilege, the psychiatrist-patient privilege. It was absolute and unconditional, not subject to any legal exception or moral override on the part of the recipient. Someone ought to write a law review article about it, but I knew it wouldn't be me.

"So when the judge asked me to help him with this, I didn't even really think about saying no. He assumed I would, and I did. I knew it wasn't strictly legal, but he's a judge, and every day I see the damage that kind of people cause."

I didn't ask him about his part in Thomas's operation, whether he included thieves in his definition of "that kind of people." Obviously he didn't, and it didn't seem politic to ask why not.

"And then one day," he continued, "the road I was on made a sharp turn to the left, and I took it. I didn't even hesitate," he said with wonder in his voice, "didn't even pause. Me, a man who always thought he did the right thing. I stepped right up and took the devil by the hand and walked with him." He paused and shook his head, as if he still couldn't believe it.

"I called the police," he said. "I called them and said Thomas was dealing crack. I didn't give them my name. I just made up stuff, and they went and arrested him. Maybe Steiner had them do it. I don't how much they have to get before they'll arrest you. But they arrested him for it, so he went down on the list."

"The list?" I asked.

"Steiner would make a list of everyone who was arrested for dealing crack, and give it to the judge. At first they would just pick those who got off, who didn't go to jail, but then they decided that was taking too long, that they were back out on the street as soon as they posted bond, selling the stuff again. So getting arrested was enough."

"How many have there been?" I asked. I knew I ought to keep my mouth shut, but I couldn't help myself, and I didn't see that it would matter much.

"With him in there," he said, gesturing toward the enclosure in the back, "it'll be fifteen. The list is a lot longer, but Steiner's pretty careful about picking them up. He says we'll get further if we take it slow."

"But they picked up Thomas?" I asked.

"Yeah, they got Thomas. He was easy, you see. I called him up and told him to meet me over here, that there was going to be a chance to buy a bunch of stuff cheap."

"Steiner knew you worked for him?"

"Yeah, I saw his name on the list and I told Steiner that I worked in his warehouse, that I thought I could get him over here. All the cops know Thomas's business, but I told Steiner I wasn't stealing stuff myself, I was just working for him. Steiner didn't care." Gifford's moral sense about whom he worked for didn't seem to be highly developed.

"Did Steiner know Thomas wasn't into drugs, that you set him up?" I asked.

"I think he suspected. But no, he didn't know. He may have thought I wanted to take over the business."

"Did you?" I asked, thinking of the dusty, unused looking warehouse.

He stared at me for a few seconds, then said, "No, I don't give a damn about Thomas's business. That business is over."

He kept staring at me like he was waiting for another question. A psychiatrist might have waited him out, let him think it over himself and bring it up in the next session. But this was my only session, so I asked it. "Why then? Why did you do it? He paid you good money to work for him, and you knew his mother. Lucy showed me a picture of you two together." A little white lie didn't seem to matter much now. "Why get him killed?"

"That's why," he said. "Because I know his mother."

I didn't say anything this time, just sat there and waited. He massaged his face with his left hand, cleared his throat, and said, "Lucy's mother used to work at the judge's brother's house. A big old place right by the country club. Lucy would go over there with her mother, help out and play some with the brother's daughter. Lucy was a pretty little thing in those days, bright eyed and smiling all the time. I'd go over there and work in the yard sometimes, when the judge didn't need me at his place. That's where I met her. I'm four years older than she is, and when I was seventeen, and she was thirteen, we fell in love. I wanted to marry her, but her mama said she was too young, that we'd have to wait. So we did. I didn't hardly touch her. But he did."

I could see a vein pounding in his forehead, and his knuckles were almost white he was gripping the shotgun so hard. I could hear his teeth grind in the stillness of the room.

"Who?" I asked quietly.

"The judge's brother," he said. "He must have been fifty years old. He was catching Lucy out in the garage, down in the basement, wherever he could, and putting his white thing up in her every chance he got. He told her he'd fire her mother from her job if she told her, so she never did. But she told me. She told me she was going to have his baby. Her mama knew she was pregnant, and she thought it was mine."

"I was eighteen by then, but I was still a boy, and a black boy at that. I didn't know what to do. It was in my heart to kill that man, except I knew it wouldn't do anything but harm to Lucy. He had quit bothering her when she started to show, or I would have. I asked Lucy to marry me, but she wouldn't do it, said he had ruined her. So I joined the army, went away for four years."

"My God," I said, "Thomas is the judge's brother's son?"

"Was," Gifford said with a bitter laugh. "Was his son. When I got back from the army, Thomas wasn't a baby no more. His face was setting into its features, and every time I looked at him I could see Baker. I was still in love with Lucy, but she had changed, grown up and grown bitter by the whole thing. And I couldn't stand to be around that child. After a while I got married to someone else, then divorced after a while. I was with other women, but it never worked long. When Thomas grew up, moved out of the house, I started going over to see Lucy again. I still see her the way she looked thirty years ago."

He looked at me for a second, as if waiting for me to comment, but I wasn't sharing my thoughts on Lucy's appearance.

"Lucy wasn't the girl I had known, but she was still Lucy, and we were happy. We never got married, and we didn't live together. We were just sweethearts again. And I thought maybe we had healed what that man had done to us. I got so I could be around Thomas without wanting to hit him, without thinking about what had happened. It had been a long time since it had happened, and the man had been dead for a long time. I thought maybe it was okay.

"Then Thomas asked me to work for him. I didn't want to, but Lucy said I ought to. The money was good, and she kept after me, so I finally said I'd do it. So I started working for him, just like I had worked for his uncle and his daddy. And then I started on this over here with the judge and Steiner. And one day, when Thomas handed me my paycheck, and drove off in that expensive car of his, leaving me to sweep up the warehouse, I knew what had to happen. It was like it had all been decided years ago, like I didn't have no choice in the matter. I had come to that turn in the road, and the devil was pushing me down it."

He stopped talking, looking spent and exhausted. The heater had cooled off all the way, and there was no sound in the building except his rasping breath. I had been trying to listen hard just to come up with some angle that might save my ass, and found myself caught up in his story. I knew that I looked like shit, with blood caked on my head, puke drying on my jacket, and the fear of death all over me. But I had never seen a man as tortured looking as Gifford. I had to know some things, even if they were only academic to me.

"Did Thomas ever know who his father was?" I asked.

"No," he said, "Lucy never told him. He asked me once last year if I knew, and I told him I didn't. He said he was wondering if it was me. I told him I wished I was. Good Lord, I wish I had been." A tear squeezed out of his left eye, and ran down his cheek.

"Were you here when he came?" I asked.

"No," he said. "That's the only one I've missed. I told the judge I was sick, and I was. I drove one of his vans over here the day before, so Thomas would see it when he pulled up and think I was here. Steiner came over to Memphis in Thomas's car after they did it and picked me up, and we came back over here for the van. Steiner put the car back in Thomas's garage about four in the morning, and I picked him up in the van." That explained the mud in Thomas's garage, and the mud and soybean stalk on the underside of the van.

Gifford sat slumped in the chair, the muzzle of the shotgun barrel resting on the floor, his right hand slack on its grip.

"Was it worth it?" I asked.

Gifford looked at me with the eyes of a brain gone beyond despair, into a land where the soil is ash, the streams run with acid and the sun never shines. "What do you mean?" he asked in a voice I could barely comprehend, a voice that came from the world his soul had entered. "Right or wrong didn't matter. It was the way it had to be."

It was now or never, I thought, but as I tensed my muscles again Gifford suddenly stood up from the chair. He blew out a big breath, and said, "And that's the way it is, and I'm going to have to live with it till I die. There ain't no use thinking otherwise."

He backed up so he was sitting on the desk, and kept the shotgun on me. "Look," I said, putting a lot of feeling into my voice, which wasn't hard to do, "you don't have to keep doing it. Why don't you quit now? Let that guy in there and me go. Don't put us on your conscience, too. You can get out of town, or you can go to the cops and turn state's evidence, get it all off your chest. That way you wouldn't get the death penalty."

"Shut up now," he said, shaking his head and pointing the shotgun at me. "Didn't you hear what I been saying? There ain't no turning back now."

"It's never too late," I said. "You could…"

"Shut up!" he almost yelled. "Shut the hell up! I don't want to talk about it no more. You say another word and I'll take this shotgun to your head again, then tape up your mouth." He was shaking, and paler by a few shades. I shut up. I didn't know what options I had left, but any of them would be harder to execute after another rap from the Browning.

He pulled the chair over toward him, turned its back to me, and put his feet in the seat and the shotgun barrel over the top of the backrest, pointed at my head. And then we sat together, each in his own overlapping world, waiting for the dawn.

I worked hard at not panicking, taking deep, slow breaths. I had no idea what I could do to get out of this situation, but I knew panic would be worse than another blow to the head. I tried to keep my thoughts in order, going over possible scenarios that might let me escape. I had a sinking feeling that I had missed my best chance by not rushing Gifford during his story, but I consoled myself by thinking that it takes a while to get used to the idea that you need to do something that will most likely end up with you being dead.

My watch was still on my wrist, and it showed that it was almost three. Gifford sat silent, his eyes pointed at me, but mostly watching something else. The only sound was my own breathing and the beat of my heart. The cold intensified, and I began to shiver, my teeth rattling together. I don't know whether Gifford noticed it, or got cold himself, but he got up and plugged the electric heater back in. I wondered how Anderson was making out in the back room.

I thought about the dependent relationship between Gifford and Baker, a type of relationship that was hundreds of years old. Gifford seemed in many ways a strong man, but he hadn't been strong enough, or independent enough, to tell the judge he was nuts, that there was no way he was going to get involved in his lunatic scheme to rid the city of its undesirables. Despite the actions of the judge's brother—Amanda's father—Gifford had still looked to the judge for guidance in legal, and maybe moral, matters. Or maybe he had just assumed that if the judge said do it, it was okay. That assumption hadn't been overridden by his own independent judgment until it was too late.

I didn't know the judge, but I knew his type. He was to the manor born, and would have the same self-assurance and certainty in the correctness of his actions as an English lord. His son's drug problem, and maybe time's slow erosion of his brain, had led him to believe that Steiner's solution was the proper course. Unlike Gifford, who had taken the same road but now knew it was the devil's highway, the judge would die believing he had done the right thing. When he asked, or told, Gifford to help him, he would have expected nothing less than habitual obedience. Other coloreds might have gotten uppity, or forgotten their place, but not Hayes. If Hayes had refused him, it would have shaken the judge's view of the world more than the discovery of his son's drug addiction.

By luck and happenstance, Steiner, Gifford and the judge were brought together, their twisted souls wrapped around each other in a strange triple helix that conceived and carried out murder in the name of the public good. The innate evil of their actions, their breach of the most fundamental social covenant, was disguised from them by the abstraction of their purpose. Of all the three, Gifford alone had become self-aware, partly because he was just doing what he was told without the same wholehearted belief in the validity of his actions as Steiner and the judge, but mostly because he had gone beyond the abstract— the murder of Thomas Tuggle made it personal.

I came out of my musing, looked at Gifford, and realized it hadn't gotten me anywhere. He sat like a rock, the muzzle of his shotgun fixed on my face. The barrel was a black tunnel, and at the other end was a lead slug or wad of pellets, setting on top of a charge of powder. With a twitch of his finger, Gifford could send the lead down the barrel and through my face and head in the blink of an eye, leaving my accumulated knowledge, experience, hopes and fears dripping down the wall behind me. It seemed like it should be harder to end a life, especially if it was mine.

18 _____

No great escape plan presented itself. The heater went on and off, Gifford occasionally rolled the chair back and forth on the concrete floor with his feet and I heard Anderson's chains rattle now and then from the back room. Before I knew it, it was five thirty. My heart leaped and my bowels cramped as the door opened and Steiner came in carrying two Styrofoam cups of coffee.

"The judge wants you to fry him some eggs," Steiner said to Gifford. "I'll watch him till the judge is ready."

Gifford stood up from the desk. "How much we doin' this morning?"

"Just the guy in back. The judge says two in one day would be unseemly, and there has to be a trial." As Gifford went out the door, Steiner smiled at me. "It's your lucky day."

Steiner set one of the cups on the table, pulled my pistol out of his belt, and walked over and placed the other cup on the floor a few feet in front of me. He backed up, keeping the muzzle of the Smith on me. "Act right and the next twenty four hours will be tolerable," he said. "If you don't, we'll have to cuff your hands behind you and tape your mouth. You might as well make it as good as you can."

I damned near said thanks out of habit, but just took the coffee instead and tried a sip. It was hot and sweet, and felt good in my stomach despite the lingering nausea. I sat back against the wall, holding it in both of my cuffed hands, and worked on it slowly. Steiner sat where Gifford had been, the pistol in one hand and the Styrofoam cup in the other, sipping coffee and staring at me.

We sat silent until the coffee was gone, then I asked, "How long do you think you can keep it up?"

"You mean our little secret here?" he asked with a smile. "Not indefinitely. At some point the judge will die, but all that will mean is I'll have to find some other place to do this. No, it will really end when some scum I'm arresting shoots me first, or somebody sees me grabbing them and the cops or the FBI catch up with us. Or who knows, maybe we'll do enough that I'll feel comfortable quitting before I get killed or shot, but I doubt that. It feels too good to stop."

"So it's just you three, huh?" I asked. "No other cops?"

"Just us three. But that's another way we could get stopped. We've had enough success that I've started to hear vigilante rumors going around the department. Nobody with any sense gives a shit. I mean, if the incidence of some fatal disease goes down, do you try to bring it back up to its former levels? Of course not. But some dumbass in the department, or some so-called community activist, may start doing more than wondering where all the crack dealers have gone. I can't rule out such idiocy. Most likely, they'll say it's a racist thing, but crack hurts a lot more poor people than rich people, and there are a lot more poor black people than poor white people in Memphis."

In a strange sort of way, I felt relieved by his statement about the close knit nature of their group. I had remembered Tommy's adamant statement out by his lake to drop my search for Tuggle, and had wondered during the night if he knew about a conspiracy, or was even part of it. Steiner didn't have any reason not to tell me the truth, though, so I figured Tommy had just heard the rumors Steiner had referred to about vigilantes, and didn't want me to get mixed up in anything. The other possibility, of course, was that there was an investigation going on into the disappearances, and Tommy had been connected enough to hear about it. Either way, it didn't implicate Tommy, but it sure as hell didn't help me, unless the investigation was going to result in a raid on the farm in the next twenty-four hours.

"So," I said. "Has everyone you've executed been black?"

"No, they've mostly been black, but we've had a couple of white guys, one involved in distribution and the other pushing to kids, and a couple of Colombians that were pretty far up the chain. I'm proud of those Colombians. Getting rid of them really made a tangible difference in the amount of stuff on the street, at least for a couple of months, and we would have never gotten them by conventional methods. They had all kinds of money, and would have gotten the best lawyers."

Beneath his cop's veneer of toughness and cynicism, I could see that Steiner was totally into the solution. I didn't think I was going to have any luck trying to convince him that I wanted to be a co-conspirator, but I also figured that if I tried to convince him to call off the whole thing, as I had with Gifford, I would quickly find myself with my hands behind my back and tape on my face. Any chances I had for escape were not good, but they would be a lot worse in that situation.

Steiner stretched and yawned. "You ruined my sleep last night."

"I bet you slept better than I did," I said.

"I bet you're right," he said. "You know, you're about to see something that ought to impress you, and I hope it will. You're our first witness, of course. You'll see justice carried out quickly and inexorably, no long years of bullshit appeals, no waste of the taxpayers' money paying lawyers and tying up the court system, or feeding and housing some animal for twenty years till he's painlessly put to sleep on a padded table in a comfortable room, with the ACLU outside with candles singing We Shall Overcome."

"If you get caught, they'll be singing it for you," I said, and immediately asked myself why I couldn't keep my fucking mouth shut.

I was afraid that I might have pushed the wrong button, but he just smiled at me. "I've thought about what would happen if I get caught. At first I thought I would probably kill myself before I would let them catch me, but then I realized that someone would need to tell our story. There have got to be a lot of people out there who feel like I do, and the support might in the long run mean more than what the three of us accomplish here. Even if I am executed, or maybe especially if I am. So you see, no matter what happens, I'm happy."

I started to say he would have a good insanity defense, but I stopped myself just in time. He was excited, and his face was shining, presumably because of the pending execution of Anderson. He got up and walked over to the back room and unlocked the chain. He kept an eye on me, but peered into the room where Anderson lay. He walked back over to the desk, still smiling, and sat down again.

"Hayes will be back soon," he said. A minute later, I heard tires approaching on the gravel from the direction of the river. They stopped, a vehicle door slammed, and then Gifford walked into the room. "Judge says it's time," he said.

"Can you handle the one in there by yourself?" Steiner asked, gesturing with the pistol toward the back.

"The way we got him tied up, that won't be no problem," Gifford said. He walked back through the wire door, and I heard him grunt, and then a scraping noise. He came out through the door backwards, Anderson's heels in his hands. Anderson's legs were tied together from above his knees to his ankles with yellow nylon cord, and his arms were strapped tightly to his body with the same cord. The tape was back over his mouth and around his head, which he was trying to hold up off the floor as Gifford dragged him. He was making muted noises, and his eyes were rolling wildly. His hope for survival had died like a paper match hissing out in the bottom of a urinal.

Gifford dragged him out the door, and I heard a grunt and a thump. "Let's go," Steiner said to me, gesturing with the pistol. I walked in front of him into the pre-dawn darkness. Gifford's pickup was right outside, and Anderson was lying in the back, with Gifford sitting on the side of the bed holding the Browning. Steiner gestured me up with the pistol, then got into the cab and started the truck.

Anderson was helpless, so Gifford kept the shotgun on me as we made the short drive to the house on the river. There was a faint line of red in the east, but most of the stars were still out, and the frost was still falling from the sky. I could hear the gabble of waking ducks out on the water in front of us.

We were at the house in a few seconds, and made a turn and pulled up on the side by the river as Steiner killed the engine. Anderson started to buck and twist as soon as the truck stopped. Gifford reached out casually with the shotgun barrel and rapped him on the forehead hard enough to draw blood, and Anderson calmed down.

Gifford waved me out of the truck, and I got down onto the gravel. The area was lit by bright floodlights from under the roof eaves. There was a space of about fifty feet between the house and the edge of the water. A dock extended out from the land on foot thick pilings that disappeared into the black water. Trees and cypress knees grew up thick from the surface of the water, which I soon realized was not the main stream of the river but a backwater shielded from the main current by brush and other vegetation.

Steiner got out of the truck and put my gun on me as Hayes leaned his shotgun against the side of the truck and pulled Anderson onto the lowered tailgate. He stooped low, got Anderson up on his shoulders, then stood up with a grunt like a weightlifter. Anderson was making noise through the tape again, but he didn't try to twist off Gifford's shoulders. Gifford carried him over to the edge of the water, next to a thick, short post sticking up out of the ground. He sat Anderson up against the post, facing the river with his head and neck sticking up above the top, and tied him against it with a thick rope. Anderson craned his head to the left, and then to the right, trying to see what was going on, then gave up, his head falling on his chest.

The red band in the east had grown noticeably higher in the sky, and at least half of the light was now coming from the sun.

There was a stack of concrete blocks beside the water, with a big chain laid across them. Steiner saw me looking, and said, "It's primitive, but that's the disposal system. There's a pool out there about twenty feet deep. Except for the few bits and pieces that get blown out into the water when we do the execution, we wrap them up tight and sink the bodies in there."

The coffee rose up in the back of my throat, and I thought I was going to vomit again. I had a sudden flash back to the article I had seen in the Wynne paper about a piece of human skull being found in the river, and wondered if it had belonged to Thomas.

There was a noise behind me and Steiner looked past my shoulder. "Good morning, judge."

"Good morning, lieutenant," a cultured Southern voice said behind me. I turned and saw a man of medium height, with silver hair visible beneath a green Tyrol hat. He was wearing a down jacket, khaki pants, and Wellington style boots with a shine that was visible even in the dim light, probably courtesy of Gifford. He looked at me with mild curiosity, and I looked back at him. He bore a slight resemblance to his niece Amanda, and to his nephew Thomas, but it was hard to see through the years that lay on him. "Judge Baker," I started to say, hoping he was not totally beyond reason, but when my mouth opened a light flared in his eyes, and he said harshly to Steiner, "Lieutenant, haven't you explained the rules to the prisoner?"

Steiner grabbed my shoulder and twisted me toward him. Jamming the muzzle of the .357 between my eyes, he said, "Don't say another word unless you're asked a question. Understand?" I nodded, and he slowly lowered the pistol. So much for reasoning with the judge, I thought.

"Are we ready to go here?" the judge asked. "I'm cold."

"Yes, your Honor, we're ready," Steiner replied.

"Let's do it, then," the judge said. It was lighter now, and when I looked up at the sound of beating wings I could see a small flock of teal rocket past overhead. I wished I could join them.

The judge walked over to where Anderson was tied, looked down at him for a second, and then said, "May God have mercy on your soul." Anderson was now shaking his head violently from side to side, and his feet were scrabbling in the dirt.

Gifford came over and got his shotgun, and took Steiner's place watching me. Steiner looked at me, "You don't mind if I use yours, do you? This is my favorite part." He held the big Smith out in front of him and walked over to the post. Anderson was looking over his shoulder and saw him coming, and started to throw his head and shoulders up and down and sideways with a manic energy, as if he could avoid the hollow point slug if he could just keep them moving. Steiner cocked my gun, and tried to follow Anderson's head with the muzzle for a few seconds, then uncocked it and walked back over to us. He had an exasperated look on his face. "Judge," he said "would you please hold the shotgun on this prisoner while Hayes gives me a hand?"

The judge nodded and Gifford handed him the weapon. Gifford and Steiner walked over to the post, and Gifford grabbed a double handful of Anderson's dreadlocks and pulled his head up straight. Gifford stepped sideways, his arms extended and straining to keep Anderson's head upright. Steiner cocked the magnum and put its muzzle against the base of Anderson's skull. There was a flash and a roar, then Hayes Gifford standing by the post with what was left of Anderson's head, severed from his neck by the high velocity slug.

Anderson's legs kicked spasmodically, and his shoulders rocked back and forth, spraying the blood that fountained up from the stump of his neck in a bright red circle. Steiner took a step back, then put his little finger in his left ear and wiggled it around, trying to restore some of his hearing. "Damn," he said loudly, looking at the mutilated head Gifford was holding, then down at the pistol in his right hand.

Gifford dropped the head with a thump and brushed at the blood spattered on his coat. A beam of sunlight shone through the branches of a cypress tree growing up out of the river, illuminating a red mist that slowly settled on the surface of the water.

I was biting back hard on the coffee, but no one else seemed unduly troubled, especially Anderson, whose body had now relaxed as all of its electrical circuits went cold. The judge walked over and put the shotgun down on the dock, and Steiner came back to stand by me. "I'm going back inside," the judge said to Steiner, and walked around the corner of the house.

Steiner stood a few feet away from me, Uncle Stan's Smith dangling in his hand. There was a spray of bright red drops on the revolver and the back of his hand. He didn't look insane, he looked happy. Happy now was the same as insane. He gave me that too familiar smile, and started to open his mouth. Before any words could come out, there was a loud bang behind him, a whistling noise and a slapping sound as something hit the house. Steiner's body jerked. He took a step toward me, blood welling up over his lip, and fell face down. Five or six holes showed in his upper back, and one in the back of his neck.

Gifford was standing by the dock, the shotgun at his shoulder, his head lifting slowly off the stock. I stood frozen, not wanting to bring attention to myself, but badly wanting the revolver still gripped in Steiner's hand. Before I could make the call, there was a sound to my left, and the judge came back around the corner of the house. "What the hell is going on, Hayes?"

Gifford stared at the judge for a few seconds, then slowly turned the shotgun barrel toward him.

"Hayes," the judge said, "what in the world?" He stuck his open left hand out toward Gifford, palm up.

I watched Hayes, trying to decide when to go for the pistol. He took a deep breath, closed his eyes, and jerked the trigger.

I was down behind Steiner, desperately grabbing for the Smith with my cuffed hands, expecting the next shot to come my way. I got the revolver out of Steiner's bloody hand and brought it up over his back in time to see the judge standing against the wall of the house, both hands gripping his belly. Gifford had his eyes open, and before I could open my mouth or pull the trigger he blew another load of buckshot into the judge's chest. The judge jerked up straight, knocking his head against the wall, then slumped forward onto the ground.

I thumbed back the hammer, rested the butt of the revolver on Steiner's back, and fixed Gifford in the sights. I had thought Steiner was already dead, but he took a long, shuddering breath that raised the pistol up and then dropped it down. Blood-dampened air blew out one of the holes in his back onto my face.

"Hayes," I said, "drop the shotgun."

He turned back to me, the shotgun held in his right hand by its grip, pointing at the ground. His face had the same wondering look that had been on the judge's just before he was shot.

"Hayes," I said again, "drop the shotgun. It's all over."

"Lucy knew you was coming over here," he said in a voice I could barely hear. "Steiner and the judge would have killed her so she couldn't talk. I had to do it. I been thinking about it since you told me, and I decided what I had to do."

"All right, Hayes," I said. "I understand. Everybody else will understand, too. Just drop the gun."

He looked down at the Browning in his hand like he had forgotten it was there, then back at me. "She's still going to know unless you're dead," he said, raising the shotgun. The top of the front sight of the Smith was fixed at the base of his sternum as I squeezed the trigger and held tight as the revolver bucked in my hand.

I stood up from behind Steiner, his lung blood bright on my hands and mixed with Anderson's on the pistol. I looked down at him and saw that both eyes were open in a glassy stare, and that his chest was still. He had died in time to be a sturdy rest for my shot.

I walked over to where Hayes had been standing, and looked at him floating facedown in the shallow backwater. There was a hole in the middle of his back you could have put a cantaloupe in. One broken end of his backbone stuck up out of the hole like a cracked stick. He rocked slowly in a widening, dissipating pool of red.

The Browning was lying in the mud on the bank where he had dropped it as the slug had back flipped him into the slough. It was empty, the action locked back on a vacant chamber.

Just then I heard a noise behind me, and turned as Henry Jackson rounded the corner, pistol in hand. He stopped when he saw me, then looked over at Steiner and the judge, and what was left of Anderson's body tied to the stump.

"You okay?" he asked.

"Yeah, sure, I'm okay," I answered.

19 _____

Henry had become concerned when I hadn't made our scheduled late night coffee meeting or answered my phone. He had left Memphis early the next morning, and had cruised up and down farm roads until he found the right one. I wasn't sure whether I wished he had come earlier or not.

I used Henry's cell phone to call a friend at home who was an assistant U.S. attorney in Memphis. Arkansas was out of his jurisdiction, but he said he would call the FBI. It wasn't that I didn't trust the local law, but I figured since the FBI would be involved eventually, I might as well bring them in on the front end. Henry and I went around to the front of the house and sat quietly on the front porch until they came.

They were there in less than an hour, three cars full of agents. I didn't know how they would take my story, but I had hardly started telling it before an agent searching the house found the judge's diary. It outlined the whole plan, and a record of all the trials and executions. After that, they seemed a lot less suspicious of me. I answered all of their questions, and told them everything I could, except that Amanda and Thomas had the same father. It wasn't any of their business, and it didn't matter to their investigation.

About noon, they called in the locals to pick up the fresh bodies and drag the river for the others. They let Henry drive me back to Memphis. One of the agents took my keys and said he would drive my truck home. Uncle Stan's .357 was tagged for evidence. They said I would get it back eventually.

I wanted to go back to my place, but Henry insisted on taking me to the hospital. I felt like shit, so I didn't argue with him very hard. At the hospital, they X-rayed my head, put a few stitches in my scalp, and told me I had a moderate concussion but no skull fracture. They cut me loose about four thirty, just as the sun was going down. Henry had left to open his business, so I got a cab downtown. It let me out on Front Street across from Amanda's office.

I stood for a minute on the sidewalk, letting my lungs clear out the hospital air, and watching the sun sink over the levee on the other side of the river. Overhead, thousands of black birds flew back from feeding in the fields in Arkansas, looking for roosting trees in town. I took a final deep breath of the clean, cold air, then went up to see Amanda.

She had a client in the waiting room, but she let me in first. I spent a half hour with her, catching her up on events since I had left her drunk and lonely in her castle. Neither of us mentioned that last meeting. I told her the same story I had given the FBI, everything but that Thomas was her brother. Maybe she already knew, maybe that was why she had pushed me so hard to find him, but maybe she didn't. If she hadn't figured it out for herself, or if Lucy hadn't told her, I didn't think it was my place to tell. That's not why she had hired me.

She kept her face impassive, showing no sign of grief or shock when I told her what had happened to Thomas. I volunteered to help her tell Lucy, but she said she would handle it. When I got through, she didn't ask any questions, just looked at her watch, thanked me for my efforts, and said she hoped I would feel better soon. The last thing she said as I went out the door was to send her a bill. It pissed me off, but not enough to tell her the whole story.

It was black night outside as I walked home, my head throbbing despite the pills they had given me at the hospital. A wind had come up, blowing the leading edge of another weather front into town. I thought randomly of the sins, past and present, that had come together today in a bloody climax. I thought of Gifford's unloaded shotgun on the bank beside the body that leaked its essence into the river that had absorbed the other condemned souls. I would piece it together in the coming days, maybe even make some sense and peace out of it, but by the time I got to my alley all I could think of was how tired, hungry and sick I was.

I barely made it up the fire escape. I unlocked and opened the door, and let myself into my office. Behind it, a light glowed from my living quarters, and a warm smell of cooking came from the kitchen. Mary walked out into the office, wearing an apron and holding a glass of red wine in one hand.

"John, you're home."

ACKNOWLEDGMENTS

I wish to thank the following for their support and assistance: my parents, Dr. Charles and Mrs. Peggy Crawford, and my brother, Larry Crawford; Ed Kaplan, for his useful suggestions on the manuscript; Bob Morris and Lucian Pera, for their intellectual property law expertise; and Jim Smith, my editor. Most of all, however, I would like to thank my sons, Charlie and Connor, for their encouragement and for allowing me time to write, and my wife, Alice, without whose support, in ways too numerous to count, this book would never have been started, much less completed.

Printed in the United States
25580LVS00001B/88-114